I0563360

HE'S MY SON

By

Jennifer Jackson

Copyright © 2025 by Jennifer Jackson

All rights reserved. No part of this book may be reproduced, distributed, or transmitted in any form or by any means, including photocopying, recording, or other electronic or mechanical methods, without the prior written permission of the publisher, except in the case of brief quotations embodied in critical reviews and certain other non-commercial uses permitted by copyright law.

Acknowledgments and Dedications

I would like to take a moment to express my heartfelt gratitude to everyone who has supported me on this incredible writing journey. This novel would not have been possible without your encouragement, belief, and inspiration.

First and foremost, I want to extend a special thank you to my daughter. You have been the guiding light in my life, and your unwavering support has been instrumental in bringing this narrative to fruition. Without you, there would simply be no "me" — thank you for always believing in my dreams and pushing me to pursue them.

I am also deeply grateful to my friends and family, who stood by me through every draft, brainstorm, and late-night writing session. Your patience, feedback, and love have fueled my passion and kept me motivated.

Additionally, I would like to acknowledge some remarkable individuals, who have played pivotal roles in this journey: Doneza Inez Smith, your insights and encouragement have been invaluable; Toni J. Robinson Jones, your creative spirit and discussions have inspired me more than you know; and Antoinette Brown, thank you for being a sounding board and a trusted friend throughout this process.

With all of your support, I have been able to pour my heart and soul into this book. I am immensely grateful for each of you, and I hope that this novel resonates with readers as much as your encouragement has resonated with me. Thank you for joining me on this adventure — I couldn't have done it without you!

About the Author

Jennifer Jackson is an award-winning author, screenwriter, and filmmaker based in Philadelphia, Pennsylvania. With a passion for storytelling that spans across various mediums, Jennifer has dedicated her life to creating compelling narratives that captivate and inspire.

After earning her degree in Fashion and merchandising, Jennifer took her first steps into the entertainment industry as an independent screenwriter and director. Her films have received accolades in over 36 film festivals, showcasing her talent for weaving intricate plots and dynamic characters.

Jennifer's debut novel, *He's My Son*, marks a thrilling turn in her writing career, blending emotional depth with the intricate drama of life's unexpected twists and delivering a gripping tale for her readers. When she's not writing, Jennifer enjoys exploring fashion, dabbling in creative arts, and spending time with her two lively kids.

A little fun fact about Jennifer:

In her spare time, Jennifer can often be found binge-watching reality TV shows, sipping tea, or getting lost in a good book. Her life motto? "Don't just follow your dreams; chase them down with a vengeance!"

You can connect with Jennifer through the following email:

- Email: hesmyson2025@gmail.com

(mailto:hesmyson2025@gmail.com)

Books by Jennifer Jackson:

He's My Son (2025)

**Upcoming projects and novels in development.

Dive into Jennifer's world of storytelling and experience the rollercoaster of emotions, relatable characters, and plot twists that keep you turning the pages!

Contents

Prologue

The crisp autumn air danced off the golden leaves scattered across the campus grounds, a reminder that seasons change, but some things remain timeless — like the friendships tangled with complex emotions and unspoken desires. Ramona, Sarah, Jake, and Marcus had all met in their first year at Eastbridge University, where ambition and dreams intermingled with laughter in the lecture halls and the aroma of coffee from the campus cafe. They were four individuals, each embarking on their distinct paths, yet their lives were intricately woven together by the threads of friendship, love, and betrayal.

Sarah Peterson was the quintessential goody two-shoes, always on top of her studies, her heart set on becoming a nurse. Her bright smile and bubbly personality drew people to her effortlessly, but it was her unwavering loyalty that kept her friends close. Jake McKinley, with his rugged charm and twinkling hazel eyes, soon captured Sarah's heart. They were a picture-perfect couple — a match made in college heaven. Jake poured his ambition into becoming a chemical engineer, enlisting in the armed forces after graduation to finance his education and serve his country. He was the perfect gentleman and Sarah loved him for it.

Then there was Ramona Whitmore, a striking beauty, whose presence could turn heads and sway hearts. Everyone in town desired her not just for her looks but also for the sharp business acumen inherited from her father, Senator Frank Whitmore — a powerful and corrupt man, who seemed to overshadow her every move. In the shadows of her illustrious family name, Ramona craved something more than just the glamorous life laid out for her by her father. Real estate beckoned her, and she had recently begun to make waves in the industry, establishing herself as a force to be reckoned with.

Beneath the surface, however, lay a turbulent undercurrent. Ramona had always been drawn to Jake, sensing a connection that went deeper than friendship. Their conversations were electric, filled with banter and unacknowledged chemistry. The nights spent studying late in the library turned into stolen moments — the kind that lingered long after they parted ways. But Jake was with Sarah, and though the friendship was strong, the tension between Ramona and Jake simmered just beneath the surface, her longing masked by friendly smiles.

As their respective paths shifted post-graduation, the landscape of their lives began to change dramatically. Jake proposed to Sarah, and in a whirlwind of joy, she said yes. Their wedding was a celebration filled with family and friends, a fairytale come to life, as she walked down the aisle in a veil of white, radiant and glowing. Unbeknownst to the delighted guests, Ramona's heart shattered as she watched the man she desired say "I do" to someone else.

During the months leading up to the wedding, Ramona found herself trapped in a business arrangement of her own — an unholy matrimony with Marcus Anderson, a dauntingly successful businessman with connections that scared her father into compliance. Marcus obviously wasn't a bad person; he was charming, ambitious, and capable in his own right. But deep down, Ramona yearned for passion, for reckless abandon, for the happiness she believed was stolen from her. Marcus was everything her father desired — except he wasn't Jake.

In a moment of desperation to seize what little time she had left, Ramona made a decision that would haunt her indefinitely. The night before her wedding, she slipped into the shadows, seeking out Jake. They met in that dimly lit café near the campus, the kind of place that held countless memories of their fleeting friendship, where laughter echoed off the walls. It was here that the air crackled with unspoken words, and in the corner booth, where they had shared dreams and secrets, Ramona succumbed to emotion.

What followed was a heated affair, a final act of rebellion against the life that she had reluctantly chosen. Hidden beneath the table, their hands clasped tightly together as they whispered fervently, lost in a torrent of feelings ignited by the impossibility of their situation. They shared more than just the thrill of desire that night; they shared dreams of what could have been — the life they could have created together. It was supposed to be their dirty little secret, a moment wrapped in secrecy, a fleeting taste of what was never meant to be.

As dawn broke, casting a soft glow over the world, Ramona woke with regret swirling in her chest. The realization of what she had done crashed down on her like a cold wave. She had tasted the sweetness of forbidden love, but it came at a steep price. The delicate thread connecting them had been irreparably frayed, and she was left to confront the chaos of her choices.

In the days that followed, the reality set in, as she prepared to walk down the aisle to Marcus — days filled with smiles, laughter, and friendly chatter. The wedding was to be a powerful display, a celebration of friendship and family. But as she donned the white gown that symbolized purity and devotion, the memory of that one night with Jake haunted her like a stubborn ghost of the past.

And so, as she took each step toward the altar, Ramona felt the weight of her choices pressing down on her shoulders. She was poised to trade one cage for another, sold to the highest bidder, but her heart still tethered to Jake's. Little did she know, the story was far from over. The twists of fate had yet to unravel, and a darker path lay ahead — a path where loyalty, love, and ambition would collide in ways she could never have anticipated.

This was not just a tale of friendships torn apart; it was a compelling saga that would test the very limits of their dreams, their passions, and ultimately, their hearts.

Chapter 1

My Best Friend

In a cozy living room filled with warmth and laughter, Ramona and Sarah were engaged in a lively conversation, catching up on each other's lives. As they sat on the couch, sipping on glasses of wine and laughing, it was clear that their bond was as strong as ever. They had been best friends since growing up in the same small town, sharing countless memories together. Ramona had always been the more adventurous and daring of the two, while Sarah was the more cautious and level-headed one. So, when Ramona began to tell Sarah about the shocking revelation that she had recently discovered, Sarah was both intrigued and slightly apprehensive.

With a shocked expression, Ramona exclaimed, "I think Mark is having an affair."

Sarah, taken aback, retorted, "That's crazy. Mark loves you." As Ramona began to express her suspicions, her emotions started to surface.

"The late-night phone calls, the mysterious disappearances, the sudden change in behavior, Mark even bought new underwear. I've been trying to get him to do that for weeks. That sounds like an affair to me," she confided in her closest friend, the words trembling as they escaped her lips.

Sarah responded, "I think you're jumping to conclusions. Just because Mark bought new underwear doesn't mean he's having an affair."

"Sarah, I'm telling you, Mark is having an affair. His behavior has been strange over the past few months," expressed Ramona.

"You can't go around accusing Mark of having an affair. You need proof," Sarah cautioned.

Ramona explained how she had started to notice strange behavior from her husband, Mark, over the past few months. He was spending more time with their next door neighbor, a man named Maxwell, and seemed to be growing distant from her. At first, Ramona brushed it off as just a friendship between the two men, but as time went on, she couldn't ignore the signs any longer.

One day, when she came home early from work, Ramona walked in on Mark and Maxwell in a compromising position in their own living room.

"Sarah, wow! I have no words."

Exclaimed Ramona, "Is that enough proof for you?" The shock and betrayal she felt were overwhelming.

"What did you do?" Sarah asked, concerned. Instead of confronting them right then and there, Ramona decided to bide her time and gather evidence.

"I need your help," Ramona replied.

"Sure, I'm always going to be there for you. Wait, you're not going to do something crazy, are you?" Sarah cautioned.

Ramona jumped off the couch and started pacing the floor like a madwoman.

"Did you hear what I said? Mark is having an affair with a man."

As Sarah watched Ramona pacing across the floor and talking to herself, a sinking feeling settled in her stomach. She couldn't help but wonder what Ramona was about to get herself into this time.

With a furrowed brow, Sarah mustered the courage to ask, "Do you have a plan"

Ramona's response sent shivers down her spine,

"No. I will come up with something. You are better off not knowing."

Sarah's puzzlement grew, but she couldn't shake the reminder, "Just remember, you're on probation, and I don't have any bail money. Besides, you still haven't paid me back from the last time you got arrested." As Ramona turned around and glared at her, Sarah couldn't help but fear the storm that was about to unleash.

The sun had long set, casting a soft glow over the city skyline. The room was dimly lit, with flickering on the table, their warm light dancing across the walls. Ramona was eagerly waiting for her husband to come home. She made up her mind to fight for their marriage, to reignite sparks that had slowly faded away over the years. With a purpose in her, she carefully selected a set of sexy lingerie, hoping to surprise him and remind him of the passion they once shared.

She adorned the lingerie and decorated the room with scented candles, their soft glow casting a romantic ambiance. A bottle of wine stood half-empty, its rich aroma filling the air and played their favorite music in the background, Ramona couldn't help but feel a mix excitement and nervousness. She had even prepared Mark's favorite meal, putting in extra effort to make it perfect. Glancing at her watch, she knew he should be walking through the door any minute now.

Ramona took a quick glance around the room, making sure everything was in place. She wanted this night to be special, to show Mark how much she still cared. But as an hour passed, and then another, her anticipation turned into worry. Maybe he had to work late, she thought, trying to calm her racing thoughts.

Twenty minutes later, Ramona found herself pacing the floor, her worry growing with each passing moment. What if something had happened to him? What if he had gotten into an accident? The once romantic atmosphere in the house, now felt heavy with uncertainty.

By the time Mark finally walked through the door, three hours had passed. Ramona's heart sank as she caught a whiff of cheap cologne and Irish spring soap. She didn't say a word, her disappointment and hurt evident in her eyes. The food she had prepared with so much love had turned cold, and the candles that once burned brightly were now mere flickers of their former glow.

Ramona took a deep breath, trying to find the patience within her. She wrapped up the food, blowing out the candles one by one. As she looked at her husband, she couldn't help but wonder what had kept him away for so long. But for now, she remained silent, waiting for him to explain his absence, hoping that her efforts to save their marriage hadn't been in vain. But Mark did not even notice the romantic setting in front of him. His mind was preoccupied with the weight of the day, the stress of work weighing heavily on his shoulders. Finally, Ramona spoke up, her voice breaking the silence that had settled between them after Mark had placed his briefcase on the table.

"Why are you coming home so late?" Ramona's voice held a hint of disappointment, her eyes searching for answers in the depths of Mark's tired gaze. Mark finally looked up at Ramona, his eyes meeting hers for the first time that evening. And that's when he noticed it - the silky black negligee she was wearing, the delicate fabric clinging to her curves.

"I went to the gym," Mark replied, his voice lacking the enthusiasm that Ramona had hoped for. Ramona folded her arms, her disappointment turning into frustration.

"Why didn't you call me?" Her words hung in the air, heavy with unspoken expectations. Mark walked towards Ramona, his steps slow and tired.

"I didn't know we were celebrating something today," he said, his voice tinged with regret. Ramona felt tears welling up in her eyes, her heart aching with the missed opportunity for a romantic evening.

"I wanted to surprise you with a romantic evening," she whispered, her voice barely audible. Mark's heart sank as he realized the magnitude of his oversight. He reached out and gently kissed Ramona's forehead, his lips lingering for a moment.

"I'm sorry, babe. If I knew that you were going to do something wonderful like this, I would have come home early," he said, his voice filled with genuine remorse. "Now, if you excuse me, it's been a long day. I'm tired, and I'm going to get ready for bed."

He walked away from Ramona. The strong fragrance of inexpensive cologne caused her to feel nauseated. In a fit of anger, Ramona hurled the vase against the wall. Subsequently, she proceeded to gather the shattered fragments of the vase from the floor. While glancing out of the window, she observed that her neighbor's attire appeared disheveled. In precise moment,

Ramona realized that her marital relationship had reached its definitive end.

The next day, Ramona and Sarah visited The Evil Eye Surveillance Spot, a surveillance store for all their spy equipment needs. As they stepped into the store, Sarah marveled at the array of equipment before them and asked, "What exactly are we looking for?" Ramona, focused on her plan, ignored her and began searching. A salesperson approached them and greeted,

"Hi, ladies, how can I help you?"

Ramona, with an intense tone, explained, "I'm looking for surveillance equipment to catch my lying, cheating, bastard of a husband."

The salesperson assured her, "Well, you came to the right place. What exactly are you looking for?"

Ramona, resolute in her stance, stated, "I need evidence to take to court to prove that my husband has been cheating on me." The salesperson proceeded to showcase the latest equipment, including recording devices and mini cameras. They even had a recording device that could fit in the compartment of a TV remote control. Ramona declared, "I'll take everything you suggested," as she reached for her credit card.

Sarah, expressing concern, interjected, "Wait, this is way too much stuff. Don't you think you're going overboard?"

Ramona retorted, "You're the one who said I needed proof," and proceeded to grab the bag and walk to the door. "By the time I finish with him, he's gonna wish he never cheated on me, because I'm gonna take every penny he has," she declared. Sarah followed behind, shaking her head and reflecting.

"Why do I always get myself into these predicaments?"

With Sarah's support and encouragement, Ramona devised a plan to catch her husband and their neighbor in the act. Ramona concealed the surveillance cameras in inconspicuous locations, such as behind picture frames, within decorative vases, and even disguised as household items like a clock or a plant. The cameras captured the intimate details of her husband and the neighbor's clandestine encounters - whispered conversations by the garden, stolen glances in the kitchen, and lingering touches that betrayed secrecy of the betrayal. The footage painted a vivid picture of the affair, and waited for the perfect moment to confront them.

That night, after finishing work Mark returned home and proceeded to kiss Ramona. She turned her head away because she still had vivid memories of what he had done with his mouth. Ramona attempted to stomach a conversation with Mark.

Ramona suggested, "Hey babe, let's do a movie night? "

Mark yawned, "Babe, I had a long day at work and I'm exhausted."

Ramona trying to convince him by rubbing on his broad chest, assured him that the movie would be fun. "Oh, sweetie, I promise, it'll be a short movie." Mark, unable to refuse her, gave her a small smile and agreed to movie night.

"I can't say no to you."

Ramona was excited, "Great! I'll get the snacks."

Mark started setting up the theater system. As Mark set up the speakers, he asked Ramona about the movie they would be watching.

Ramona said, "I want it to be a surprise?"

Mark taking off his jacket and sitting on the couch, waited for Ramona to join him. She turned to him and suggested inviting Maxwell for the movie night. Mark looked at her strangely and asked why. Ramona explained that she thought it would be a good idea, since Maxwell rarely leaves his house, and she wanted to be friendly with their neighbor.

Mark reluctantly called Maxwell to ask if he wanted to join them for movie night. Shortly after, Maxwell arrived at the door and Mark offered him a beer. Maxwell expressed his gratitude for the invitation, and Ramona assured him that he would be entertained. Maxwell asked for its title. Ramona happily replied that it was called

"The Secrets That Bonds Us."

Mark turned off the lights and Ramona started the movie, causing a shift in the room's atmosphere. As they watched, both men began to sweat and feel uncomfortable due to the explicit content on the screen. Mark abruptly turned off the TV, and Maxwell hastily left the house, still hearing the sounds of moaning and groaning outside. Ramona had even positioned a small screen for the neighbors to witness the betrayal. Maxwell was deeply upset and couldn't believe what had just happened. In her anger, Ramona threw anything she could find at Mark, as he ran out the door.

And when that moment finally came, Ramona was able to expose the affair and put an end to the deception that had been happening right under her nose.

As she finished recounting the whole ordeal to Sarah, Ramona couldn't help but feel a sense of relief and empowerment. She had taken control of the situation and stood up for herself, refusing to be a victim of betrayal any longer. And with Sarah by her side, she knew that she could face whatever challenges lay ahead with strength and resilience.

As Sarah listened to Ramona's shocking revelation, she couldn't help but wonder what other were lurking beneath the surface. Little did she know, this was just the surface of a tangled web of deceit and betrayal that would unravel before their very eyes.

Suddenly, the door swung open, interrupting their conversation. It was Sarah's son, Jackson, returning home from college. Sarah's heart skipped a beat. The sight of her son, his face beaming with genuine joy, filled her with an indescribable happiness. She couldn't help but rush towards him, wrapping her arms tightly around him in a warm embrace.

Sarah had always been a devoted mother to Jackson. From the moment he was born, she poured all her love and attention into raising him. They had formed an unbreakable bond over the years, especially after the tragic loss of Jackson's father in a car crash the previous summer.

Jackson's father and Sarah were married at a young age. After completing high school, the couple pursued higher education. Sarah was studying nursing, while Jackson's father, Jake, was studying chemical engineering. Both of them worked full-time to support themselves. However, Sarah had to leave her studies when she became pregnant. The couple discovered that their baby had some health issues, leading to Sarah being placed on bed rest by the doctor.

Unable to work due to her pregnancy, Jake took on a second job to provide for his family. This resulted him getting very little rest, as he attended school during the day and work at night. A year later, he fell asleep while driving. Sarah's life changed drastically, when she lost her husband. She was left alone to raise her baby boy, and without the support of Ramona, she would have been lost.

After the accident, Sarah and Jackson had leaned on each other for support. They became each other's rock, finding solace in their shared grief. Jackson, being the only man left in the house, took on the responsibility looking after his mother and ensuring their household continued to run smoothly.

As Jackson prepared to leave for college, Sarah felt a mix of pride and sadness. She knew it was time for him to spread his wings and pursue his dreams, but the thought of being alone without her son by her side was overwhelming. She had always relied on Jackson's strength and presence, and the idea of facing life without him seemed daunting.

However, Sarah understood that she had to let Jackson go. She wanted him to have the opportunity to grow and discover himself, just as his father would have wanted. So, with a heavy heart, she bid him farewell and watched as he embarked on this new chapter of his life.

At that moment, all the worries and fears melted away. Sarah felt a surge of excitement, knowing that her son was home, even if just for a little while. Jackson swung her around, their laughter filling the room, as they reveled in the joy of being together again.

As they settled back onto the couch, Sarah couldn't help but marvel at how much Jackson had grown. He was no longer the little boy she had raised, but a strong, independent, young man. She admired his tenicity and resilience, knowing that he had faced his own challenges, while away at college.

Despite the distance, Jackson had always made an effort to stay connected with his mother. He would call her every day, sharing stories of his classes, friends, and adventures. He would even bring his dirty laundry home, a small reminder of the days, when they would tackle household chores together.

And of course, Jackson's healthy appetite remained unchanged. Sarah would always prepare his favorite meals, ensuring that he felt the warmth and comfort of home whenever he returned.

As they sat there, talking and laughing, Sarah couldn't help but feel a sense of gratitude. She was grateful for the time that they had together, grateful for the love they shared, and grateful for the strength they had found in each other during the darkest of times.

At that moment, Sarah knew that no matter where life took them, their bond would always remain unbreakable. Jackson would forever be her favorite boy, and she would always be his biggest supporter. Jackson wrapped his arms around her. His voice filled with genuine joy as he greeted his favorite girl.

But amidst the joyous reunion, Jackson couldn't shake off the newfound feelings stirring within him. He could not help but notice the Ramona's eyes sparkled when she laughed, or the way her smile lit up the room. He himself captivated by her presence, his heart beating faster with each passing moment. As he looked at Ramona, he realized that his affection for her had transformed into something deeper, something he had never experienced before. It was as if a switch had been flipped, and he saw her in a whole new light.

Sarah introduced her son to Ramona. Apologizing for her rudeness, Ramona recognized Jackson and tried to shake his hand, but he hugged her instead. Ramona commented on how she hadn't seen him since he was a child, and complimented him on his appearance. Jackson said her name in a deep voice, causing Ramona's heart to race. Sarah insisted that Ramona stay and join them for dinner, but Ramona declined, saying they had a lot of catching up to do and promised to call Sarah the next day. Ramona hurriedly left the house, closing the door behind her as her heart skipped a beat.

Jackson's admiration for Ramona had grown steadily over the years. From an age, he had witnessed her unwavering kindness and warmth, always there for his mother in times of need. But as he grew older, he became more infatuated to her. Not just his mother's best friend, Ramona became a woman, who had experienced her own fair share of heartache and loss.

Ramona was known for her strength and resilience. When Jackson was a young boy, he referred to the couple as Aunt Ramona and Uncle Mark. Their marriage initially seemed full of love and joy. They had established a happy home together, but over time, he, too, had sensed a shift in their relationship. The love they once shared began to fade, but he never expected Uncle Mark to be on the down low.

He couldn't help but wonder, if there was a chance for something more between them. But with their complicated history and the fear of losing another loved one, would Jackson be willing to take the risk and pursue a relationship with the woman, who had become so much more than just his Mother's best friend?

Chapter 2

Secret Lovers

After the encounter in Jackson's living room, he never thought about Ramona. One day, however, their paths crossed and she found herself drawn to him in a way she had never before. She seen him around town, but never had the courage to approach him. Ramona was captivated by his piercing brown eyes and the way he moved. As the hours turned into days and the days into nights, a profound transformation unfolded before his eyes. With each passing moment, he found himself captivated by the subtle shifts in Ramona's demeanor. What was once a laughter tinged with a hint of sorrow had blossomed into a genuine, unadulterated joy that radiated from her very being. The heaviness that once clouded her eyes, burdened by grief, had been replaced by a newfound sparkle, a resilient glimmer that spoke volumes of her strength. In those enchanting moments, he couldn't help but be spellbound by her beauty and the profound connection he felt with her.

But it wasn't until one fateful evening, as they sat together on the porch, sharing stories and memories, that Jackson realized his feelings had evolved beyond admiration. He found himself captivated by Ramona's strength, her ability to find light in the darkest of times. He saw her as a beacon of hope, a reminder that even in the face of tragedy, it was possible to find happiness again.

Jackson's crush on Ramona took him by surprise. He had never expected to develop such feelings for his mother's best friend. But as he reflected on their shared experiences of loss and heartache, he realized that their connection ran deeper than he had initially thought.

It was a warm Tuesday night, the air heavy with the scent of summer. The full moon high in the sky, an ethereal glow over the quiet street. Not a soul could be seen inside the houses that lined the road, their inhabitants hidden away in the comfort of their homes.

Jackson strolled leisurely down the sidewalk, his hands buried deep in the pockets of his jeans. He had just left his mom's house, where she had lovingly prepared his favorite dish, lasagna. The taste still lingered on his tongue, a comforting reminder of home.

As he continued his solitary walk, lost in his own thoughts, a commotion broke the silence. Ramona emerged from her house, her loyal companion Coco bounding excitedly beside her. But in a moment of distraction, the mischievous dog darted off the porch and down the street, his paws pounding against the pavement.

Ramona's heart raced as she called out Coco's name, her voice filled with worry and desperation. Panic surged through her veins as she chased after her beloved pet, her feet pounding against the concrete. But just as she feared Coco would disappear into the night, a figure emerged from the shadows, swift and determined.

It was Jackson.

His eyes fixed on the runaway dog, and with a burst of energy, he sprinted after Coco, his long strides closing the distance between them. In one swift motion, he scooped up the mischievous canine, saving him from the dangers of the street.

Relief washed over Ramona as she reached Jackson's side, her breath coming in ragged gasps. Gratitude filled her eyes as she looked up at him, her deep, dark brown orbs shining with appreciation. She thanked him profusely, her voice filled with genuine gratitude for his timely intervention.

But as their eyes locked, something shifted in the air. Time seemed to stand still as Jackson found himself captivated by Ramona's gaze. There was an undeniable connection, an unspoken understanding that transcended mere gratitude. And At that moment, a spark ignited, setting their hearts ablaze.

They began to talk, their conversations flowing effortlessly as they discovered the depths of each other's souls. Secret meetings became their refuge, hidden away from prying eyes, where they could explore not only their minds but also the contours of their bodies. The affair consumed them, becoming an intoxicating blend of passion and desire.

For Ramona, it felt like she was living in a dream, every stolen moment with Jackson an eternity of bliss. The world around them faded into insignificance as they reveled in the intensity of their connection. But little did they know, their indiscretions will be mentally intoxicating.

Jackson is sitting at the breakfast table, lost in a daydream about his passionate affair with Ramona, his mother, Sarah, engaging him in conversation. She serves his favorite breakfast — buttermilk pancakes, eggs, sausages, and freshly squeezed orange juice — as Jackson's mind wanders to memories of Ramona's soft, ruby red lips on his body's lower region. Sarah places the plate in front of Jackson, who, though eternally grateful for his mother's cooking, is still lost in thought. As he pours syrup on his pancakes, Sarah yells and turns around, noticing the mess he's made.

"What are you doing?" She quickly grabs a dishcloth to clean it up. Jackson snaps out of his daze.

"I'm sorry!"

Sarah laughs, teasing him about a girl being the cause of his distraction. "Who's the girl?"

Jackson denies it, "I don't know what you are talking about" Claiming Sarah is the only girl in his life and hugs her.

As they continue to talk, Sarah's phone rings, Ramona's name flashing on the screen. Sarah answers the call and after a moment Jackson, too, finds out that Ramona called since she needed help to move furniture for a dinner party. Sarah promises to send Jackson over after he finishes his breakfast.

"I don't think that is a good idea."

Jackson, feeling nervous and conflicted, continues eating his breakfast, while Sarah insists that he go to assist Ramona. Reluctantly, he volunteers, not knowing that he's being unwittingly sent into a lion den by his mother.

Jackson stepped out of his house, the taste of breakfast still lingering in his mouth. His mother's voice echoed in his ears, nagging him about helping Ramona. He hurriedly made his way down the street, growing sense of regret gnawing at his conscience. How could he have let himself get involved with his mom's best friend? It was a mistake, a moment of weakness that now haunted him with every step.

As he approached Ramona's house, his hesitation grew. Should he ring the doorbell? Should he face the consequences of his actions head-on? Before he could make a decision, the door swung open, revealing Ramona standing there, a knowing smile on her face. She had seen him on the ring cam, catching him in the act of arriving.

"Quick, come in," Ramona urged, her voice filled with urgency. "My guests will be here soon." Without a word, Jackson closed the door behind him and began helping Ramona rearrange the furniture. Exhausted, they both collapsed onto the couch, but Jackson's unease only grew as Ramona's hand began to caress his thigh.

He felt his nerves intensify. "Thanks for helping me," Ramona whispered, her voice laced with gratitude. "I would've never gotten this done without you."

Jackson's mouth went dry, his mind racing for an escape. "I should be going now," he stammered, attempting to rise from the couch. He knew he should push her away, put an end to this dangerous game they had been playing. But as her body pressed against his, he couldn't deny the electric current that surged between them.

 "I cannot do this anymore," Jackson managed to say, voice strained with both yearning and guilt. "You are my mother's friend." He knew deep down that this was wrong, that their connection was magical. But as Ramona climbed on top of him, her breath hot against his ear, all rational thoughts seemed to evaporate.

"If this is wrong," Ramona murmured, her voice barely audible, "I don't want to be right." At that moment Jackson gave into temptations.

Little did he know, this illicit affair would set in motion a series of events that would forever change their lives.

As the heat between them intensified, Jackson's body glistened with sweat and his desire was palpable. Ramona felt her own temperature rising as she boldly unzipped his pants, the anticipation building with each passing moment. Without hesitation, they moved closer to the table, their passion igniting a reckless abandon within them. In a bold and daring move, Ramona swept all the dishes onto the floor, signaling their mutual desire to give in to their primal urges. Jackson seized her in a fervent embrace, their bodies entwined as they succumbed to the raw, unbridled passion that consumed them on the table.

The hot and steamy affair led them to the bedroom. As they moved closer to each other, the air between them seemed to crackle with electricity. His hands touched her waist, pulling her in close, and their lips met in a passionate kiss.

Jackson's hands explored her body, caressing her curves, as her lips trailed down his neck. His breathing grew heavier as her tongue moved lower and lower.

The heat between them was almost unbearable, as his hands caressed her body, exploring every inch of her skin. She could feel his desire for her, as his hands moved lower and lower, each touch sending a wave of pleasure through her body.

He moved inside her and they both gasped as their bodies moved together in perfect harmony. His thrusts grew faster and faster as they moved closer and closer to the edge. Finally, they both reached their climax and collapsed in each other's arms, exhausted and blissful.

They lay tangled in each other's arms, and the weight of their secret love affair finally began to settle in. Ramona and Jackson knew they couldn't keep their passion hidden forever. The question lingered in the air, heavy with uncertainty, how would they navigate the treacherous waters of revealing their forbidden love to his mother.

Jackson abruptly woke up and hastily got out of bed, accidentally tripping over his shoe and falling to the floor. Ramona, noticing his actions, asked him where he was going. After quickly fixing his clothing, Jackson expressed regret and stated that he needed to leave. Ramona approached him and tried to reassure him that their actions would remain a secret. However, Jackson insisted that their encounter could not be repeated and abruptly left the room. Ramona, feeling frustrated, threw a pillow at the door as her dog looked on in confusion.

It's a Friday evening and Sarah is filled with an unexpected burst of energy. Restless and bored to stay cooped up in the house, she reached out to her best friend, Ramona. Ramona glanced at her caller ID and rolls her eyes, not particularly thrilled about talking to Sarah at the moment. Especially, not after the recent sexual encounter she had with her son, Jackson. Reluctantly, Ramona pushes the call button, her voice laced with a hint of annoyance as she answers.

"Hey, girl! It's after nine, is everything okay?"

Sarah, in her usual cheerful tone, responds, "Everything is fine. I haven't heard from you in a while."

Ramona's irritation grows as the conversation continues.

"Girl, you know me, I'm always busy," she retorts.

But Sarah searches for a distraction, a reason to keep engaging with her best friend, and glances at the papers scattered across her dining table.

"Do you feel like going out for a nightcap?" she asks.

Ramona is shocked by the suggestion. "What? You want to go out?" Sarah, equally surprised, questions Ramona's response.

"Why did you say it like that?"

Ramona, with a hint of resignation, replies, "Sure, I have nothing else to do."

Sarah's excitement is palpable as she exclaims, "Great! Meet me at Jake's place."

Ramona disconnects the call, whispering to herself, "Why Jake's place?"

Fifteen minutes later, Ramona arrived at Jake's place. She approached Sarah with an insincere smile on her face. Sarah had taken the initiative to order beverages for both of them. Ramona leaned in and patted Sarah on the back.

"I took the liberty of ordering drinks," Sarah responded.

Ramona was perplexed as Sarah was not typically inclined towards nightlife or social gatherings. Sarah was more of a homebody Ramona remained puzzled by this sudden meeting and began to feel anxious. Could Sarah have discovered the sexual encounter Ramona had with her son Jackson just a few hours ago?

Ramona gave Sarah a small smile and said, "Thank you for the drink. Sarah, this is out of character for you. Why did you choose Jake's place? You don't usually drink."

Sarah was speechless.

Ramona, on the other hand, appeared calm

Sarah made a bold career transition over the years, shifting from nursing to interior design. She has always had a keen eye for home decor.

"I know, but I needed to leave the house. I have a significant project's presentation tomorrow, and I'm feeling nervous."

Ramona, on the other hand, appeared calm.

"Girl, you've got this. You are the best interior designer in Philadelphia." Sarah noticed that Ramona seemed radiant.

"Ramona, you look different."

Ramona hesitated for a moment, before responding,

"Oh, really? How so?"

Sarah studied her friend's face, noticing a certain radiance that she hadn't seen before.

"Well, your eyes seem brighter, and there's a certain glow about you. It's like you're... happy."

Ramona's smile faltered slightly, and she quickly averted her gaze.

"Oh, it's probably just the lighting in here. You know how dimly lit Jake's place can be."

Sarah wasn't convinced. She had known Ramona for years, and this sudden change in demeanor was unusual. But before she could press further, their drinks arrived, distracting them momentarily. As they clinked their glasses together, Sarah couldn't shake the feeling that something was off. She decided to tread carefully, not wanting to ruin their night. But deep down, she couldn't shake the nagging suspicion that there was more to Ramona's sudden arrival than met the eye.

Ramona holds her wine glass while Sarah peruses the dinner menu.

"I'm famished! I can't decide what to order. Everything on the menu looks so appetizing," Sarah remarks.

Ramona pushes the menu aside and says, "Sarah, there's something I need to discuss with you."

Sarah becomes concerned and asks, "What's wrong? Are you feeling unwell?"

Ramona explains, "No, it's not that."

Sarah breathes a sigh of relief.

"Then what is it?"

Ramona takes a deep breath and says, "I've decided to ask for a divorce from Mark."

Sarah is shocked and questions, "Are you certain about getting a divorce?"

Ramona lowers her head and replies, "Yes, the betrayal runs too deep."

Sarah sympathizes, saying, "I understand, Ramona, but you've been married to Mark for 20 years. Are you ready to give that up?"

Ramona smiles and says, "Yes, I'm sure. Besides, I've started seeing someone else and the sex is fulfilling."

Sarah covers her mouth in surprise and exclaims, "I knew it! It's written all over your face."

Ramona blushes and admits, "I wanted to tell you, but I didn't want to jinx it. Sarah, you should start dating again."

Sarah laughs and responds, "I'm not ready for that just yet."

"How much longer do you intend to wait?" Ramona inquired.

Sarah covered her face with her hand.

"The dating scene has significantly changed over the past two decades. Therefore, I am doubtful that there is a suitable partner for me out there," Sarah expressed.

Ramona responded, "How can you be certain if you are unwilling to make an effort? Besides, as the saying goes, 'if you don't use it, you'll lose it.'"

Sarah glanced around the room discreetly to ensure no one was eavesdropping.

"God, leave it to you to say something like that. And in public, too!" Sarah remarked in a resigned manner.

Ramona picked up her phone and sent a flirtatious text message to Jackson. She promptly placed the phone back down to resume her conversation with Sarah.

"I mean, I've been single for so long, don't even know where to begin." Ramona leaned in closer, her voice filled with excitement. "Well, I have someone in mind for you. His name is Ethan, and he's a friend of the guy I've been seeing."

Sarah raised an eyebrow, intrigued. "Really? Tell me more about him."

Ramona grinned mischievously.

"He's tall, dark, and handsome, with a fantastic sense of humor."
Ramona glances around to see if anyone is listening, then leans
in closer to Sarah. "Let's just say, he'll have you speaking in
tongues. Lord knows you could use a little of that. I really think
you two would hit it off." Sarah's jaw drops in surprise. She's
embarrassed, but Sarah can help to feel a of pounding in her
chest.

"Well, maybe it's time for me to take a leap of faith and give
love another chance."

Ramona clinked her glass against Sarah's.

"To new beginnings, my dear. Cheers!"

As they toasted, Sarah couldn't help but feel a glimmer of hope
for what the future held. Little did she know, this dinner
conversation would be the catalyst for a journey she never
expected.

Chapter 3

The Betrayal

It had been a long day for Sarah, filled with meetings, deadlines, and the constant demands of her job. Exhausted, she finally decided to take a quick break and escape into the virtual world on her phone. As she sat down on her couch, she unlocked her phone and began scrolling through her inbox, hoping to find a momentary distraction from the chaos of her day.

Messages from friends, family, and colleagues filled her screen, each one vying for her attention. But amidst the sea notifications, one particular message caught her eye. It was from an unfamiliar number, devoid of a name or any context. Curiosity piqued, Sarah hesitated for a moment before opening it, unaware of the storm that was about submerge her.

Her eyes widened in disbelief as she read the explicit words adorned the screen. Confusion and shock washed over her, leaving her frozen in her place. Could this be happening? Who would send such a message to her?

As her mind raced to make sense of the situation, a sinking feeling settled in the pit of her stomach. It was then that she noticed the attachment, a video file that accompanied the message. Trembling, she hesitated for a moment, her thumb hovering over the play button. She knew deep down that whatever lay within that video would forever change her life. With a shaking hand, Sarah pressed play, her heart pounding in her ears. The screen flickered to life, revealing a scene that shattered her world in an instant. It was a video of her son and her best friend Ramona in a compromising sexual position. Ramona record their sexual affair. Sarah is devastated, her best friend, her confidante, and the last person she would ever suspect of such a betrayal.

Sarah's breath caught in her throat as she watched the explicit nature of the video unfold before her eyes. The shock and disbelief were overwhelming, threatening to consume her entirely. How could Ramona, someone she trusted implicitly, be involved in something so unspeakable? Questions swirled in her mind, but answers seemed elusive, leaving her drowning in a sea of confusion and despair.

As the video came to an end, Sarah's world shattered into a million pieces. The trust she had placed in her friend, the safety she had felt within her own home, all crumbled in an instant. With tears streaming down her face, she clutched her phone tightly, her mind racing with a mix of emotions — anger, betrayal, and an overwhelming need for justice.

Sarah knew that her life would never be the same again. The path ahead was uncertain, filled with darkness and pain. But one thing was clear — she would stop at nothing to uncover the truth, to protect her son from going down the road of heartache and destruction.

Sarah sat on the couch, her mind filled with anger and confusion. The door creaked open, and Jackson, walked in, sweaty from his evening jog. He attempted to hug his mother, but instead, she gave him an evil stare.

Sarah walked closer to Jackson, her eyes burning with fury.

"Where did you go?"

Jackson furrowed his brows, trying to understand what his mother was getting at.

"I went for a jog, like I do every night."

"Why?"

"What's wrong with you?" Jackson asked, shock by her coldness.

"No, what's wrong with you? Have you lost your mind?" Sarah snapped back, her voice filled with disappointment.

Confused, Jackson took a step back. "I don't know why you're so angry. What did I do?"

Sarah yelled at him, her voice filled with accusation. "So, you're a porn star now?"

Jackson's confusion turned into shock. He couldn't comprehend why his mother would say such a thing. "Mom, what are you talking about?"

Sarah pushed her phone into Jackson's chest, her hands trembling with anger. "Look at this video!"

Jackson reluctantly took the phone and pressed play. As the video played, his mouth right along with his heart dropped to the floor. He couldn't believe what he was seeing.

Sarah's voice trembled with hurt. "How could you do this to me? She is my best friend!"

Jackson desperately tried to explain the situation to his mother. "Mom, I didn't mean to hurt you. It just happened. I never wanted to betray you."

Sarah yelled at him, her voice filled with pain. "I do not want you to see her ever again. Do you hear me?"

Jackson cautiously entered the kitchen, his voice trembling as he spoke. "Mom, where did you get that video? I don't remember recording anything with that woman."

Sarah turned to face him, her eyes filled with a mixture of anger and disappointment. Without a word, she walked over to him and delivered a sharp blow to the back of his head. The pain jolted through Jackson's body, but he knew he deserved it.

"How could you be so stupid, Jackson?" Sarah's voice was filled with frustration. "Ramona is not who she seems. She's the blackmail queen, and now you're tangled up in her web."

"I'm sorry, Mom," Jackson whispered, his voice filled with remorse. "I didn't know. I don't know what to do."

 Sarah's glare softened slightly, but her anger was still evident. "Get out of my face," she snapped. "I will take care of this situation."

Jackson approaches the staircase while Sarah remarks, "You reek of betrayal. Go and take a shower." Sarah proceeds to the kitchen and pours herself a glass of red wine. Consumed by anger, she finds herself unable to shed tears. She now faces the daunting task of confronting Ramona

Feeling defeated, Jackson turned and walked towards the stairs. As he climbed them, he couldn't help but feel the weight of his mistakes pressing down on him. He knew he had to find a way to make things right, to protect his mother from the consequences of his actions.

Once in his room, Jackson closed the door behind him and sank onto his bed. He felt a mixture of shame and fear.

Jackson, devastated by his mother's reaction, never saw Ramona again. He wished he could turn back time and make different choices, but it was too late. He had lost not only his mother's respect but also a part of himself.

The next day, Sarah mustered up the courage to confront Ramona. "Ramona, we need to talk," she said her voice filled with a mix of anger and sadness. Ramona, sensing the urgency in Sarah's tone, replied,

"What's wrong? You sound upset."

Sarah took a deep breath, realizing this was not a conversation to be had over the phone. "This is not something we can discuss over the phone, Ramona," she explained. Without waiting for a response, Sarah quickly hung up, leaving Ramona bewildered and curious about what could be so important.

Driven by a sense of unease, Ramona wasted no time and drove straight to Sarah's house. As she approached the door, her heart raced with anticipation. Sarah swung the door open with a glaring attitude, her eyes filled with a mix of anger and hurt. Ramona stepped into the house, feeling a sudden wave of discomfort wash over her. Something was definitely not right.

Sarah wasted no time in getting to the point. "Do you have something to tell me?" she asked, her voice laced with accusation. Ramona's mind raced, trying to make sense of the situation.

"Tell you what? What is going on?" she replied, her confusion evident. Sarah's frustration grew, her patience wearing thin.

"I don't have time to be playing these cat and mouse games with you," she snapped.

Ramona's puzzlement deepened, her mind searched for answers. Sarah's next words hit her like a ton of bricks.

"Why are you having sex with my son?" Sarah's accusation hung in the air, leaving Ramona speechless. She struggled to find the right words, her mind racing to comprehend the gravity of the situation. Sarah's anger was palpable, her eyes burning with a mix of betrayal and disbelief.

"Don't even try to deny it," she continued, her voice strained with emotion. "Why would you do something like this?"

 Ramona was dumbfounded by the question, her mind racing to find an explanation. She became defensive, her voice filled with a mix of guilt and defiance.

"We've been seeing each other for a while," she finally admitted, her voice barely above a whisper. "I didn't do anything wrong."

 Sarah now properly furious replies, "He's my son."

Ramona approached Sarah, her heart pounding in her chest as she tried to find right words to say. "Look Sarah, I know you're upset. But Jackson is a grown ass man," she began, her voice trembling slightly.

Sarah's tear-streaked face turned towards Ramona, her eyes filled with a mix of betrayal and hurt. "You were supposed to be my friend, I trusted you. I was always there for you, even when your ass was in trouble. I was there for you, and this is how you repay me? By screwing my son?"

Ramona's voice dripped with sarcasm, her words laced with bitterness.

"I'm sorry," Ramona managed to say, her voice barely above a whisper. Sarah moved closer to Ramona, her anger radiating off her in waves.

"You are a heartless bitch," Sarah spat, her voice filled with venom. Ramona was shocked, unable to believe that Sarah was talking to her that way. They had been through so much together, and now it seemed like everything was falling apart.

With all the commotion downstairs, Jackson heard the raised voices and quickly ran down to see what was going on. He stood between the two women, not knowing how to go about the situation. He knew he had to diffuse the situation before things got even more hostile. Ramona reached out and touched Jackson's shoulder, her eyes pleading with him.

"Can you please tell your mother that we are in love?" she asked softly.

Suddenly, there was a loud slap that echoed through the room. Ramona's face stung with pain as Sarah's hand connected with her cheek. The room fell silent, the tension thick in the air. Sarah's voice was filled with rage as she shouted.

"You trifling bitch, stay away from my son!" Jackson quickly stepped in, blocking Sarah's path as she tried to hit Ramona again. His voice was firm, yet filled with sadness.

"Ramona, I think you should leave," he said, his eyes pleading with her to understand.

Sarah yelled, "Get the hell out my house." Ramona starts walking towards the door. She blows Jackson a kiss. "I will see you tomorrow, my love," she expresses. Sarah makes another attempt to get a go at Ramona, but Jackson intervenes by restraining her before any contact is made.

Consequently, their friendship undergoes an irreparable change.

Chapter 4

Misery Deserves Company

Ramona lounges on her sofa, watching an episode of City Couture Confessions, snacking on her samosa as she waits for her food delivery from Serenity Grove Bistro. Abruptly, a knock at the door startles her from her relaxed state. Assuming it's the Savior Eats delivery person, she opens the door without much thought. However, it turns out to be her ex-husband, Mark. Ramona, displeased by his presence, confronts him, questioning his motives. Mark insists he's there to retrieve his belongings, but Ramona, uninterested in engaging with him, directs him to the basement to collect his things. Once Mark is in the basement, Ramona locks the door behind him.

Ramona stood there, her heartbeat loud in her chest as she watched Mark disappear into the depths of the basement. She couldn't believe he had the audacity to show up unannounced, expecting her to welcome him with open arms. The nerve of him, thinking he could just waltz into her life after everything he had done.

As she locked the basement door, a mix of anger and satisfaction washed over her. It was a small victory, but one that felt so sweet. Mark deserved to be locked away, just like he had locked away her trust and shattered their marriage. Turning away from the basement door, Ramona took a deep breath, trying to calm the storm of emotions swirling inside her. She knew this was just the beginning, that there were still battles to be fought and wounds to be healed. But for now, she relished in the feeling of reclaiming her power, of taking control of her own life.

Walking back to the living room, Ramona sank back onto the sofa, her eyes fixed on the television screen. The show she had been watching before Mark's unwelcome arrival continued to play, but her mind was elsewhere. Thoughts of the past, of the pain and infidelity, mingled with thoughts of the future, of the strength and resilience she had discovered within herself.

After some time, Ramona's food from Serenity Grove Bistro arrived, but she had lost her appetite. The samosa sat untouched on the coffee table, a reminder of the interrupted peace, she had been enjoying just moments ago. But she refused to let Mark's unexpected visit ruin her day any further.

Picking up the remote, Ramona turned off the television, silencing the noise of City Couture Confessions. She needed a moment of silence, a chance to gather her thoughts and find her center once again. And as she sat there in the quiet of her living room, she couldn't help but feel a glimmer of hope, a flicker of excitement for the new chapter that lay ahead. Ramona knew that locking Mark in the basement was just the first step in her plot of revenge.

Jackson sat in his car, his hands gripping the steering wheel as he called Ramona's number. Every moment of the past few hours played over and over in his mind, intensifying his anger and confusion. His mother house became a war zone, where friendships fell apart and trust broken.

Ramona used to be very close to his mother, but now their relationship was destroyed. She asked him to come over to her place, saying there was something important to discuss. However, Jackson could sense there was something deeper going on. The way she looked at him, the subtle glances and lingering touches, indicates a desire he wants no part of.

As he entered her house, the air felt heavy with tension. Ramona wasted no time in trying to seduce him, her advances met with a firm rejection. He couldn't understand why she would even attempt such a thing, knowing the consequences it would bring. Anger burned within him as he demanded answers.

"Why did you record our encounter?" Jackson's voice carried a clear tone of frustration, his eyes desperately seeking any sign of remorse on Ramona's face.

She hesitated, her gaze shifting away. "I... I don't know. It was a mistake, Jackson. I never meant for it to go that far."

His anger grew stronger as she provided no explanation. "And the text you sent to my mother? Was that a mistake, too?"

Ramona's voice trembled as she tried to justify her actions.

"Yes, it was an accident. I didn't mean to involve her, I swear."

Ramona grabbed Jackson's hands, attempting to explain the situation. However, he flinched from her with a feeling of disgust.

Ramona pleads, "Please, allow me to explain. Your mother and I went out for a late-night drink, and right after our sexual encounter, too."

Jackson's anger begins to escalate.

"Ramona," he interrupts.

Startled, Ramona quickly responds, "Alright, alright."

She proceeds with her explanation, "During our conversation, your mother noticed a sort of glow about me. And I mistakenly sent a text meant for you to your mother, as she was the last person I had conversed with on the phone."

Jackson becomes livid, exclaiming, "How could you be so irresponsible? Don't you check your call log before sending a text to someone?"

Ramona expresses deep remorse, saying, "Babe, I have sincerely apologized."

Jackson's patience wore thin and determined. He firmly said. "I can't see you anymore, Ramona. This ends here."

But as he turned to leave, a sudden thump echoed from the basement, freezing him in his tracks. He glanced back at Ramona, his eyes narrowing with suspicion.

"What was that noise?"

She took a brief moment to hesitate before providing a weak explanation. "It's just the washing machine, Jackson. Nothing to worry about." Jackson quickly exit Ramona's house without a word.

It had been two weeks since he broke up with Ramona, yet anger and a sense of betrayal still consumed Ramona's heart. She couldn't believe eyes as she watched him, Jackson laughing and mingling with another woman. The sight was like a dagger through her chest, fueling a rage she had never known before.

Unable to bear the sight any longer, Ramona stormed out of the coffee shop, her mind racing with thoughts of revenge.

Ramona entered to her office, staring at the closed door, Ramona couldn't help but feel a pang of sadness. Going back to work was supposed to distract her from the pain she had been feeling, but it seemed to only amplify it. The tears that had filled her eyes earlier threatened to spill over once more.

But Ramona was determined to push through. She had built a reputation as a successful real estate broker, and she wasn't about to let personal struggles get in the way of her career. She wiped away the tears, took a deep breath, and forced herself to focus on the task at hand. Just as she was about to dive back into her work, there was a knock on her door. The receptionist informed her that her 2:00 PM appointment had arrived. Ramona straightened her posture and put on her professional smile, ready to meet her clients.

The Wilson family entered her office, and Ramona greeted them warmly. She offered them all seats and coffee, a small gesture that seemed to put them at ease. Mr. Wilson began explaining their search for a condominium for their daughter, while Ramona observed the young lady sitting across from her. There was something about her that struck a chord with Ramona, a familiarity that she couldn't quite place. She racked her brain, trying to remember if they had crossed paths before, but nothing came to mind. Perhaps it was just a passing resemblance to someone she knew.

As Mrs. Wilson expressed her concern for her daughter's safety, Ramona reassured them that they had nothing to worry about. She prided herself on her knowledge of the city and its neighborhoods, and she was confident in her ability to find the perfect place for their daughter.

By the ends of the meeting, the Wilson family seemed comfortable with their decision to have Ramona as their broker. They thanked her for her time and left the office, leaving Ramona alone once again. As she watched them walk away, Ramona decided to go home early.

She dashed down the street, a lady caught her attention. There was something about her, something familiar.

It was as if a switch had been flipped in Ramona's mind, and suddenly, she knew. It was the Wilson girl who she saw at the coffee shop with Jackson.

Jackson's betrayal had ignited a dark side in Ramona, leading her to come up with an idea. She proceeded to walk down the street in an attempt to catch up to Allison. Ramona approached the lady and politely said,

"Excuse me, Miss Wilson. Do you remember me? I am Ramona from Skyline Central Realtors."

Initially startled, Miss Wilson soon recognized Ramona and replied, "Yes, my parents and I visited your office earlier to inquire about a condominium." Ramona pretended to be out of breath as she continued,

"I have been trying to reach your parents for the past two hours. I have found a perfect place for you."

Excited by this news, Allison responded, "That's wonderful!" Ramona gave her a sly smile and added,

"The owners are eager to sell the property as soon as possible, as they have received other offers. We need to act swiftly."

Allison reached for her phone to call her parents, but Ramona interrupted, shouting,

"No, how about I show you the property first? If you like it, then you can call your parents."

Initially hesitant, Allison eventually agreed,

"There's no harm in seeing the place first. We can take my car."

Ramona nodded, her smirk widening.

As they walked towards Allison's car, Ramona couldn't help but feel a sense of satisfaction. Her plan was falling into place perfectly. Allison unknowingly walked into her trap, Ramona knew she had the upper hand.

They arrived at the property, a beautiful condo nestled in the heart of the city. Ramona unlocked the door and gestured for Allison to step inside. As they explored the rooms, Ramona couldn't help but notice the excitement in Allison's eyes. She knew she had found the perfect bait.

"This place is amazing," Allison exclaimed, her voice filled with awe. "I can't believe we stumbled upon such a gem."

Ramona's smirk grew wider.

"Yes, it truly is a hidden treasure," she replied, her voice dripping with deceit. "And the best part is, the owners are desperate to sell. They've already received multiple offers, but I have a feeling they'll be willing to negotiate with us."

Allison's eyes widened with anticipation.

"Really? That's incredible! We have to act fast then."

Ramona nodded, her mind already calculating the next steps of her plan.

"Exactly. We need to make an offer they can't refuse. And with your parents' approval, we can seal the deal before anyone else has a chance."

Allison hesitated for a moment, her phone still in her hand.

"I should really call my parents first," she said, her voice filled with a hint of caution.

Ramona's smile faltered for a split second, but she quickly regained her composure.

"Of course, Allison. But wouldn't it be better to show them the property first? Let them see it with their own eyes before making any decisions?"

Allison pondered for a moment, her trust wavering. But ultimately, her excitement got the better of her.

"You're right,"

Ramona suggests that Allison should contact her parents in the home office. Allison begins dialing the when suddenly, Ramona approaches her from behind with a cloth containing a potent substance. Ramona swiftly places the cloth over Allison's mouth, causing her to lose consciousness and fall to the floor. Ramona is plans was set in place.

She would make Jackson suffer, just as he had made her suffer. She didn't think twice before snatching the young girl, driven by her anger and desperation to carry out unspeakable actions.

Deep within the confines of Ramona's basement, the girl endured unimaginable torture, her cries for help echoes through the cold, damp walls. But she was not alone. Ramona's missing husband, a secret unknown to the world, was also trapped in that forbidden to place. Ramona had become a monster, a twisted soul consumed by vengeance.

That evening, Ramona made the decision to confront the intruders in her basement. She switched on the light, causing it to flicker, and the wooden steps creaked under the weight of her red 6-inch heels. Eventually, at the bottom of the steps where she discovered two individuals who were bound. In one corner stood her ex-husband, while in the other corner was a girl from the coffee shop. The young girl appeared bewildered and unaware of the situation. Ramona removed the tape from her ex-husband Mark's mouth, prompting him to question her actions.

Ramona remained silent. She then approached the other girl and forcefully removed the tape from her mouth. The young lady immediately began pleading for her life, requesting to be released. Ramona responded with laughter, stating that both individuals needed to conserve their energy as they would be staying there for a while. Mark pleaded with Ramona, urging her to release the innocent young lady. Ramona, with an evil laugh, retorted that the young lady was not innocent, as she had stolen her man.

Confused, the girl asked, "What man?"

Ramona's eyes narrowed as she glared at the girl.

"Don't play dumb with me," she said. "I saw you flirting with Jackson at the coffee shop. You think I wouldn't notice? Well, now you're going to pay for it."

Her eyes widened in fear, her voice trembling as she spoke.

"I swear, I didn't know you guys were together. We were just talking, I promise."

Ramona, her anger boiling over. "Talking? Is that what you call it? You think I'm stupid? I know what you were doing, trying to steal him away from me."

Mark, still tied up in the corner, interjected desperately.

"Ramona, please, this is insane. Let her go. This has nothing to do with her or Jackson, remember? Besides, Jackson is your best friend son. We can work this out. "

Ramona ignored him, her focus solely on the girl.

"You know what? I don't care if you knew him or not. You're going to suffer just like I did."

Tears streamed down the girl's face as she pleaded once more.

"Please, I didn't mean any harm. I didn't know Jackson was your boyfriend. I'm sorry."

Ramona's laughter filled the basement, echoing off the cold walls.

"Sorry? Sorry won't change anything. You've ruined my life, and now it's time for you to experience the pain I've endured."

As Ramona reached for a knife on a nearby table, the girl's eyes widened in terror.

"No, please! I'll do anything, just let me go!"

But Ramona was consumed by her rage, her heart filled with vengeance. She lunged towards the girl, the knife glinting in the dim basement light.

But Just as she was about to strike, a sudden ring of the doorbell shattered the silence, freezing her in her tracks.

Chapter 5

Obsessed

Margaret Anderson, the mother of Mark, was seated comfortably in her preferred rocking chair within confines of her own residence. Engaged in knitting a blanket for her neighbor's newborn daughter, Margaret glanced at the clock and realized it was past noon. Typically, Mark would call her at this time to remind to take her morning medication. However, once again, he failed to do, causing her to become concerned. Setting aside her knitting needles, Margaret reached for her mobile phone and checked her messages, hoping to find a missed call from her son. To her surprise, there were no messages or calls from him. Margaret made the decision to call Mark, but he did not answer.

However, she was unable to leave a voicemail due to his full mailbox. This behavior was uncharacteristic of Mark, prompting Margaret to visit Ramona's house in order to ascertain if Mark had returned home. Typically, Mark would utilize a ride-sharing service for her, but Margaret was unfamiliar with this process and instead opted to call a taxi. Eventually, she arrived at Ramona's house and knocked on the door, only to be met with a hostile expression on Ramona's face.

Mrs. Anderson was at the door, her eyes filled with worry and desperation. Ramona, filled with bitterness, had trapped her ex-husband in the basement as an act of vengeance. Margaret's heart sank as she saw the expression on Ramona's face. It was a look she had never seen before, and it sent a shiver down her spine. Something was terribly wrong.

"Ramona, is everything alright?"

Margaret asked, her voice a bit shaky with concern.

Ramona's eyes darted nervously, avoiding Margaret's gaze.

"Oh, Mama Anderson," she finally managed to say, her voice strained.

"Ramona, hi, I need to talk to you."

For a moment, Ramona's anger wavered as she watched the woman's trembling hands clutching onto a faded photograph of Mark. The lines etched on her face told a story of sleepless nights and endless searching. Ramona's heart, though hardened by years of resentment, couldn't help but ache for the pain she saw in those eyes.

As the door creeped open, Ramona hid the knife behind her back, and maintained a calm exterior. She greeted Mark's mother with a forced smile, her grip on the knife tightening. She had complete knowledge of where Mark was, hidden in the depths of her basement, away from anyone's sight. Ramona had no choice but to convince her that he was not with her.

"Mama Anderson, what a surprise," Ramona said, her voice laced with false cheerfulness. "To what do I owe this unexpected visit?"

Mark's mom's eyes darted around the room, searching for any sign of her missing son. Ramona could see the desperation in her gaze, the hope that maybe, just maybe, Mark would be here. But Ramona was determined to keep her secret hidden, to maintain control over the situation.

"I...I'm sorry to bother you, Ramona," Mrs. Anderson stammered, her voice quivering. "But I haven't seen or heard from Mark in days. I've been searching everywhere, calling everyone he knows, and no one has seen him. I thought maybe he would be here."

Ramona's heart skipped a beat, her grip on the knife tightening. She knew she had to be careful with her words, to convince his mother that Mark was not with her and without raising suspicion.

"Oh, Mrs. Anderson, I haven't seen Mark in weeks, I thought he was with you," Ramona replied. She paced back and forth in Ramona's living room, her worry growing with each passing minute. Her son, Mark, had always been responsible, but something seemed off. Mark was a creature of habit, always calling her, to make sure she took her medicine on time. He hadn't answered her calls or responding to her messages, and making her anxious.

"Maybe I should report him missing,"

She mumbled to herself, her voice filled with concern. Ramona, her ex-daughter-in-law, watched her with a furrowed brow, sensing the distress in her voice.

"No, no, don't jump to conclusions," Ramona said, trying to reassure Mrs. Anderson.

"You know your son is always out of town on business. Maybe he's just caught up in a project and forgot to let you know."

Mark's Mother sighed, her worry deepening.

"But he always lets me know when he's leaving," she replied, her voice tinged with frustration. "This time, it's different. I can feel it."

Ramona's patience wore thin, her own exhaustion creeping in.

"I'm sure he'll be calling you soon," she said, her tone strained. "I have to get up early in the morning. If I hear from him, I will tell him to call you, okay?" With a gentle push, Ramona guided her towards the front door, hoping to alleviate her mother-in-law anxiety.

As the door closed behind Mrs. Anderson, Ramona let out a frustrated sigh.

"I hate mama's boys."

She muttered under her breath, her irritation seeping through her words. With a forceful slam, she shut the door, leaving the silence of the empty house.

As Margaret entered her home, the silence seemed deafening, the absence of Mark's voice echoing through the empty rooms.

She picked up her phone again, hoping against hope that he had called while she was away. But the screen remained blank, devoid of any missed calls or messages. Margaret's worry deepened, and she felt a sense of urgency wash over her.

With trembling hands, she dialed the number of the local police station. As she explained the situation to the officer on the other end, Margaret's voice cracked with emotion. "Please, you have to help me find my son. Something isn't right. He would never just disappear like this."

The officer assured her that they would do everything they could to locate Mark, and Margaret clung to that glimmer of hope.

As the days turned into weeks, Ramona's obsession with Jackson grew stronger. She had convinced herself that if she could just keep him hidden away from the world, he would come to love her. Her misguided actions had escalated from innocent attempts to get his attention to full-blown stalking.

Ramona had planned every detail of her operation. She had set up a hidden room in her basement, complete with a bed, food, and water. She had even installed cameras to monitor Jackson's every move. It was as if she had created her own twisted version of a love nest.

On the other hand, Jackson was growing concerned about Allison's sudden disappearance. They had hit it off at the coffee shop, and he couldn't understand why she had stopped responding to his calls and messages. Unaware of the situation, he did not know that Allison was trapped in Ramona's basement, her pleas for help going unanswered.

Over time, Jackson's life unraveled. He lost his job because of his distracted and erratic behavior. His friends grew concerned as he became more withdrawn and paranoid. He couldn't shake the feeling that he was being watched, but he did not know just how close to the truth he was.

One evening, as Jackson sat alone in his apartment, he received a mysterious package. Inside was a video recording of himself, taken from the hidden cameras in Ramona's basement. The footage showed him going about his daily routine, unaware of the eyes that were watching him.

Jackson felt his heart tighten with fear as he came to understand the intensity of Ramona's obsession. He couldn't tell his mother about the situation. But Jackson did not know how to break free from Ramona's clutches by himself either. Her careful manipulation prevented any successful attempts to seek help.

A few days later, and it was now evening time, and Jackson was lying in his bed, caught up in a basketball game playing on the television. The sound of sneakers squeaking on the court and the roar of the crowd filled the room, creating a comforting mood. But his peaceful evening took an unexpected turn when a cryptic message from Ramona flashed across his phone screen.

"I see you."

Startled, Jackson's heart thundered as he jumped out of bed, his mind racing with questions. He rushed over to the window, hoping to catch a glimpse of Ramona's car parked outside. Unfortunately, he couldn't see any signs of her in the night's darkness. Paranoia crept into his thoughts, and he felt a shiver run down his spine.

Just as he was about to dismiss the message as a prank, another notification chimed on his phone. This time, it was a video. Trembling with a mix of fear and anger, Jackson reluctantly pressed play. The screen illuminated with an eerie glow, revealing a video himself lying in bed, unaware of being watched.

Fury surged through his veins, and he typed a response to Ramona, his fingers twitched with each keystroke. "Leave me alone, you psycho!" he texted, before hurling his phone against the wall in frustration. The phone shattered into pieces, scattering across the floor.

Jackson's mind raced, trying to make sense of the situation. How was Ramona able to see him? Was she really watching him, or was this some sick game she was playing? He began tearing through his room, searching for any hidden recording devices, destroying his once clean room.

As he tore apart his belongings, his eyes caught a glimmer of white light emanating from his high school football trophy, placed on a shelf. With a blend of curiosity and apprehension, he approached it. With trembling hands, he removed the platform supporting the trophy, revealing a hidden compartment within.

His heart pounding, Jackson's eyes widened in disbelief as he discovered a mini camera inside the trophy. The realization hit him like a ton of bricks. Ramona had been spying on him all along, invading his privacy in the most insidious way possible. Deception and anger surged within him, fueling a single-mindedness to uncover the truth behind Ramona's twisted game.

With the camera in hand, Jackson vowed to confront Ramona and put an end to her torment. Little did he know, this was only beginning a dark and dangerous journey that would test his sanity and push him to the brink of his own fears.

The next morning, the gray sky covered the small town of Eastwood, casting a gloomy mood on the streets. Jackson, his face etched with resolve to see this through, made his way towards Ramona's office. Ramona, a well-respected real estate agent and a pillar of the community, was known for her professionalism and integrity. She had built a reputation that commanded respect from everyone in town.

As Jackson entered the office lobby, he noticed Ramona engaged in a conversation with other agents. The atmosphere was buzzing with the usual chatter and the sound of ringing phones. Making his mind about confronting her, Jackson walked through the glass door and swiftly grabbed Ramona by the arm. The people in the office, sensing the tension, and growing concerned.

Ramona remained calm and assured her colleagues that everything was okay. With a calm yet firm voice, she suggested they take the conversation into her office. Jackson, seething with anger, followed her silently, his eyes fixed on her every move.

Once inside the office, the tension between them was intense. Jackson's fury was evident as he yelled, his voice echoing off the walls, "Look here, you crazy bitch! I told you, it's over. Don't call or text me ever again." Ramona tried to console him by placing her hands on his chest. But her attempt only fueled his rage.

In a moment of blind anger, Jackson pushed Ramona against the wall, his actions causing a commotion that caught the attention of the office security. They rushed into the room, their presence a stark reminder of the line that had crossed. Concern etched on their faces, they asked Ramona if she was okay. She nodded, her eyes filled with a mix of fear and desperation.

Before storming out of the room, Jackson issued a final warning, his voice dripping with venom, "If you don't leave me alone, I will go to the police." With those words hanging in the air, he disappeared through the door, leaving behind a shaken Ramona and her confused colleagues.

Security personnel escorted Jackson out of the building in order to ensure the safety of Ramona and the other employees. As the rain fell, he made his way to his car, the door and expressing his frustration by banging his hand on the steering wheel. He pondered how he had become entangled in such a chaotic situation. Ramona, who was once a pleasant woman, now appeared to have transformed into an evil person.

An hour later, the agents at Skyline Realty Estate were standing around, engrossed in their usual gossip. The office buzzed with whispers and hushed conversations, until suddenly, the doors swung open, revealing a dark and handsome gray-haired gentleman accompanied by his security detail.

Ramona, preparing for her next appointment, when she heard a commotion outside her office, looked up in surprise as her father barged in.

"Father, what are you doing here?" She asked cautiously, knowing his sudden appearances rarely meant anything good.

"Do I need a reason to see my only daughter?" Frank responded, his voice calm but laced with tension.

"Of course not, Father," Ramona replied, forcing a smile as she walked towards him. She barely had time to embrace him before Frank motioned to his security detail to wait outside. The moment they left, his demeanor shifted drastically. Without warning, he grabbed her and shoved her against the door, his face inches from hers, filled with anger.

"Why do you always continue to embarrass me?" he spat, his voice low but venomous.

Shocked and trying to maintain her composure, Ramona asked, "What are you talking about?"

Slowly, she backed away, putting distance between them.

Frank's anger boiled over.

"You're running around with some 22-year-old boy. Have you no shame? He's your best friend's son!"

Ramona, trying to remain calm, placed some papers into her briefcase. "My love life is none of your concern, Father."

Frank's face twisted with fury. "Did you forget who you're talking to?"

Ramona shot back sarcastically, "Not at all. You remind me every time we see each other."

Frank's voice softened but remained stern. "I'm about to announce my campaign for mayor. I can't afford distractions like this."

Ramona met his eyes with a calm resolve. "I'll handle it, Father."

He sat on the edge of her desk, his tone shifting to one of concern, though still laced with his usual condescension.

"Ramona, I'm worried about you. Your track record with men is terrible. First, you divorce your gay husband, and now you're with some boy half your age."

Ramona gently patted her father on the back, trying to diffuse the tension. "Stop worrying, Dad. I won't embarrass you or tarnish your public image."

Satisfied, Frank smiled and stood. "Now that's settled, let's go have lunch."

Ramona, still composed on the outside, declined, "I'll have to take a rain check. Can we do lunch tomorrow?"

Frank kissed her on the forehead. "Sure, just call my secretary and set up an appointment."

As he left the office, Ramona sat back in her chair. The moment the door closed behind him, her facade crumbled. Tears welled up in her eyes as she struggled to contain her fear and anguish. Alone, she cried, the weight of her father's power and control suffocating her.

Chapter 6

Drunken Love

Ramona was coming home from a late night meeting, her heart filled with a sense of accomplishment. The sale of a house had just earned her a generous commission, and the weight of success lifted her spirits. As she cruised the dimly lit streets, the music blared from her car speakers, filling the night air with her favorite tunes. The rhythmic beats seemed to match the rhythm of her elated heart.

But then, in a split second, her euphoria shattered like glass. Ramona's eyes caught sight of Jackson's car parked on the side of the road. A surge of anger flattered through her veins, erasing all traces of her previous joy. Without a second thought, she abruptly reversed her car, screeching to a halt beside Jackson's vehicle.

Her fury manifested in swift, violent actions. Ramona stormed out of her car, her feet pounding the pavement as she approached Jackson's tires. Kicks rained down upon them, a physical release of her pent-up frustration. But that wasn't enough. She needed to release more pain.

With a determined stride, Ramona marched back to her own car and popped open the trunk. Her hands fumbled for a moment before finding what she sought — a heavy pipe. Clutching it tightly, she returned to Jackson's car, her rage fueling her every move. The pipe crashed against the windows, shattering the glass into a thousand glittering pieces. The sound echoed through the night, a symphony of destruction.

Breathing heavily, Ramona discarded the pipe, its metallic clang against the pavement ringing in the quiet of the night and puncturing her fury. Her anger still burned, demanding further recourse. She withdrew her keys from her pocket, their jagged edges glint in the dim light. With deliberate intent, she dragged them across sleek surface of Jackson's car, leaving deep, permanent scratches in her wake.

Suddenly, a flicker of light caught Ramona attention. She turned her head, her eyes widening as she noticed the glow emanating from nearby house. Panic surged within her, realizing that her reckless actions had not gone unnoticed. The neighbor had been awakened by the commotion, and Ramona knew she had to flee before they emerged from their house.

In a frantic rush, she sprinted back to her car, her breath heaving. The engine roared to life as she jammed the key into the ignition, her foot pressing hard on the accelerator. The tires screeched against the asphalt as she sped away, leaving behind a trail of shattered glass and damaged metal.

Ramona's mind raced, a whirlwind of regret and fear what had possessed her to unleash such fury? As the night swallowed her car, she vowed to herself that this would be a turning point. No longer would anger dictate her actions. It was time to confront the demons within, to find a way to heal the wounds that had driven her to this destructive path.

Half an hour later, Ramona's car pulled into the driveway, the engine humming softly as she brought it to a stop. The weight of regret settled heavily upon her shoulders, her blood rushing in her ears. She reached into her bag, her fingers trembling as they closed around the cold metal of her keys. Pausing for a moment, she took a deep breath, trying to steady herself before facing the consequences of her actions.

With a heavy sigh, Ramona opened the car door and stepped out onto the pavement. The evening air felt thick and suffocating, mirroring the turmoil within her. As she walked towards her house, her steps seemed to echo with the weight of her guilt.

Ramona threw her keys onto the table, the sound of them clattering against the wood echoing through the empty house. She absentmindedly placed her handbag on the couch, her mind consumed by the events that had led her to this moment. Her reflection caught her eye in the hallway mirror, and she couldn't help but notice the disheveled state of her hair and clothes. Beads of sweat dotted her forehead, evidence of the internal struggle she had been battling.

She stood before the mirror, her eyes locked with her own reflection. Ramona's voice quivered as she began to speak, the words escaping her lips in a whisper. "I can't believe I destroyed Jackson's car," she muttered, her hands instinctively rising to cover her mouth, as if trying to contain the remorse that threatened to spill out.

Her shoes were kicked off haphazardly, forgotten on the floor as she paced back and forth, the weight of her actions pressing down upon her.

"I have to make this right," she breathed out, her voice cracking with emotion. Tears welled up in her eyes, blurring her vision as she struggled to find a way to undo the damage she had caused.

Her steps grew heavier as she made her way towards the basement, a sense of desperation guiding her. "I can't take this anymore," she muttered, her voice filled with a mix of anguish and remorse. With each step, her decision seemed to solidify, until she reached the bottom of the stairs, her hand hovering over the light switch.

But then, her gaze fell upon a wedding picture displayed on a nearby table. Ramona turn back around and decided to go to bed instead.

Over time Ramona's behavior had grown increasingly malicious, bordering on sinister, which Jackson had initially dismissed as a phase or her having personal problems. But when she started targeting him directly, he knew he had to take action.

The final straw came when he found his car vandalized the next morning when he had confronted her in her office, with a chilling message scrawled across the windshield,

"You're next."

Determined to put an end to Ramona's reign of terror, Jackson had gathered all the evidence he could find. Photos, videos, witness statements — he had it all organized in a folder, ready to present to the police. But as he stood in the station, facing the skeptical officers, his confidence wavered.

Ramona had always been a cornerstone of the community, known for her charitable work and friendly demeanor. It was unbelievable to think that a person with such an outstanding reputation could be capable of such maliciousness. The officers dismissed Jackson's claims, chalking it up to paranoia or a personal vendetta.

As he exited the Ninth District police station, a sense of defeat overwhelmed him, and as if mirroring his mood, dark clouds gathered in the sky. While heading to his car, the rain poured down, soaking his pale face.

Jackson sat in his car, his hands gripping the steering wheel, his heart hammered in his chest. He had just left the police station, feeling angry and unheard. The weight of Ramona's stalking had become unbearable, and he had hoped that seeking help from the authorities would bring him some relief. But they had dismissed his claims, brushing them off as figment of his imagination.

He noticed a lit bar as he was driving, Jackson couldn't help but feel a sense of desperation wash over him. He knew he couldn't continue living in fear, looking over his shoulder, wondering when Ramona would strike next. He needed someone to believe him, to understand the danger he was facing.

With a heavy sigh, he pushed open the car door and stepped out onto the pavement. The chilly night air bit at his skin, but he barely noticed. Tenaciousness fueled his every step as he made his way towards the entrance of the Pete's Bar. Perhaps here, in the dimly lit corners and hushed conversations, he would find someone who would listen, someone who would take his claims seriously.

Jackson sat on the bar stool, his mind consumed by a whirlwind of and emotions. The weight of his troubles seemed to press down on him, visible in the lines etched on his face and the wear in his eyes. The bartender, a perceptive soul with a kind heart, noticed Jackson's distress and struck up a conversation.

"Rough day?" the bartender asked, his voice laced with genuine concern.

Jackson sighed heavily, grateful for the opportunity to unburden himself. "You have no idea," he replied, his voice tinged with a hint of bitterness that he could not suppress.

The bartender nodded sympathetically, understanding the weight of unseen battles.

"First one's on the house," he offered, sliding a drink across the counter towards Jackson.

Jackson mustered a weak smile, appreciating the gesture. "Thanks," he muttered, taking a sip and feeling the warmth of the liquid course through his veins.

As the minutes ticked by, the alcohol began to take its toll on Jackson. His speech slurred, and his demeanor grew increasingly belligerent. Concerned for his well-being, the bartender approached him cautiously.

"I'm sorry, buddy, but I think it's time to cut you off," the bartender said gently, hoping to diffuse the situation before it escalated further.

Jackson's eyes widened with anger, his voice rising in defiance.

"I don't need you telling me what to do! Just give me another damn drink!"

Realizing the situation was spiraling out of control, the bartender motioned for the security guard to intervene. The burly figure approached, ready to diffuse any potential conflict. Jackson, sensing the gravity of the situation, decided it was best to leave before things escalated further.

But as he made a move towards the exit, the security guard swiftly intercepted him, snatching his keys from his hand. In a moment of desperation, Jackson swung a punch at the guard, hoping to break free from his grasp. However, the guard's reflexes were sharp, and he deftly blocked the blow, causing Jackson to stumble and crash onto the floor.

The commotion caught the attention of Mrs. Anderson, who was sitting at a nearby table waiting for a friend. She reached for her phone and dialed Sarah's number. She needed to let her know that her son had been arrested.

As the phone rang, the old lady's heart thumped in her chest. She wondered how Sarah would react to this news.

Finally, she answered, her voice filled with concern.

"Hello?"

"Sarah," Mrs. Anderson said, her voice trembling slightly.

"It's me. I'm at Pete's bar. I just saw your son. He's been arrested."

Sarah did not recognize the voice on the other and the phone. She wondered how Sarah would react to this news. Finally, she answered, her voice filled with concern.

Sarah did not recognize the voice on the other end of the phone. It was unfamiliar, distant and yet somehow urgent. Mrs. Anderson had to remind Sarah who she was, and the mention her son's name sent a shiver down Sarah's spine. "Sarah, I am Mrs. Anderson, Mark's mother," she said, breaking through the confusion.

"Ramona is my ex-daughter-in-law."

Sarah's mind raced, trying to place the connection. Mark, Ramona, Mrs. Anderson... It all clicked into place. Mark was Ramona ex-husband, and Mrs. Anderson, is a sweet elderly lady, who owns the local bakery store on the corner. Ramona and Sarah have not been communicating for several weeks. What will be the reason for Mrs. Anderson's call to Sarah is unclear.

"I apologize, Mrs. Anderson. May I ask what you mentioned regarding my son, Jackson?" Sarah asked nervously.

There was a pause on the other end of the line, as if Mrs. Anderson was gathering her thoughts. Then, with a heavy sigh, she began to explain the situation. Jackson, Sarah's son, had been arrested at Pete's bar. The words hit Sarah like a punch to the gut, leaving her breathless and disbelieving. As Mrs. Anderson continued to recount the details, Sarah's mind raced with a mix of emotions. Anger, disappointment, and concern swirled within her, threatening to overwhelm her senses. But amidst the chaos, she felt a glimmer of gratitude towards Mrs. Anderson for reaching out and informing her about her son's situation. Without a second thought, Sarah hung up the phone and immediately jumped into her car.

The drive to the 9th district police station was a blur, her mind consumed with worry for her son. She couldn't help but wonder how Jackson had ended up in this situation, and what it meant for his future. Arriving at the police station, Sarah's heart beat loudly in her ears as she rushed inside. She navigated the maze of corridors, her eyes scanning the faces of officers and detainees alike, until she finally reached the front desk. With a thready voice, she asked about her son. Minutes felt like hours as Sarah waited anxiously for news. Finally, a weary-looking officer approached her, confirming that Jackson was indeed in custody.

Sarah's disappointment in her son's behavior weighed heavily on her, but her desire to help him remained unwavering. As they walked out of the police station together, Sarah's mind was filled with a mix of emotions. She knew that the ride home would be a silent one, as both mother and son grappled with the oppressive air surrounding them. But amidst the disappointment, Sarah held onto a glimmer of hope that this would be a turning point for Jackson, a wake-up call that would lead him down a better path.

Finally, a weary-looking Officer Richardson approached her, confirming that Jackson was indeed in custody. It took them a while but they got through all the processes that required her to take Jackson home.

As they walked out of the police station together, the silence in the car was deafening, but Sarah knew that the real conversation would come later, in the privacy of their home. As she gripped the steering wheel tightly, she couldn't help but wonder how they had reached this point, and what it would take to bring her son back from the edge.

As Jackson struggles with the decision to reveal the truth about Ramona's stalking to his mother, the weight of his silence threatens to consume him.

Will he finally come clean and risk everything, or will he continue to keep the dark secret?

Chapter 7

No Help In Sight

The next morning, Jackson stumbled his way to the kitchen, his head aching from the hangover from drinking so much the night before. As he entered, he found his mother vigorously banging pots and pans together, creating a symphony of clanging sounds. It was clear she was trying to teach him a lesson. It was a mockery of how she usually worked in the kitchen, fluid and composed.

Normally, the smell of his mother's cooking would have made his mouth water, but this morning, it only made his stomach churn.

"Mom, must you be so loud?" Jackson groaned, his voice filled with discomfort.

Sarah turned to face him, a stern expression on her face. "That's what happens when you over drink, Jackson," she replied, her voice laced with disappointment.

"I would never drink again," Jackson muttered, regret filling his voice.

In an attempt to help him with his hangover, Sarah poured him a cup of coffee. Little did Jackson know, she had added a secret ingredient to alleviate his suffering.

"Here, drink this," she said, pushing the cup towards him.

Curiosity got the better of him, and Jackson took a hesitant sip of the coffee. Instantly, he spat it out, his face contouring in disgust.

"What is this? It tastes horrible!" He exclaimed, his voice filled with disbelief.

"Do you want your hangover to go away?" She asked, her tone firm.

Jackson didn't answer, but instead, he continued to drink the nasty concoction, hoping it would provide some relief. Sarah watched him closely, her eyes filled with concern.

"Jackson, I'm very disappointed with you. This is not like you. Now, tell me what's going on," she demanded, her voice tinged with worry.

Jackson struggled to find the words as he sat across from his mother at the kitchen table. The weight of his secret was becoming unbearable, and he knew he couldn't keep it hidden longer. Ramona had been stalking him for weeks, and it had taken its toll on Jackson. So he spilled everything that had been happening over the past few weeks to his mother.

"And you're just now telling me?" His mother asked, concern evident in her voice. Jackson ran a hand through his hair and took a sip of the coffee his mother had made for him. He sighed, trying to gather his thoughts.

"I thought I could handle it," he finally admitted, his voice barely above a whisper.

Sarah, who had been sitting quietly beside him, spoke up.

"I thought I told you to leave her alone," she said sternly, her eyes filled with disappointment. Jackson tried to explain himself, the words stumbling out of him in a rush.

"I haven't talked to her since you two had that altercation last month," he said, despair creeping into his voice.

"Jackson, what have you gotten yourself into?" His mother's face revealed concern as it softened. She asked, her voice laced with worry.

"You can't handle this alone. Ramona is a master manipulator, and she has men wrapped around her finger."

"I went to the police," he complained, his voice shaking with resignation and upset. "But they didn't believe me. They said there wasn't enough evidence."

Sarah chimed in, her voice filled with frustration. "Ramona always had the system in her back pocket. She knows how to play the game."

"I don't know what to do," Jackson admitted, his voice barely audible.

Sarah's voice rose, filled with anger. "You will not do a damn thing," she said. "I will handle Ramona."

"Mom, I need to take a walk to clear my head."

Jackson stood up, his mind racing with thoughts of Ramona and the danger she posed. He needed to get himself together and the anxiety of everything with Ramona and his hangover was not helping.

He stepped out of the house, the cool breeze brushed against his face from the chaos that had consumed his thoughts.

But as soon as he stepped out of the house, a car came hurtling towards him, its headlights blinding his vision. Panic surged through Jackson's veins, and he jumped out of harm's way.

"Look out!" Sarah's urgent words broke through the chaos.

It was Ramona's car, He realized, his mind racing to comprehend the danger that had just unfolded before him. Sarah, the constant protector, rushed to her son's side, her face marked with worry.

"Are you okay?"

Ramona's car had missed Jackson, but the close call left him shaken. Sarah extended a helping hand to Jackson, providing comfort during the commotion. His injuries were a few scratches and bruises, nothing too serious. He would live to see another day.

"Let's go, Jackson,"

Sarah's voice was firm, her will unwavering. Confusion clouded his thoughts as he tried to comprehend her words.

"Where are we going?"

"To the police station,"

Sarah declared, her voice tinged with a mix of anger and revenge. We're going to file a restraining order this time.

They walked towards the police station. Jackson's mind cleared, the fog of fear disappearing. With each step, He felt a newfound strength building within him, fueled by the unwavering support of his mother by his side. It was time to take a stand, to reclaim his life from the clutches of Ramona's obsession.

And so, with determination in Jackson's heart and a glimmer of hope in his eyes, He embarked on this journey towards freedom, ready to face whatever the devil throws at him.

Margaret has not heard from her son, Mark. Her attempts to reach the police station were unsuccessful, Margaret made the decision to personally visit the station. She contacted her neighbor to inquire if he could accompany her, but unfortunately, he was unavailable. Margaret had to call a taxi to go to the station. Upon her arrival, she approached the front desk and was greeted by an officer who inquired about the purpose of her visit.

Margaret expressed her desire to report her son, Mark, as missing and proceeded to explain the situation.

However, Officer Richardson responded by laughing at her, causing Margaret to become increasingly upset. Detective Miller intervened and addressed Margaret by her surname, Anderson, reminding her that they had previously informed her that they would contact her if any information regarding her son became available. Mrs. Anderson expressed her frustration with Detective Miller,

"I told you he's been missing for three days and it's unusual for him not to contact me."

Detective Miller responded, "Perhaps Mark was simply enjoying himself with a female companion or had chosen not to communicate with his Mommy."

This remark infuriated Margaret, prompting her to assert herself and state that she dared Detective Miller to make such a statement. Also, she mentioned, "I believe Mark's ex-wife, Ramona, is involved in his disappearance. She's been causing trouble for him ever since their divorce."

Detective Miller raised an eyebrow, clearly skeptical. "Mrs. Anderson, we can't jump to conclusions without any evidence. Have you tried reaching out to his ex-wife?"

Margaret sighed, feeling frustrated with the lack of support from the police. "Yes, I've tried calling her multiple times, but she won't cooperate with me. I just have a gut feeling that something is wrong."

Detective Miller sighed, his tone softening slightly.

"Look, Mrs. Anderson, I understand your concern as a mother, but we need concrete evidence before we can launch a full investigation. I promise you, we will keep an eye out for any information regarding your son."

Margaret nodded, her eyes welling up with tears.

"Please, Detective Miller, I just want to find my son. He's never gone this long without contacting me."

Detective Miller's expression softened further, and he placed a comforting hand on her shoulder.

"I'll do what I can, Mrs. Anderson. In the meantime, try to stay strong. We'll keep searching for Mark."

Margaret nodded, grateful for any possibility of hope. As she left the police station, she couldn't shake the feeling that something was terribly wrong. Determined to find her son, Margaret vowed to take matters into her own hands, even if it meant uncovering painful secrets along the way.

As Margaret exited the police station and made her way to Tasty Treats, a small bakery that she owned on the corner. She attempted to call her son once more, but this time the operator informed her that the phone number had been disconnected. As her hope dwindled, she couldn't shake the feeling that her ex-daughter-in-law was involved in her son's disappearance.

Margaret sat on the steps, her heart heavy with despair, a familiar face caught her eye. It was Ramona, walking briskly towards her. Margaret's exhaustion turned to fury as she realized that Ramona held the key to finding her son. Margaret rose from the steps, gave the woman who had torn her family apart, the evil eye.

Ramona walked past Mark's mother without sparing her a glance, uninterested in conversation. She entered her place of business, knowing a presence loomed behind her. It was Officer Richardson, trailing close, as he often did. A shady cop, yet someone Ramona had relied on time and again. He had a crush on her, but the feeling was far from mutual. Richardson was short, overweight, and drove a beat-up car—far from the type to pique her interest. Still, Ramona had learned to use his infatuation to her advantage, flirting just enough to get what she needed.

"Hey, gorgeous," Officer Richardson greeted, his voice dripping with false confidence.

Ramona turned, her face twisting in disgust. "What do you want, Officer Richardson?" she asked coolly.

He grinned. "How about letting me take you to dinner tonight?"

She rolled her eyes. "I'm a busy woman, Richardson. I don't have time for this."

His smile didn't falter. "Oh, I know you're busy. In fact, a sweet little old lady came into the station today... to file a missing person report."

Ramona froze, then slowly crossed her arms. Her voice dropped. "Cut the games. What do you really want?"

"I told you," he smirked, "let me take you to dinner."

"I have other plans," she replied, her patience wearing thin.

Richardson chuckled darkly. "Oh really? What could be more important? Running over Jackson again? You might want to think twice before answering."

Ramona's expression shifted, the cold front melting away into faux coyness. She stepped closer, her voice softening as she leaned into the flirtation. "Fine. Where do you want to meet?"

His smirk widened. "Oceanfront Tavern. Eight o'clock. Don't be late." With that, he swaggered out, leaving Ramona seething in his wake.

As Ramona turned around, she realized everyone in the office was staring at her. Annoyed, she snapped, "What are you all looking at?" The room quickly shifted, with people turning away, though a few stifled laughs could be heard behind her back. Fuming, Ramona stormed into her office and slammed the door shut.

Leaning against her desk, she muttered to herself, "A date with him? Really?" She couldn't shake the thought. "He's taking me to Oceanfront Tavern?"

Her brow furrowed. "How can Richardson even afford that place? Only the rich and famous go there." She frowned deeper, pacing around her office.

"He better not stick me with the bill."

Then, something dawned on her. "Wait... how did he know about the car situation?"

The realization settled heavily. She had no choice but to go on this date.

Back at the police station, just as Officer Richardson returned to his desk, he overheard two people speaking with Officer

Carter about filing a missing person report. Sensing an opportunity, Richardson cut in smoothly. "Thanks, Officer Carter, but I'll take it from here."

He turned his attention to the distressed couple. "How can I help you?" he asked, his tone professional.

The man, Mr. Wilson, cleared his throat nervously. "It's our daughter, Allison. She's missing. We need to file a report."

Richardson nodded, trying to keep his expression neutral. "Of course. Let me gather some details from you."

After he took down the information from the Wilson's, Richardson's expression darkened. He discreetly pulled out his phone and sent a quick text to Ramona: *What did you do now?*

Sliding his phone back into his pocket, he continued filling out the paperwork, a smirk playing at the edge of his lips. This was going to be interesting.

Chapter 8

We Demand Justice

Jackson and his mother promptly proceeded to the local police station following his latest traumatic encounter with Ramona. Her former best friend's attempt to harm her son by using her vehicle had startled Sarah. Jackson courteously held the door open for his mother as they entered the police station. Sarah entered with a stern demeanor, demanding justice for her son. Upon reaching the front desk, Sarah insisted on speaking with an officer.

The officer stationed at the front desk advised them to wait patiently, as someone would be available shortly. Frustrated, Sarah forcefully placed her hands on the desk, expressing her urgency to speak with someone immediately. Just as the officer was about to reprimand Sarah, a detective approached them. The officer introduced himself to the two individuals, and inquired about how he could assist them. Sarah explained the situation involving Ramona and her son, while Jackson expressed his need for a restraining order.

As Sarah gave her account of the events, Detective Miller listened attentively, his expression growing more serious with each passing moment. He assured them they had come to the right place, and he would do everything in his power to ensure their safety.

After taking down all the information, Detective Miller informed Jackson they would need to file a formal report and gather evidence to support their claims. He wrote information and assured the two that they would be with them every step of the way.

As they sat down to fill out the paperwork, Jackson couldn't help but feel a mix of relief and anxiety. Relief that they were taking action against Ramona, but anxiety about what might happen next. He glanced in his mother's direction.

Hours passed as they recounted the events, providing as much detail as possible. Detective Miller commended them for their cooperation and assured them they were doing everything they could to ensure their safety. He promised to keep them updated on the progress of their case and urged them to reach out if they needed anything.

As Jackson and Sarah walked out of the police station, their minds were still reeling from the events that had just unfolded. He knew that the road ahead would be challenging, but he also knew that they were not alone in this fight. With the support of his mother and dedication, he felt a glimmer of hope that justice would prevail. However, their focus shifted to a person sitting on the steps, crying uncontrollably. It was Mrs. Anderson, a familiar face in their small town.

Sarah, always one to offer comfort, approached Mrs. Anderson with a light tap on her shoulder.

"Mrs. Anderson, is something wrong? Why are you crying?" she asked, her voice filled with genuine concern.

She turned around, her tear-streaked face revealing a mix of sadness and something more. As her eyes met Sarah's, a flicker of recognition passed between them. Jackson, standing beside his mother, watched the exchange with growing confusion. He had no idea what was going on.

Sarah, maintaining her calm demeanor, turned to Jackson and quietly instructed him to help Mrs. Anderson up. Jackson, still bewildered, did as he was told, extending a hand to the distraught woman. She took it gratefully, her grip tight and trembling.

Once Mrs. Anderson was on her feet, she took a deep breath and explained why she had been at the police station. Jackson and Sarah listened in shock as the elderly woman revealed she had filed a missing person report for her son, Mark. The weight of her words hung heavy in the air, leaving an eerie silence in their wake.

Sarah, her voice filled with sympathy and urgency, turned to Jackson and explained just who Mrs. Anderson was related to.

"She is Ramona's mother-in-law," Sarah whispered, her eyes filled with concern.

"And she also told me that you were at Pete's Bar and that you were arrested."

Jackson's mouth dropped open, his mind struggling to process the information. He remembered being at the police station the day before, but the details were hazy, clouded by a fog of confusion and alcohol. The gravity of the situation began to sink in, and he felt a knot tighten in his stomach.

As if sensing their confusion, Mrs. Anderson's trembling voice broke through the silence.

"I believe Ramona has something to do with my son's disappearance," she confessed, her words heavy with emotion.

Sarah's eyes widened, her mind racing to connect the dots. Ramona, their mutual acquaintance, had always seemed harmless, but now a cloud of suspicion hung over her. The pieces of the puzzle were slowly falling into place, revealing a disturbing picture.

Without hesitation, Sarah turned to Mrs. Anderson. "Please, come back to the house with us," she urged.

"We need to talk and figure out what's going on. It seems like Ramona is starting to be more than just a nuisance."

Mrs. Anderson acknowledged that Ramona was becoming a concern. She told Sarah, "I'd love to come to your house to talk, but I need to stop by the bakery first. I can meet you at your house after that."

Sarah replied, "That's silly, my son and I have nothing else to do. We can go to the bakery with you."

Jackson chimed in, "I'm fine with that. I could go for one of your famous chocolate cheesecakes."

Sarah gave him a playful look and said, "Kids these days are always thinking about food." Mrs. Anderson chuckled as they walked down the street.

As they made their way to Mrs. Anderson's bakery, a sense of unease settled over the trio. He never imagined that his mother's once-close friend would turn into his worst nightmare. The once familiar streets now seemed shrouded in mystery, and the truth they were about to uncover would change their lives forever.

At Tasty Treats, the scene in the bakery was chaotic. When they walked in, they were met with a mob of people. Mrs. Anderson pulled one of her employees aside and asked, "What's going on? Why is it so crowded in here?"

The young girl explained, "Derrick called in sick, and we're short-handed with a ton of orders."

Mrs. Anderson was pleased to see so many customers, but she hadn't expected such a rush on a Saturday.

Linda added, "It's the football season, and everyone is ordering snacks for parties."

Another employee mentioned, "A restaurant critic raved about your famous Philadelphia Eagles Kicks, and now everyone is flocking here."

Mrs. Anderson turned to Sarah and apologized, saying she couldn't leave as her son Mark was supposed to handle the football promotion. Sarah surveyed the busy bakery and told Mrs. Anderson, "You can't manage all of this alone. Jackson and I will help you."

Sarah put on an apron, and Jackson, giving his mother a strange look, began eating a cheesecake. Sarah playfully tapped him on the back of his head, and he quickly put the cake down to assist behind the counter.

That evening, Ramona came to a decision that would forever change the lives of those trapped in her basement. With a plate of food in hand, she descended the stairs, and something akin to desperate boldness thrummed under her skin. The captives, Mark and Allison, watched her approach with fear etched across their faces.

Ramona's hands shook as she peeled the tape off Mark's mouth, his voice breaking the silence.

"Ramona, this is crazy. Why are you doing this?"

His words hung heavy in the air, begging for an answer that she refused to give. Ignoring him, she crossed the room, her eyes fixed on Allison, who was suffering from the effects of dehydration.

With a swift motion, Ramona removed the tape from Allison's mouth, and the young woman's pleas for her life filled the room. Fear and desperation dripped from every word, but Ramona's anger drowned out any sympathy she might have felt towards her in that moment. She screamed at Allison, demanding her silence, threatening to seal her mouth shut once more.

In a surprising act of bravery, Mark stood his ground for the both of them, defending the younger woman. "Ramona, this is ridiculous. Just let the girl go. This is between you and me." His words hung in the air, a plea for reason amid chaos. But Ramona's rage consumed her, and she rushed towards him, slapping him across the face.

"Shut up!" She shouted, her voice laced with pain.

"Why are you standing up for her?"

His response cut through her like a knife. "I'm not standing up for her. She's innocent and has nothing to do with this."

The weight of his words stabbed at her wounded heart, exposing the truth she had tried to bury.

Tears welled in Ramona's eyes as she struggled to find her voice. "What about me, Mark? Don't I deserve to be happy? I gave you twenty years of my life, and you cheated on me with a man."

The words hung in the air, heavy with the weight of a loveless marriage and her shattered heart.

Ramona stood at the bottom of the creaky wooden stairs, her breath caught in her chest as the words echoed in her mind, appearing in their once blissful marriage. How had she been so blind? How had she not seen the cracks forming beneath the surface?

With a heavy sigh, Ramona turned around to face Mark, her eyes filled with a mix of anger and hurt.

"By the way, Mark," she said, her voice dripping with sarcasm, your mother stopped by the other day." She watched as his expression shifted, a flicker of concern crossing his face.

"She was so worried about her baby boy," she added, her words laced with bitterness.

As Ramona ascended the rickety stairs, Mark's voice pleaded with her, desperation seeping through his words.

"Ramona, please, leave my mother out of this," he begged, his voice cracking with emotion. But it was too late for pleas and apologies.

She paused on the steps, her gaze piercing through him.

"You should have thought about that before you had an affair with your next-door neighbor," she retorted, her voice cold and cutting. With one final slam of the basement door, Ramona left Mark standing there, his guilt and regret consuming him. Mark quickly ran over to Allison. He tilted her head back so she can drink a sip of water.

Ramona made her way into another room, her eyes scanning the space. It was a replica of the love nest she had created for Jackson, her lover. A pang of sadness washed over her as she realized the life they had built together was nothing but a facade.

As she stood there, surrounded by the remnants of a love that had long since faded, Ramona made a silent vow to herself. She would find her own happiness, away from the lies and deceit that had plagued their marriage. And with the fire burning inside her, she took her first step towards a new beginning, leaving behind the shattered pieces of a love that had once been her everything.

Ramona decided to take a long, hot shower, hoping it would clear her mind. As the water streamed over her, she closed her eyes, trying to wash away the stress and frustration of the day. The steam enveloped her, but no matter how hot the water was, it couldn't drown out her thoughts.

The dinner with Officer Richardson loomed large in her mind. How could she get through the night without losing her temper or exposing too much? She hated feeling trapped, yet she knew she had no choice. The man knew too much — far more than she was comfortable with. And now, with the missing person case swirling around, the stakes were even higher.

Ramona leaned her forehead against the cool tiles, letting the water cascade down her back. "How did I get into this mess?" She whispered to herself. She had always been so careful, but now everything seemed to be closing in on her.

As the heat of the shower soothed her tense muscles, Ramona took a deep breath. She had to play this right. One wrong move, and everything she had built could crumble.

Ramona stepped out of the shower, wrapping a towel around herself. As she walked into her bedroom, she noticed her phone screen lighting up with a new message from Officer Richardson. Opening it, her eyes widened in disbelief. The message was cryptic—a photo of handcuffs and the time: 8 P.M.

She let out a frustrated sigh and threw her phone onto the bed, the tension building in her chest. What game was he playing now? The message felt like a twisted game, a reminder that he had the upper hand.

Shaking off the unease, Ramona walked over to her closet. She pulled out a silky chiffon dress, its soft fabric slipping through her fingers. It was elegant but understated — perfect for the evening ahead. She knew she needed to look the part, to maintain control of the situation, even if it was spiraling out of her hands.

After slipping into the dress, she moved to the mirror, applying her makeup with precision. Smoky eyes and a bold lip. Her expression was calm, but inside, her mind was racing. She finished by styling her hair, sleek and polished, as if it was her only armor for the night ahead.

Finally, satisfied with her appearance, Ramona grabbed her purse and headed out the door. The Oceanfront Tavern awaited her, along with Officer Richardson — and whatever dangerous game he intended to play.

Chapter 9

The Dinner From Hell

Fifteen minutes later, Ramona arrived at the Oceanfront Tavern. The warm glow of the restaurant's lights and the elegant ambiance surprised her. It was more luxurious than she had imagined, with soft music playing in the background and the sound of waves crashing in the distance.

As she walked through the door, her eyes scanned the room until they landed on Officer Richardson, seated at a table by the window. He stood up the moment he saw her, his eyes widening as he took in her appearance. Ramona forced a smile, playing her part.

"Good evening, Officer Richardson," she said, her voice polite but distant.

He grinned, unable to hide his admiration. "Hello, gorgeous. Please, call me Gary." He pulled out a chair for her, attempting to be chivalrous.

Ramona sat down, offering a quick, "Thank you." She glanced around the restaurant, trying to focus on anything but his gaze. "This place is beautiful."

Richardson beamed, leaning in slightly. "A beautiful restaurant for a beautiful woman."

Ramona's smile tightened as she tried to remain composed. She knew she had to keep up the act, but every moment with him felt suffocating. The game was just beginning, and she had to stay sharp.

Ramona continued the conversation, trying to mask her irritation with a light tone. "I've always wanted to dine here, but I can't afford it."

Gary smirked. "To be honest, neither can I."

Ramona's mouth dropped in disbelief. She whispered under her breath,

"I'm not paying for this."

Gary burst out laughing. "Relax. The restaurant owner owes me a favor. We're covered."

Her expression shifted from surprise to suspicion. She narrowed her eyes slightly. "Why are we really here?"

Before he could answer, a waiter approached, asking if they were ready to order drinks. Gary waved him off. "Come back in a few minutes, we're still deciding."

As the waiter walked away, Gary leaned back in his chair, his playful smirk returning. "I wanted to wait until we had a few drinks, before getting down to business, but you're always so persistent, aren't you?"

Ramona sat up straighter, her gaze sharpening. "I'm not here for games, Gary. What's this really about?"

His smile faded slightly, replaced by something darker, more serious. "We'll get to that soon enough. But first, let's enjoy the evening, shall we?"

Gary waved the waiter back to their table. "The lady would like to place her drink order," he said, turning to Ramona with a knowing smile. Ramona ordered a glass of red wine, her voice steady but uninterested. The waiter then turned to Gary, who ordered a whiskey. "I'll be back with the drinks shortly," the waiter said, before walking away.

Gary leaned back in his chair once more and his eyes roamed in her general direction before they fixed on her face. "You really need to smile more. You have such a beautiful smile."

Ramona forced a polite smile, though it didn't reach her eyes. "Thank you, but lately, I don't have much to smile about."

Gary's expression softened. "Yeah, I know. I'm sorry to hear about your divorce."

Ramona's eyes darkened at the mention of it. "If you don't mind, I'd rather not talk about that jerk."

Gary nodded, trying to be sympathetic. "I totally understand. His loss... and my gain."

Ramona's expression shifted, her disgust clear even as she tried to hold back her true feelings. "I'm sorry," she said, her tone sharper, "but let's be real here—you're just not my type."

Gary flinched slightly, his playful demeanor faltering for a moment. But he quickly recovered, offering a tight-lipped smile. "Well, I like a challenge," he said, trying to brush off the rejection, but Ramona could see the crack in his confidence.

Ramona turned her gaze to the window, watching the waves crash against the shore, wishing she were anywhere but there.

The waiter returned with their drinks, placing Ramona's wine and Gary's whiskey on the table before stepping away. Gary took a sip, and with a sly smile, said, "That ex-husband of yours really did a number on you, huh? Solidified that heart of stone."

Ramona's response was cold and biting. "I'm glad we're divorced. He's a pathetic mama's boy."

Gary leaned in slightly, his voice dripping with mock sincerity. "I thought you liked boys. Didn't you take on a younger lover?" His words hung in the air, taunting her.

Ramona shot him a glare so sharp it could have cut glass. She didn't respond right away, pretending she had no idea what he was talking about. Instead, she took a long, deliberate sip of her wine.

Gary chuckled, not fooled by her act. "Come on, Ramona. Everyone in town knows about it. You're getting real sloppy."

She set her glass down carefully, refusing to take the bait. But Gary pressed on, his voice lowering. "I get it. You're angry. I mean, your ex did decide to, uh, switch teams."

Ramona's hand tightened around her glass, her knuckles whitening. Gary's smirk grew, clearly enjoying watching her squirm, but Ramona took a deep breath, trying to regain her composure.

She gave him a chilling smile. "I don't see how my past is your business, Gary."

Gary shrugged, his eyes glinting with amusement. "Oh, it's not. But it's hard to ignore when you're making headlines in a small town. Don't worry, though. I'm not here to judge. I'm just here to… help."

Ramona leaned back, her posture cool and defiant. "Help?" She asked, her voice dripping with sarcasm. "Or blackmail?"

Gary just smiled, swirling his whiskey, not denying a thing. Then he leaned forward, and when he spoke his tone was smooth but probing. "Why so defensive, Ramona? You need my help, whether you want to admit it or not."

Ramona crossed her arms, still trying to keep her composure. "And what exactly do I have to do for this so-called help? I told you, I have everything under control."

Gary let out a low laugh, shaking his head. "Control? Really? You're sleeping with your best friend's son, you wrecked Jackson's car, your ex-husband is missing, and now your client's daughter is missing too. Yeah, you're doing *great*."

He took a sip of his drink, letting the weight of his words settle in.

Ramona's calm exterior cracked slightly. She took a deep breath and exhaled slowly. "Fine. What do I have to do?"

Gary smiled, relaxing back in his chair, clearly enjoying her surrender. "Nothing, gorgeous. I'll take care of everything."

Ramona forced a smile, eager to move past this uncomfortable conversation. "Good. Now, can we order dinner? I'm starving."

Gary chuckled, raising his glass. "Sure, but first, let's make a toast."

Ramona raised an eyebrow, puzzled but unwilling to show hesitation. "Okay... to what?"

Gary lifted his glass higher, his eyes locking with hers. "To secrets... and keeping them buried."

Ramona's stomach twisted, but she raised her glass, clinking it against his. As they sipped their drinks, she realized just how deep into Gary's web she had fallen.

The waiter returned to the table, ready to take their orders. Ramona quickly placed hers, followed by Gary. After jotting it down, the waiter took the menus from the table and assured them, "I'll be back with your food shortly."

As soon as the waiter left, Ramona leaned forward, her voice low. "Are you going to let me in on this plan, Gary?"

Gary grinned, keeping a casual posture. "Let's just say, I'm going to take care of your problems — permanently."

Before she could ask more, the waiter came back, setting their food down in front of them. The dishes looked as good as they smelled, a temporary distraction from the tension lingering in the air.

Gary's tone shifted to something more serious as he cut into his steak. "I need to know everything you've done, Ramona. Don't leave out any details."

Ramona hesitated, her fork hovering over her plate. She was skeptical, unsure how much she should trust him. But the pressure was mounting, and Gary already knew too much. Slowly, she began to reveal some of her darkest secrets — things she hadn't told anyone else. She kept her voice steady, testing the waters and watching for his reaction.

Gary listened carefully, nodding as she spoke, and when she finished, he set his glass down and gave her a reassuring smile. "Don't worry your pretty little head about it. I'll take care of everything from here. Now, eat. The food's going to get cold."

Ramona smiled for the first time that evening, feeling a strange sense of relief. Despite the danger, there was something oddly comforting about Gary's confidence. As they continued eating, the tension between them eased, and soon they were laughing and joking like old friends.

For a moment, Ramona let herself enjoy the company, momentarily forgetting the twisted path she was walking down.

Ramona smiled as the evening began to wind down. "This has been a wonderful evening, but I have to get up early tomorrow," she said, subtly signaling it was time to end the night.

Just as she spoke, the restaurant owner, Raphael, came over to their table. "How was the meal tonight? I hope everything was satisfactory," he asked with a warm smile.

Ramona replied, "The dinner was amazing. Thank you."

Raphael gave a slight bow. "Thank you, my lady."

Gary chimed in, "Yes, my compliments to the chef."

Raphael grinned. "So does that mean my debt is paid off?"

Officer Richardson nodded. "Yes, indeed."

Raphael, still smiling, asked, "Can I offer you some dessert?"

Ramona shook her head with a laugh. "I couldn't eat another bite."

Gary, however, waved the waiter over. "We'll take it to go."

A few minutes later, the waiter returned with doggy bags, including their dessert packed neatly inside. Gary stood up, signaling the end of the evening, and offered, "I'll walk you to your car."

Once they reached Ramona's car, Gary opened the door for her. She slipped inside, adjusting herself in the seat as he closed the door behind her. Leaning down to the window, he said, "I'll call you tomorrow so we can go over the plan."

Ramona gave him a small nod. "Agreed."

With that, she started the engine and drove off into the night, her mind swirling with everything that had unfolded. Gary's promise lingered, but so did the unease.

On the drive home, Ramona couldn't shake the feeling of how different Gary had seemed tonight. She always thought of him as a big, sleazy scumbag — someone she barely tolerated. But beneath his rough exterior, she now saw a glimmer of charm. Still, despite the unexpected shift in her perception, she knew deep down that they could never work as a couple. The thought of it felt impossible.

As she finally pulled into her driveway, her phone buzzed with a text from Gary:

"I hope you got home safe. I had a good time tonight. Hope we can do it again. Goodnight."

Ramona read the message and hesitated for a moment, before replying with a short but polite response. After sending the text, she tossed her phone back into her handbag and got out of the car, taking her keys from the ignition. She unlocked the door and stepped into the quiet of her house.

Once inside, she headed straight for the bathroom to undress and wash away the long, exhausting day. After slipping into her bed, she grabbed the remote and turned on the 10 O'clock news, the low hum of the TV filling the room. Before she realized it, her eyelids grew heavy, and she drifted off to sleep, her mind still spinning with thoughts of Gary and the tangled web that she was caught in.

Chapter 10

We Have Something In Common

Sarah and Jackson welcomed Mrs. Anderson in their home after a long exhausting day at the bakery. Their hearts heavy with the weight following a long frustrating and depressing morning at the police station. As they guided her to the kitchen table, Sarah couldn't help but notice the tremble in Mrs. Anderson's hands. Eager to provide comfort, she gently placed her own hand over Mrs. Anderson's, silently assuring her that this was a safe place.

Sarah noticed Mrs. Anderson starting to gather her things, sensing that the conversation about Ramona couldn't wait any longer. She smiled warmly, trying to ease the tension before diving into the difficult topic.

"I don't know how you do this every day," Sarah said, hoping to start on a lighter note.

Mrs. Anderson, or Margaret as she had just insisted, chuckled softly.

"Honestly, I didn't know if we'd pull it off either. Ever since that restaurant critic gave us a glowing review, business has picked up by 20%."

Sarah nodded in agreement. "Well, your son's a genius — that football promotion he came up with really did the trick."

Before Mrs. Anderson could respond, Jackson chimed in from across the room, munching on one of Mrs. Anderson's famous cookies.

"No, Mom, it was her cooking that did the trick. These cookies are the bomb!"

The two women laughed as Jackson continued to enjoy the cookies with childlike enthusiasm. Mrs. Anderson glanced at her watch and sighed.

"Well, it's getting late. I really should be heading home, but thank you for helping out today, Sarah."

Sarah stepped closer, a gentle look in her eyes.

"It was our pleasure, Margaret," she replied. Then, lowering her voice a little, she added, "I know it's late, but we still need to talk about Ramona. I promise it won't take more than a few minutes."

Mrs. Anderson's expression shifted, her smile fading as the weight of the subject settled in. "Ramona," she said quietly. Then a moment later relented. "Okay, I have a few minutes."

Sarah took a deep breath, knowing that the conversation ahead wouldn't be easy, but it had to happen.

Though Jackson seemed preoccupied with his phone, his attention divided between the conversation at hand and whatever held his interest on the screen. Sarah couldn't help but feel a pang of frustration, wanting his full presence in this moment of need. But she pushed the thought aside, focusing on Mrs. Anderson and the questions that burned within her.

"Why do you think Ramona has something to do with your son's disappearance?"

Sarah asked, her voice filled with genuine concern. Mrs. Anderson's eyes immediately welled up with tears as she struggled to find the words.

"I haven't seen Mark in three weeks," Mrs. Anderson finally managed to say, her voice quivering with a mix of fear and sorrow. Sarah's heart ached for her, the pain of a mother's uncertainty palpable in the room. Sarah pressed further, her voice gentle yet persistent.

"When was the last time you talked to him?"

Mrs. Anderson's tears flowed freely now, her voice choked with emotion.

"The last time I spoke to him was when he told me he was going to Ramona's house to get the rest of his things. I haven't heard from him since then."

Sarah's mind raced, connecting the dots and sensing the unease surrounding Ramona's involvement. She turned her gaze towards Jackson, hoping for his support and attention. But he remained fixated on his phone, seemingly oblivious to the weight of the conversation unfolding before him.

Sarah exchanged worried glances with Mrs. Anderson, she couldn't help but wonder what had captured Jackson's attention so completely. Was it a mere distraction, or was there something more to his dctachment? With a heavy sigh, she decided to address it later, for now, their focus needed to be on finding answers for her and bringing her son home. Mrs. Anderson eyes filled with worry.

She had went to the dimly lit police station to file a police report, her heart heavy with the weight of her son's disappearance. But deep within her, a nagging feeling had still persisted, a gut instinct that whispered a name — Ramona. She couldn't shake the belief that Ramona had something to do with her son's vanishing, a feeling that resonated in her old bones.

In the moment, Sarah, even though concerned about her friend, glanced over at Jackson, who was lost in his own thoughts.

"Boy, are you listening?" Sarah's voice broke through the silence, urging Jackson to join the conversation. He looked up, his eyes clouded with confusion.

"I'm so sorry," he stammered, "but I'm confused about this text that I received."

Sarah's frustration grew, and she raised her voice. "Can't you see, Mrs. Anderson is heartbroken? What could possibly be so important that you're distracted right now?"

 Jackson's gaze shifted, torn between the text message and the distress in the room. "I'm sorry," he muttered, "I just... I don't understand."

Mrs. Anderson, understanding the younger generation's attachment to their phones, sighed softly. "I have grand kids, they're always on their phones," she said, her voice tinged with empathy.

Sarah, however, was not as forgiven. And as the tension lingered, Mrs. Anderson's eyes wandered, and she noticed something familiar about the two young individuals sitting beside her.

"I happened to notice you two were also at the police station," she remarked out of nowhere, her voice filled with curiosity.

Sarah, eager to explain their presence, began recounting the events that had led them there.

"Ramona," Sarah began, her voice filled with a mix of anger and concern, "Tried to run over Jackson with her car." But even as Sarah said it, Mrs. Anderson wasn't surprised.

94

"Why in the world would she do that?" said, his voice trembling with fear. Coming to expect this sort of thing from her ex-daughter-in-law now.

"Because she's crazy," Jackson replied, his tone laced with bitterness.

"Well, we have something in common in regards to Ramona, then."

Sarah agreed, her eyes darting around the room nervously.

"We need to do something. It's obvious the police are not going to help us."

Sarah looked over at Jackson, who was still clutching his phone tightly.

"Put that phone down, Jackson," she pleaded. "We need to handle this ourselves."

Jackson hesitated for a moment, torn between his instinct to call for help and his trust in Sarah.

"Mom, I'm sorry, but I can't just put the phone down. We need backup."

Mrs. Anderson, curious and concerned, interjected, "What are we going to do?"

Sarah's resolve shone through her eyes as she got up from the table.

"We're going to Ramona's house," she declared.

Mrs. Anderson raised an eyebrow, skeptical. "Do you think that's wise?"

Sarah paused, her mind racing with possibilities. "Yes, besides, there's strength in numbers."

Mrs. Anderson chuckled, a hint of sarcasm in her voice. "That's true, but she has numbers too. Six-six-six, to be exact."

Sarah couldn't help but laugh, a nervous release of tension. "Well, we'll just have to rely on our own strength then."

They got up from the table, Sarah grabbed Mrs. Anderson's handbag, knowing they might need any resources they could get their hands on. The three of them set off towards Ramona's house, their hearts pounding with a mix of fear.

As they walk towards the door, the feeling of dread intensifies. Jackson's unease is palpable, and they cannot shake the feeling that something evil awaits them inside. One thing is for certain — wherever lies behind those doors, the devil not prevail.

They quickly stormed out of the house, urgency in every step. Jackson fumbled with the keys, locking the door behind them as Sarah help Mrs. Anderson into the car. "Jackson, hurry up!" Sarah shouted, already buckled in and ready to go.

Jackson sprinted to the car and slid into the passenger seat, shutting the door as they sped off. As the car whizzed down the road, Jackson turned to his mother. "I don't think we should be going to Ramona's house," he said hesitantly.

Mrs. Anderson, with a nervous laugh, agreed. "I have to admit, it's after 10 P.M., and besides, everyone knows vampires attack at night."

Sarah burst into laughter from the driver's seat. "We'll be fine!" she said, amused by Mrs. Anderson's playful anxiety.

But Mrs. Anderson wasn't quite done. "Maybe we should stop at the grocery store first," she said earnestly.

Sarah, puzzled, glanced at her in the rearview mirror. "Why?"

Mrs. Anderson leaned forward conspiratorially. "We need to buy some garlic — for protection. What if she bites us or something?"

Sarah's laughter filled the car, the ridiculousness of the situation too much to contain. "Oh, Mrs. Anderson, you are crazy!"

Jackson, however, wasn't laughing. He turned to his mother with a serious expression. "Mom, she's right! Ramona *does* bite."

Sarah nearly choked on her laughter, caught between amusement and disbelief, as the strange tension of the night continued to swirl around them.

Jackson smirked, a mischievous glint in his eyes. "You don't understand, Mom. Ramona's crazy! She was scratching, biting — leaving all kinds of marks on me. That woman is a freak!" He looked proud of himself, a small, smug smile creeping across his face.

Mrs. Anderson's jaw dropped, absolutely shocked by her son's admission. Sarah, unable to contain her frustration, whipped around from the driver's seat and glared at Jackson. "Boy, I am your mother! I did *not* need to hear that. This is exactly why you're in trouble. Now, keep it in your pants!"

Mrs. Anderson, still in disbelief, gasped. "Oh my Lord! Sarah, I *told* you! The woman's unhinged. She's eating your son — *literally*! She's into cannibalism!"

Sarah, wide-eyed and horrified, covered her mouth. "Margaret!" she exclaimed, half-laughing, half-shocked at Mrs. Anderson's wild assumption.

Just as they pulled up to Ramona's house, the tension in the car shifted from absurd to uneasy. The house loomed ahead, quiet and dark. Sarah took a deep breath, trying to steady her nerves. "We're here," she announced, her voice tense.

But before anyone could move, Mrs. Anderson raised her hand in alarm. "Wait! I think I've got a cross in my purse!"

Sarah groaned softly, rubbing her forehead, trying to hold back a laugh. "Margaret, this isn't an exorcism."

Mrs. Anderson, rummaging through her purse, muttered, "Better safe than sorry."

Sarah parked the car, exhaling heavily as she got out and walked around to help Mrs. Anderson. Jackson, in typical fashion, slammed his car door, sending a ripple of noise through the quiet neighborhood. The barking dogs followed immediately, piercing the night air.

"Must you make so much noise?" Sarah hissed at him. "Ramona has nosy neighbors, and they'll call the police on us in a second."

Jackson shrugged, trying to brush it off. "Well, maybe we could use the police right now."

Mrs. Anderson, always ready with a dramatic line, chimed in, "And tell them what? That the devil is out here snatching people's souls?"

Sarah shot her a confused glance, then turned back to Jackson. "Margaret's not wrong, in a weird way. The police won't do anything without proof."

Jackson shook his head, reluctant. "Alright, Mom, but I still think this is a bad idea."

Sarah tried to calm their nerves, her voice steady but tinged with unease. "It'll be fine. I know Ramona. I know how she thinks."

Mrs. Anderson, never one to let a moment pass, threw in a sarcastic jab. "You didn't know she was sleeping with your son, though."

Jackson turned his head, guilt spreading across his face. Sarah shot him an unreadable look that lingered. "Yes, well, we all have our crosses to bear," she said, her tone heavy with resignation. "Let's just get this over with."

They started walking up the steps to Ramona's front door. Mrs. Anderson clutched her purse, her voice hushed but dramatic as ever.

"Speaking of crosses, I've got mine right here. I just wish we had some holy water to rebuke the devil."

Sarah rolled her eyes, muttering under her breath, "Why, Lord, do I always end up in these situations?"

Taking a deep breath, she raised her hand and knocked firmly on Ramona's door, bracing herself for whatever lay on the other side.

Ramona didn't answer the door. Jackson, eager to escape the tension, quickly said, "She didn't answer. Let's go," as he darted down the steps.

Mrs. Anderson, always dramatic, muttered, "Maybe the bat is out lurking around town, looking for more victims."

Sarah rolled her eyes, glancing around the quiet neighborhood. "Boy, get your ass back up these steps. Margaret, you must've been something else in your heyday."

She nodded toward the garage. "Besides, her car's still parked here."

Margaret smirked, undeterred. "Knock again. I got your back!"

Sarah knocked once more, her fist hitting the door with a bit more urgency. The dogs in the neighborhood responded, barking louder and more frantically. Suddenly, a light flickered on inside the house. The sound of footsteps could be heard approaching the door, and the tension mounted.

Margaret's eyes widened. "Oh hell, she's out of her coffin!" she whispered dramatically, clutching her purse tighter.

And then the door creaked opened.

Chapter 11

The Mysterious Barrett

It was a loud thump coming from the basement. Ramona's heart raced as she glanced at the security camera feed, seeing three familiar faces approaching her steps. Panic surged through her as she realized they were already at her doorstep. Before she could react, Sarah, a close frenemy of Ramona's, snatched Jackson's phone from his hand. Irritated, Jackson protested, but Sarah silenced him with a stern look.

Confusion clouded Jackson's face as he read a text from Allison, a girl he had apparently stood up on a date. His voice trembled as he relayed the message to us,

"Mom, Allison said she never wants to see me again."

Sarah, always quick to take charge, dismissed the issue for later, promising to discuss it with Jackson. But before we could delve into the matter, Ramona, swung open the door, her tone laced with annoyance.

"What do you want? You do know what time it is?"

Ramona's words dripped with hostility as Sarah forcefully barged into her house. "We need to talk"

Ramona crossed her arms, glaring at Sarah and clearly shocked, retorted, "I don't remember inviting you into my house."

Mrs. Anderson, standing behind Sarah, muttered, "Sarah, don't get too close. She might not have all her shots."

Ramona's eyes flashed with anger. "Shut up you old bat!"

She took a step closer to Mrs. Anderson, her voice dripping with hostility. Mrs. Anderson wasn't the one to back down. "Who are you calling an old bat? You're the one who hangs upside down in her closet."

Before things could blow even more out of proportion, Sarah quickly stepped between them, holding out her arms to keep the peace. "Margaret, please," she pleaded, trying to calm her down.

"Ramona, just tell us where Marcus is, and we'll leave. That's all we need."

Mrs. Anderson, Ramona's ex-mother-in-law, cut through the tension, her voice firm and demanding, "Cut the bullshit, Ramona. Where is Marcus?"

Ramona's response was cold and detached, "I told you a few days ago, didn't I? I don't know where he's at. Your son is none of my concern. We are divorced, remember?"

Attempting to diffuse the escalating situation, Sarah stepped in, her voice calm yet urgent,

"Mrs. Anderson, I'll handle this." Then she turned to Ramona, "Marcus is missing."

Ramona's indifference only fueled Sarah's suspicion. Ramona's eyes flicked to Sarah, her voice low and cold.

"I'm only going to tell you this once. I don't know where Marcus is. Now, get out of my house before you really make me angry."

But just as the tension reached its peak, a loud thump echoed through the house, causing them all to freeze in their tracks.

Sarah's eyes widened as she questioned the source of the noise. Sarah, losing her patience, pushed Ramona out of the way.

"We're not leaving until you tell us what's going on."

Ramona, seemingly unfazed, nonchalantly replied, "I was doing laundry."

The air grew heavy with unspoken questions and mounting suspicion. Jackson looked at Ramona and said, "You sure do a lot of laundry."

Ramona, with a calm smile, replied, "Cleanliness is next to godliness. Now, excuse me, I must get back to my laundry."

As Mrs. Anderson's voice echoed through the air, a voice shouted, "The devil is a liar. Tell me, where is my son?"

Sarah, feeling a sense of urgency, started to walk towards the basement, but Ramona quickly stopped her.

"Where do you think you're going?" she asked. Jackson's eyes wandered around the room, until they landed on a red barrette. It was the exact same one that Allison had in her hair. Shocked, Jackson interrupted the conversation between Ramona and Sarah.

"Mom, mom, we should let Ramona continue to do her laundry," he urgently pleaded, trying to get his mother and Mrs. Anderson out of Ramona's house. However, Sarah was determined.

"Not until I get some answers. What are you hiding, Ramona?"

Mrs. Anderson, noticing the terror in Jackson's eyes, intervened.

"Sarah, Jackson is right. We should be going now."

But Sarah was not convinced. "No, she tried to kill my son!" Jackson pulled his mother out of the house, and as they left, Mrs. Anderson warned, "This is not over."

Ramona slammed the door shut behind them.

The three of them walked down the steps, their voices filled with anger and concern. Sarah words hung in the air, her tone fueled with suspicion, "Ramona is hiding something."

Mrs. Anderson, her face etched with worry, responded, "She is crazy, and we have to let the police handle it."

Jackson, his voice steady and determined, chimed in, "Mom, she is right. Ramona's elevator don't go to the top floor. Besides, I have to talk to you about Allison."

Sarah couldn't help but interject, her frustration evident, "Boy, so what if the girl dumped you? Get over it."

Jackson, undeterred, explained, "I think Ramona has something to do with Allison."

Confusion clouded Sarah's face as she questioned, "Jackson, what are you talking about?"

Mrs. Anderson, attempting to calm the tension, intervened, "Wait a minute! Let him speak."

Sarah reluctantly allowed Jackson to continue. He took a deep breath and revealed, "I've been trying to call Allison for the last couple of days, but she hasn't been returning my phone calls."

Sarah's confusion deepened, her voice tinged with worry, "What are you saying, Jackson?"

Mrs. Anderson's eyes widened as realization dawned upon her, "Jackson, I saw your face in the house. You think the two situations are connected?"

Jackson nodded solemnly, his gaze fixed on the ground. Sarah's voice trembled as she processed the implications, "Are you telling me Ramona kidnapped Allison?"

Jackson's nod confirmed her worst fears. Panic surged through Sarah's veins as she exclaimed, "We have to call the detective."

Mrs. Anderson shook her head.

"We have to call on a higher power. Because that bitch is crazy."

Jackson shook his head, "Ramona is definitely up to something."

Sarah sighed, frustrated. "I know, but there's nothing we can do about it now. We need to get Margaret home."

"But, Mom, what are we going to do about Ramona?" Jackson asked, his voice filled with concern.

"We'll talk about it in the car," Sarah said, trying to keep her composure.

As they turned to leave, Mrs. Anderson chimed in with a sly smile, "Just give me enough time to find my silver bullets."

Sarah laughed. "What happened to the sweet old lady from this morning?"

Mrs. Anderson gave Sarah a deadpan look. "What sweet old woman?"

Shaking her head, Sarah helped Mrs. Anderson into the car, chuckling under her breath as she thought about the bizarre turn of events.

Little did they know, as they sped through the darkened streets that the truth were about to uncover would not only save Allison, but also unravel a web of secrets that would change their lives forever.

Ramona stormed up the stairs, her heels clicking sharply on the wood, and snatched her phone from the nightstand. She dialed Officer Richardson with trembling fingers. The phone barely rang before Gary answered with his usual smugness.

"Hey, gorgeous! You miss me already?" His voice was thick with sleaze, causing Ramona to roll her eyes in disgust.

"No, Gary. I have a problem," she snapped, her tone sharp.

Sensing the tension, Gary's voice shifted. "What did you do now?"

Ramona inhaled sharply, trying to calm her anger. "It's about the issue we discussed earlier."

Gary's laugh was humorless. "That's not a problem, Ramona. That's a disaster you created."

Her patience was wearing thin. "Are you going to help me or not?"

There was a pause on the other end before Gary replied, his tone slightly exasperated. "Alright, just tell me what's going on?"

Ramona began explaining the confrontation she had with Sarah and Mrs. Anderson, her voice rising with each sentence.

Gary's shout through the phone startled her. "Are you crazy?! You let them in your house?!"

"Not voluntarily! I'm not some old lady they can just push around," Ramona hissed. "That witch Margaret practically bullied her way in."

Gary's tone dropped, more serious now. "Do not poke the mama bear."

Ramona scowled, her fingers tightening around her phone. "What the hell is that supposed to mean?"

"Just... don't provoke Mrs. Anderson. Leave her to me. I'll handle this," Gary said, his voice laced with caution.

Ramona was still fuming. "Whatever," she spat.

"I'll call you tomorrow with a plan," Gary assured her.

Before she could respond, the call ended. Ramona threw her phone onto the bed, feeling the heat of anger pulse through her body. Steam might as well have been coming out of her ears. She was tired of everyone treating her like she was the one in the wrong. But this time, she promised herself, she'd come out on top—no matter what it took.

Chapter 12

Evidence Don't Lie

The next day, Detective Miller arrived at Sarah's house, ready to tear into the mysterious case that had been brought to his attention. As he stepped onto the porch, Sarah greeted him with a warm smile, offering a cup of coffee and grateful for the gesture, he kindly declined, eager to get down to business.

To his surprise, Mrs. Anderson, the woman he had encountered in just days before, was also present. Her piercing eyes met his, and she wasted no time in reminding him of their previous encounter. "Yes, I'm the crazy old lady that was in your office the other day," she stated matter-of-fact.

Detective Miller was shocked by her bold accusation. "I did not say that you were crazy," he defended himself. "I merely suggested that you can't go around making wild accusations without any evidence."

Sarah interjected, her voice filled with urgency. "Our accusations are not wild, Detective. Ramona is up to something, and I believe she's hiding something in her basement that she doesn't want anyone to know about."

Detective Miller's eyebrows furrowed in confusion. "Wait, how do you know she has something in the basement? And if I recall correctly, you have a restraining order against her."

Sarah's voice rose with frustration. "Well, I had to do something! She's been terrorizing us for months. You said we have to let you do your job, so here we are, seeking your help."

Jackson, stood up abruptly, his face etched with concern. "What's the point of waiting for her to have everyone in her basement? We need to act now!"

When that got him no response, Jackson yelled, "I have proof that Ramona had something to do with Allison Wilson's disappearance."

Detective Miller had a puzzled look on his face. "Did you say Allison Wilson?"

Jackson nodded vigorously. "Yes, Allison Wilson."

Detective Miller's mind raced, trying to make sense of the situation. Confusion clouded his thoughts as he realized there was more to this case than he had initially anticipated. Determined to uncover the truth, he took a deep breath and addressed the anxious people before him.

"Alright, let's start from the beginning. Tell me everything you know, and we'll figure this out together."

Detective Miller took a moment to process the information being thrown at him. Sarah's accusations, Mrs. Anderson's claims of being labeled as crazy, and the mention of a possible hidden secret in Ramona's basement all swirled around in his mind. He had to get to the bottom of this, but the pieces of the puzzle were not fitting together quite yet.

Taking a deep breath, Detective Miller decided to approach the situation with caution. He needed to gather more information before jumping to any conclusions. With a uncertain but firm look in his eyes, he turned to Sarah and Mrs. Anderson and said, "I will need to investigate this further. Can you both provide me with any evidence or leads that may support your claims?"

Sarah and Mrs. Anderson exchanged a knowing glance before nodding in agreement. It was clear that they were both convinced of the truth behind their suspicions. As Detective Miller prepared to delve deeper into the mystery at hand, he couldn't shake the feeling that there was more to this case than met the eye. And he was willing to go to whatever lengths to uncover the truth, no matter what it may reveal.

Sarah, tried to explain what Jackson was talking about. "When we were at Ramona's, Jackson noticed Allison's red barrette." He pulled out his phone and showed the detective a picture of the hair barrette. "This is the same exact one she wore on our date."

Mrs. Anderson, Ramona's ex-mother-in-law, chimed in, her voice filled with urgency. "Is that enough proof, Detective Miller? We've been telling you for weeks that Ramona is up to something!"

Detective Miller sighed, his expression grave. "Unfortunately, that is not enough evidence. However, Allison's parents came to the police station today to report her missing. It seems we have a case on our hands."

Mrs. Anderson's eyes widened. "I told you that I wasn't crazy! Ramona is involved in this, I just know it."

Jackson's mind raced with horrifying possibilities and anxiety churned in his stomach. "What if she has everyone locked up in her basement?"

Detective Miller held up his hand, trying to calm the frantic group. "Okay, everyone just calm down. I will send two uniformed police officers to Ramona's house to talk to her. In the meanwhile, I advise all of you to stay away from Ramona until we have more information."

The truth lay hidden in the shadows, and Jackson was resolute in his quest to reveal it, regardless of the consequences.

Later at the police station, Detective Miller was discussing the case with Captain Casey. "Something isn't adding up with this Ramona person."

Captain Casey, See how preoccupied with paperwork on his desk, responded, "Whatever you do, make sure you dot your I's and cross your T's. She's a very powerful person."

"I will, Captain," Miller assured him as he started to leave.

"To be on the safe side, send two officers to Ramona's house," the Captain added.

As Miller walked down the hallway, he saw Officer Richardson and called out, "Did you file the case for the Wilson girl?"

"Yes," Richardson replied dismissively.

"But I don't think there's much to it. She sounds like a rich, spoiled brat trying to get attention."

Miller raised an eyebrow. "Did you at least look into it?"

Richardson shrugged. "No, I have higher-priority cases."

Richardson paused, sensing the tension. "Nothing about the complaints seemed suspicious to you?" he asked again.

"No, why? Did something happen?" Richardson replied, now slightly curious.

Miller gave him a pointed look. "Don't worry about it. I'll handle it. Come here for a moment."

Before Richardson could walk away, Miller asked another question. "You also took the Anderson complaints, correct?"

"Yes, sir," Richardson confirmed, his tone clipped.

Detective Miller nodded. "I'm going to send two uniformed officers to Ramona Whitmore's house."

Richardson hesitated for a moment, then quickly offered, "I can go since I'm familiar with the complaints."

Miller, in a sarcastic tone, replied, "No, that won't be necessary. Since you have so many *high-priority* cases tonight, I wouldn't want to *bother* you with this one."

His eyes lingered on Richardson, the unspoken criticism hanging in the air as he walked away.

Ramona, they're sending two officers to your house—Moore and Sanchez. They're looking for something, a red barrette. Be ready.

He hit send and slipped the phone back into his pocket, his mind racing. His heart pounded as he thought about what could happen if they found something at Ramona's place. There was no turning back now — he was in too deep.

Meanwhile, Detective Miller watched Richardson leave, suspicion clouding his expression as he continued briefing the officers. "Be thorough and report anything unusual. We can't leave any stone unturned with this one."

Two hours later, Officers Sanchez and Moore arrived at Ramona's house. She opened the door with a pleasant smile. "Good afternoon, officers. How can I help you?" she asked.

"May we come in?" Officer Sanchez inquired.

Ramona nodded, opening the door wider to let them inside. Once they were in, she offered, "Would you like something to drink?"

The officers politely declined. Moore then got straight to the point, "We understand there's been some concern about your ex-husband Marcus, and a few reports have come in. We're just checking in to see if you can provide any more information. When was the last time you saw him?"

Ramona smiled calmly as she engaged with Moore, while Sanchez discreetly scanned the room, looking for anything out of place. She crossed her arms, leaning against the doorway, her voice casual.

"I haven't seen Marcus in weeks. He hasn't been a part of my life for a while now."

As Moore continued asking questions, Sanchez wandered through the living room, his eyes scanning every corner. He subtly checked for anything out of place, any signs of disturbance. The house was immaculately clean, almost too perfect, which only made him more suspicious.

Suddenly, something caught his eye—a red fabric peeking out from under a pile of magazines on the coffee table. He discreetly lifted the magazines and uncovered a red hair barrette. His heart quickened.

"Moore, I think I found something."

Sanchez subtly moved a stack of magazines, revealing a red hair barrette on the coffee table. Moore, noticing the action, walked closer and stood beside Sanchez. Ramona, keeping her composure, asked calmly, "Is something wrong, Officer?"

Clearing his throat, Moore spoke up, "Mrs. Whitmore, do you know an Allison Wilson?"

Ramona tilted her head, pretending to think for a moment. "Allison Wilson? No, the name doesn't ring a bell."

Sanchez glanced at Moore before stepping forward. "Are you sure, Mrs. Whitmore? We were informed that her parents are clients of yours."

Ramona nodded. "Oh, yes. The Wilsons are indeed clients. But I have many clients, Officer. You can't expect me to know them all on a first-name basis."

Moore responded, "I'm sure you do. However, her parents filed a missing person report two days ago."

Ramona widened her eyes, feigning shock. "That's terrible. I had no idea. I'm so sorry to hear that."

Sanchez didn't let up. "We have witnesses who say you were the last person to see her."

Ramona's demeanor shifted as she became more defensive. "What are you implying, Officer? Are you suggesting I had something to do with her disappearance?"

Moore quickly interjected, his tone calm and measured. "We're not accusing you of anything, Mrs. Whitmore. But in the missing person report, it states that Allison was last seen wearing a red barrette."

Ramona stood up, her voice rising slightly. "And what does that have to do with me?"

Sanchez pointed to the red barrette on her coffee table. "It just so happens that there's a red barrette right here."

Ramona folded her arms, her voice steady but tense. "If you must know, Allison left it at one of the condos she was viewing. It's nothing more than that."

Moore, with a skeptical tone, asked, "Why didn't you return it to Allison?"

Ramona, maintaining her calm, replied, "Officers, I am a very busy person. I don't have the time to return every little item my clients leave behind. Now, if you'll excuse me, I have to get ready for my next appointment."

Sanchez nodded, though clearly not fully satisfied. "Well, thank you for your time, Mrs. Whitmore."

Ramona led the officers to the door, offering a polite but forced smile. As they stepped outside, Moore turned back and added firmly, "Just don't leave town."

Once outside, Sanchez turned to Moore. "She's definitely hiding something."

Moore nodded in agreement. "Yeah, she's definitely hiding something."

Once Officer Sanchez and Moore left Ramona's house, she quickly called Officer Richardson.

"Gary, I thought you were going to help me," she said urgently.

Officer Richardson replied, I gave you a heads up. I mentioned that two officers would be coming to your house."

Ramona's voice trembled as she spoke, "They're accusing me of kidnapping Allison Wilson.

"Officer Richardson tried to calm her down, saying, "Ramona, calm down. They have no evidence on you." Ramona couldn't contain her anxiety and began pacing around the house.

"They found the girl's barrette," she exclaimed.

Officer Richardson's voice rose in frustration,

"What the hell, Ramona? How can you be so sloppy? I told you they were coming to look for the barrette!"

Ramona shot back, her voice filled with anger, "Who do you think you're talking to?"

Gary's voice took on a sharp edge as he warned, "Ramona, watch your tone. You are forgetting who's keeping you out of jail.

Ramona asked, "What should we do now?"

Officer Richardson's tone turned serious, "We have to get rid of Allison."

Ramona was shocked, "Get rid of her? I don't want to kill her."

Officer Richardson replied coldly, "Do you want my help or not? Meet at Jake's Place at 9:00 PM, and we'll figure this out."

Ramona could feel her pulse racing. She didn't like being talked to this way, especially by someone like Gary. But the situation was spiraling out of control, and she needed to act quickly.

As Gary hung up abruptly, Ramona threw her phone down on the couch and stared at it, her mind churning. The weight of the situation was becoming unbearable. She never imagined things would go this far, and now Gary was suggesting they "get rid of" Allison? That wasn't what she signed up for.

She paced around her living room, muttering to herself. "I didn't come this far just to lose everything because of some damn barrette." But what could she do now? With Gary growing more unpredictable, she knew she had to stay one step ahead—if not, he might turn on her just as quickly as he'd helped her before.

She glanced at the clock. 7:15 PM.

There wasn't much time left until the meeting at Jake's Place. She needed a plan—and fast.

Back at the police station, Officer Sanchez, Officer Moore, and Detective Miller sat in the captain's office, the air thick with tension.

Sanchez spoke up first, "Ramona is really unpredictable. We can't afford to underestimate her. She acts calm, but she's dangerous."

Moore added, "She had the girl's red barrette hidden under some magazines. That's not just forgetfulness; that's intent."

Detective Miller, leaning back in his chair, replied with a hint of frustration, "I get it, but we still don't have any real proof. Just finding the barrette isn't enough to make a solid case."

Sanchez pressed further, "She *has* the barrette in her house, though. That's suspicious as hell."

Miller rubbed his temple. "Yeah, but a high-powered attorney could easily argue that Allison left it there. Ramona even said she didn't have time to return it, which gives her plausible deniability."

The three men began debating, voices rising, until the captain cut in. "Enough. Detective Miller's right. We can't move too fast on this. Ramona's father is a powerful politician, and we don't need a lawsuit on our hands. We need more evidence—real evidence—before we can make any serious moves."

Sanchez sighed, "So, what now? Do we just sit back and wait?"

The captain nodded grimly. "Unfortunately, yes. We need her to make a mistake. But mark my words, we'll be ready when she does."

Detective Miller leaned forward. "Can we at least get a warrant to search her house more thoroughly?

The captain hesitated, then replied, "I'll think about it. But remember, everything we've discussed stays in this office. I've got a feeling we've got a snitch in the department, and we can't risk any leaks."

The room fell into a heavy silence as the weight of the situation sank in. Everyone knew the next move could make or break the case.

Back at Ramona's she knew she had to be cautious. The police were already suspicious of her involvement in Marcus' disappearance, and Gary could easily turn on her to save his own skin. She couldn't risk being recognized, not tonight.

Heading to her closet, she reached up to the top shelf, pulling down the old dark brown wig she had worn for a Halloween party years ago. It was a far cry from her usual blonde hair, but that was exactly the point. She tossed the wig onto the bed, then rummaged through her clothes until she found a loose-fitting shirt and baggy jeans, the kind of outfit that would hide her signature hourglass figure. The disguise was coming together.

She stood in front of the mirror, quickly applying minimal makeup to cover her features, opting for neutral tones to make her look more plain. The finishing touch was a pair of oversized glasses, ones that would draw attention away from her facial features but still allow her to see everything going on around her.

When she looked in the mirror again, she barely recognized herself. Gone was the glamorous woman everyone knew. In her place stood a nondescript figure—someone who could easily slip in and out of places without attracting a second glance.

Ramona exhaled sharply, feeling a small sense of relief. She was ready. Grabbing her purse, she headed to the door, her mind racing. Gary couldn't set her up. He wouldn't dare. He needed her just as much as she needed him. But still, she wouldn't take any chances.

She slipped into her car and started the engine, heading towards Jake's Place. The drive took longer than expected, and with every passing minute, the tension grew. Finally, she pulled up outside the bar, her heart pounding in her chest.

Ramona arrived at Jake's Place, the dim lights casting long shadows across the parking lot. Her hands tightened on the steering wheel as she parked the car, and took a deep breath to calm her racing heart. She scanned the area from inside the vehicle, making sure there were no signs of cops or anyone else who might recognize her. Ramona adjusted her glasses, took a deep breath, and stepped out of the car. This meeting could change everything. She had hoped for a quiet meeting with Gary, but it seemed fate had other plans. The Eagles' game had drawn in a larger crowd then she had anticipated.

She inhaled deeply, calming herself before stepping out of the car. She had to be careful. Meeting Gary could either secure her position or be the moment everything crumbled. But she was prepared. Gary was in just as deep as she was, and if he thought for a second that he could turn on her, she'd be ready to pull him down with her.

Ramona pulled up the hood of her jacket and walked toward the entrance of Jake's Place. The door creaked as she entered, the stale smell of beer and cigarettes filling her senses. She scanned the dimly lit room, her gaze landing on Gary sitting in the far corner booth, looking impatient.

He didn't notice her at first, but when she approached the table, his eyes flickered with surprise. "Ramona?" he asked, trying to keep his voice low but tinged with shock.

She slid into the booth across from him. "Yeah, it's me," she said quietly, pulling down her hood. "I told you I wasn't taking any chances."

Gary's eyes narrowed as he leaned in closer. "Good. Now, let's plan our next move?" he said, with a tense voice.

"Shall we order some drinks?"

Gary discreetly signaled the waiter to come over, who inquired about their drink orders.

After taking their orders, the waiter returned with their drinks a few minutes later. Ramona swiftly finished her drink and requested another, urging Gary to keep them coming.

Sensing her eagerness, Gary intervened, moving the glass away from her.

"You need to slow down," he cautioned.

Ramona, undeterred, remarked, "This situation is intense. I don't know what to do."

Gary gently touched her hand, offering reassurance.

"I understand your apprehension, but you must trust my judgment. Your decisions are becoming too risky," he advised.

"I have no choice but to trust you," Ramona conceded.

"I've got your back! It's time to set the plan in motion," declared Gary.

Curiously, Ramona inquired, "What plan are you referring to?"

Gary smirked and replied, "We need to get Rid of Allison."

Ramona froze for a moment, her hand resting on the glass, as Gary's words sank in. "Get rid of Allison?" she whispered, her voice unsteady. "I thought you said we wouldn't hurt her."

Gary leaned forward, his tone smooth but firm. "We're not talking about hurting her, Ramona. But Allison is a loose end. If we don't handle this the right way, it's all going to blow up in our faces."

Ramona's heart pounded, and she glanced around nervously, making sure no one was listening. "I just... I don't know. This wasn't supposed to go this far." She took another quick sip of her drink, her eyes darting back to Gary. "What's your plan, exactly?"

Gary's smirk remained in place, his confidence unsettling. "Allison needs to disappear—permanently, but not in the way you think. We move her somewhere no one will ever find her. She'll be alive, but she'll be out of our way. We can make it look like she just ran off. Once we do that, the heat will die down, and you won't be a suspect anymore."

Ramona's breath caught. "You want to make her vanish?" she asked, her voice barely above a whisper. "That's risky, Gary. What if something goes wrong?"

Gary's expression darkened, his grip tightening on his glass. "Nothing will go wrong if you do exactly what I tell you to do. We're out of options, Ramona. It's either this or prison for both of us. Are you in or not?"

Ramona hesitated, the weight of the situation pressing down on her. She knew she was in too deep to back out now. With a shaky breath, she nodded. "I'm in," she said quietly. "But this better work, Gary. If it doesn't, we're both done for."

Gary's smirk returned. "Trust me, Ramona. This is the only way out. Meet me at the warehouse tomorrow night. We'll take care of everything."

Ramona nodded, but her gut twisted in fear as she silently questioned if she could trust him at all.

"Fine," she said quietly. "But if anything goes wrong, Gary, it's not just me you'll have to worry about. You're in just as deep."

Gary smirked, taking another sip of his drink. "I wouldn't have it any other way."

Gary placed the drink on the table and pulled out a small vial of liquid from his pocket. "Oh, one more thing. Give her this," he said, sliding the vial across the table.

Ramona rolled her eyes in frustration. "What the hell is this?" she asked, her voice laced with irritation.

"You ask too many questions," Gary replied, his tone cold and dismissive. He took one last sip of his drink and stood up. "I'll call you tomorrow," he said nonchalantly before turning and walking out of the bar, leaving Ramona sitting there, staring at the vial in disbelief.

Chapter 13

Get Rid Of Her

The following morning, Ramona woke up feeling a heavyweight pressing down on her. The current situation with Allison weighed on her mind as she got out of bed to fix breakfast. Every moment felt like a ticking time bomb. She hesitated, staring at the vial Gary had given her the previous night. Doubts consumed her—she didn't know what the substance would do to Allison, and Gary, ruthless and cold, clearly didn't care. She stuffed the vial back into her pocket and headed towards the basement, but just before she opened the door, her phone rang. It was Gary.

With a sigh, she pressed the green button. "Hello?" she answered.

Gary's voice was sharp. "Ramona, quick. Turn on the news."

Her heart sank as she walked back into the kitchen, putting the tray of food she had prepared for Mark and Allison on the counter. She grabbed the remote and switched on the TV. There they were—Mr. and Mrs. Wilson, standing in front of the police station, addressing the media. Ramona's stomach churned.

"What the hell are we gonna do now?" she asked, her voice trembling.

Gary's voice remained calm, almost too calm. "Relax, don't do anything stupid."

"How can you be so calm, Gary? They're offering a reward for her safe return. People are going to start asking more questions," Ramona said, panic rising in her voice.

"This situation is a cakewalk for me," Gary replied coolly. "We'll handle it tonight."

The phone went silent for a moment, and Ramona felt herself spiraling. "Ramona, did you hear what I said?" Gary's voice snapped her back to reality.

"I can't do this," she stammered, her nerves frayed.

Gary's tone grew harsher. "Ramona, get yourself together. I'm sending two men over there at 7 P.M., make sure everything is ready."

Ramona didn't respond immediately. She felt trapped. "Ramona, did you hear me?"

"Yes, I heard you," she finally replied, her voice barely a whisper.

"Don't forget to give Allison the stuff I gave you," Gary reminded her.

Ramona's anxiety flared again. "How do I know it won't kill her?"

Gary's patience snapped. "I don't have time for this bullshit!" he shouted, and the call abruptly disconnected.

Shaking, Ramona went to the refrigerator and grabbed some orange juice. She poured the clear liquid substance into the juice, stirring it slowly as dread crept up her spine. What was she about to do? She picked up the tray of food, her hands trembling, and made her way to the basement.

As she descended the steps, the weight of her decisions bore down on her like never before.

Mark lifted his head, locking eyes with Ramona. His voice was strained but firm as he said, "Enough is enough. You've proved your point. It's time to let us go."

Ramona's eyes narrowed, her tone cold. "You're in no position to tell me what to do, Mark."

"Okay!" Mark replied, his frustration evident. "But you're not going to get away with this."

"Shut up, Marcus!" Ramona snapped, her voice rising in anger.

Mark kept pushing, his gaze flicking to Allison. "Just let the girl go. By now, someone is definitely looking for her."

Ramona hesitated, her expression hardening. "You're right," she finally said, her voice dripping with sarcasm. She walked over to Allison, who looked terrified and weak, bound in her chair.

With a twisted smile, Ramona bent down, placing the tray on Allison's lap. "I'm gonna let you go," she whispered, her eyes dark as she glanced at the glass of orange juice she had just spiked.

"Before I let you go, I'll give you something to eat. You need to keep your strength up," Ramona said calmly, her voice almost motherly. Allison's eyes widened with fear as she shook her head. "No! I'm not hungry."

Ramona smiled sweetly. "At least drink some juice. I don't want you to get dehydrated before your parents come to pick you up."

Allison looked at her skeptically, unsure of what to believe. "My parents are coming to pick me up?"

"Yes, darling, they are," Ramona replied, her tone dripping with false kindness.

As Ramona walked away, Mark shot her a hard look. "What are you up to, Ramona?" he asked, suspicion thick in his voice.

Ramona paused at the top of the basement stairs, turning to look at Mark with a sarcastic smile. "Like you said, Mark, Allison has nothing to do with this situation." She quickly slammed the door, cutting off his response.

She immediately called Gary. "It's done!" she said, her voice tense.

Gary's voice was cold on the other end of the line. "Did you make sure she drank all of the juice?"

"Yes, Gary, I'm not stupid!" Ramona snapped.

"Good. My men will be there in two hours," Gary replied, his tone chillingly calm.

Back in the basement, Allison began rocking back and forth in her chair, her head starting to droop as the drug took effect. Her vision blurred, and she fought to keep her eyes open, but it was no use. Mark noticed her condition worsening and called out to her, but before long, Allison had slumped over, unconscious.

Mark struggled desperately against his bindings, trying to loosen the ropes to get to her, but it was no use. "Damn you, Ramona," he muttered under his breath, feeling powerless.

Two hours later, a knock came at the back door. Ramona glanced at her watch. It was exactly 7 o'clock. She walked towards the door and opened it, revealing two men dressed in black with masks covering their faces. Without a word, they rushed into the house, stormed down the basement steps, and punched Mark in the face, knocking him out cold. One of the men quickly tied up Allison, wrapped her in a blanket, and carried her out of the house.

Ramona watched from the doorway as they loaded Allison into a car. Her heart pounded in her chest as she slammed the door behind them. She immediately called Gary.

"What the hell was that?" she demanded, her voice trembling.

"Meet me at the warehouse," Gary said, his tone dismissive. "I'll text you the directions."

Ramona hung up, feeling a mix of fear and uncertainty settle in her gut.

Ramona grabbed her coat, slung her handbag over her shoulder, and fumbled inside for her glasses. With a deep breath, she turned off the lights and locked the door behind her. The weight of the situation pressed heavily on her mind as she walked to her car. Her hands trembled as she turned the key in the ignition, the engine humming to life.

She pulled out of the driveway slowly, her eyes flicking nervously between the road and the rearview mirror, scanning for any signs of being followed. Every mile closer to the warehouse heightened her anxiety, but she forced herself to stay calm. After what felt like an eternity, forty minutes had passed, and she finally arrived at the desolate location.

The warehouse loomed in front of her like a silent monster, the decaying exterior blending into the night. She parked the car a little distance away, taking a moment to steady herself. As she stepped out of the vehicle, the air hit her, thick with the smell of decay and dampness. Her shoes echoed on the cracked pavement as she approached the entrance.

The eerie quiet of the place was unsettling. Taking a deep breath, she reached for the rusted door handle and pulled it open.

Ramona pulling her coat tighter against the chill in the air. The warehouse loomed ahead, dark and foreboding, its worn exterior illuminated only by faint moonlight. The smell of rotten fish hit her as soon as she got close, making her wrinkle her nose in disgust. The eerie sound of dripping water echoed through the building, amplifying the unsettling atmosphere.

She pushed open the squeaky door, her breath catching in her throat. "Hello?" she called out, her voice echoing back at her. The silence that followed only heightened her anxiety. She stepped further into the room, the dim light barely illuminating her path.

As she moved deeper into the warehouse, she saw three men standing over Allison. Her heart sank. Allison was lying on the cold concrete floor, partially clothed, her frail body still and vulnerable. The men hovered over her like vultures, and Ramona's stomach churned.

"What the hell is going on here?" Ramona demanded, her voice wavering as she tried to maintain control.

One of the men, who seemed to be in charge, turned towards her slowly. "Gary said to make sure she doesn't talk," he said coldly, his face hidden in the shadows.

Ramona felt a wave of nausea, realizing how far this situation had spiraled out of control. "I didn't agree to this," she whispered, her voice barely audible.

The man took a step toward her, his tone icy. "You don't get a choice anymore, Ramona. You're in this as deep as we are."

Ramona glanced at Allison, her guilt weighing heavy. She had gotten in over her head, and there was no turning back now.

A few moments later, Gary walked into the dimly lit warehouse, looking every bit the mobster in his tailored suit and cold demeanor. "Hello, gorgeous," he said with a smirk.

Ramona quickly marched up to him, her face stern. Without warning, she slapped him hard across the face.

Gary's smirk widened, "Oh, I like it rough," he teased, clearly unfazed. Ramona, livid, hissed, "What the hell, Gary? I didn't sign up for this bullshit. Don't play games with me!"

Gary calmly walked over to the men who had brought Allison, handing them a thick wad of cash.

"Thanks. I'll take it from here," he said. The men turned to leave, but before they could exit, Ramona grabbed one by the arm. "Wait! Why is she undressed?" Her voice was sharp, accusatory. The man looked uneasily at Gary, hesitant to answer.

Ramona pressed on, her voice trembling with disgust, "Please tell me you didn't rape her."

The second guy scoffed. "Relax, lady. We don't get down like that." His words did little to calm Ramona, who still eyed them warily, unsure if she could believe him. "You didn't "

The other man interjected, "No, we're professionals. She's fine."

Gary, now impatient, pointed toward the door. "I said you can go—now." The men quickly disappeared, leaving Ramona pacing around the warehouse, her frustration building.

"You had those men storm into my house like they were about to rob me!" she snapped.

Gary, completely unconcerned, casually sat in a chair, flipping it backward and straddling it. "I had to make it look like a robbery. Just in case this plan didn't work." He shrugged, as if it were the most obvious solution in the world.

Ramona's voice rose in panic, "Why did one of your men punch my husband in the face?"

Gary burst into laughter. "You're kidding me, right? After everything, that's what you're worried about?"

Ramona glared at him, her frustration boiling over. "You're an ass, Gary. What do we do now?"

Still grinning, Gary's eyes darkened. "We have to get rid of Allison."

No!" Ramona yelled, her voice echoing through the warehouse. "I told you, we're not killing her!"

Gary's smirk faded as he stood up. "Then what's your plan, Ramona? We can't let her go. You know too much is riding on this. Because time is running out sweetheart."

As water started dripping down the cracked walls of the warehouse, the sound only added to Ramona's growing anxiety. She paced back and forth, muttering to herself, trying to gather her thoughts.

"Let me think," she said, almost to herself. Gary watched her with a raised eyebrow, his patience wearing thin.

Suddenly, Ramona stopped in her tracks, her face lighting up with a spark of realization. "I have an idea."

Gary straightened in his chair. "I'm listening."

"Let's set up Jackson," Ramona said confidently, her voice stronger now. "He's perfect. He's been a problem for you, hasn't he? We can pin all of this on him. The break-in, Allison's disappearance, everything. He'll have no way to prove his innocence."

Gary smirked, impressed. "Jackson, huh? Yeah, that could work. The guy's been a thorn in my ass. Ramona, you are one crazy bitch."

Ramona narrowed her eyes as Gary spoke, the weight of his words lingering in the air.

"Ramona, you're one cold-hearted bitch," he repeated, smirking, then continued. "Now, are you sure you want to set up your young lover? He's your best friend's son, after all."

Ramona took a deep breath, her expression hardening. "I'm sure. He's reckless, unpredictable, and he's been getting too close to everything. It's either him or me, and I'm not going down for this."

Gary chuckled darkly. "You really are ruthless when your back's against the wall."

"Just make sure it's done cleanly," Ramona said, her voice cold and detached. "He can't trace it back to us."

Chapter 14

Operation Set Up

Ramona's heart raced as she gripped the steering wheel, her palms sweating as she watched the flashing lights of the police vehicle outside her home. Panic surged through her body. Is Gary setting me up? She thought, her mind running wild with possibilities.

She slowly pulled into the driveway, trying to maintain her composure, but her hands were trembling as she reached for her phone. Her thumb hovered over Gary's contact, her heart thrumming under her skin, loud as she pressed the call button. The ringing echoed in her ear, each second feeling like an eternity.

No answer.

Her breath quickened, and she could feel her anxiety building. The same thoughts swirling in her head again and again. What if Gary had betrayed her? What if everything was falling apart? Just then, her phone buzzed. It was a text from Gary: "Calm down. It's part of the plan."

Ramona stared at the message, her mind racing. Part of the plan? She tried to steady her breathing, but the sight of the police officers moving about in front of her house kept her nerves on edge. She put her phone away, grabbed her handbag, and slowly stepped out of the car. With each step toward the house, her mind whirled with questions.

Stay calm. Act normal, she told herself.

Approaching one of the officers, Ramona forced a calm expression.

"Good evening, Officer," she said, her voice steady despite the chaos inside her. "This is my house. What's going on?"

The officer turned to her and asked, "Are you Ramona Whitmore?"

Ramona hesitated for a second before answering, "Yes, I am. What's happening?"

"Mrs. Whitmore," the officer replied, "we got a call from one of your neighbors who witnessed someone breaking into your home."

"Ramona feigned shock, her acting skills kicking in. "Breaking in? I didn't receive any alerts from my security system."

The officer nodded. "The alarm was disarmed, but everything seems to be in order. Would you like us to take a look inside?"

"Yes, of course," Ramona replied, following the officer into the house. As she walked inside, her eyes darted around. Everything appeared normal, just as she had left it.

"I don't see anything missing," she said, glancing around, trying to keep her voice even.

Just as she was starting to feel some relief, Officer Richardson arrived. He knocked on the door and introduced himself before pulling Ramona aside and speaking in a low voice.

"Mrs. Whitmore, we're investigating a series of burglaries in the neighborhood. I'll need to ask you a few more questions," Richardson said before lowering his voice further. "Also, I need you to send Jackson a text from Allison's phone."

Ramona's heart skipped a beat. "Why?" she whispered, confused and unsettled.

"Just do it," Richardson insisted. "Text him to meet you at the warehouse at 3rd and Lombard. Tell him you need to talk." officer Richardson closed his notepad. Then he walked closer to the door.

"Alright then, Mrs. Whitmore. We'll be in touch if we need anything else." Ramona forced a smile as Officer Richardson gave his final reminder. "Do you have any more questions?"

Ramona nodded, her expression calm despite the turmoil inside. "No, Officer Richardson, no more questions. Thank you for your help," she replied evenly.

As the officers made their way out, Officer Richardson paused at the door, turning back.

"Make sure you lock up and put your security alarm on, Mrs. Whitmore. We wouldn't want another incident.

She forced a smile, trying to steady her breathing. "Of course, officer. I'll do that." As she paced through the quiet, empty house, her phone buzzed again.

This time, it was Gary: "Send the text to Jackson. Now."

Ramona hesitated, but with no other option, she nodded. She retrieved Allison's phone from her handbag and typed the message, her hands shaking the entire time: "Jackson, I need to see you. We need to talk. Meet me at the warehouse at 3rd and Lombard."

Before heading to her bedroom, Ramona checked her phone again. Gary's text still flashed on the screen: "It's part of the plan." She couldn't shake the feeling that things were spiraling out of control, but with no choice, she prepared herself for the next move.

Taking a deep breath, she pressed send and hoped the nightmare would soon be over.

Ramona stepped into the bathroom and turned on the faucet, letting the water run until it was hot. She could feel the steam rising around her, creating a barrier between her and the world outside. The sounds of the house faded away as she took a deep breath, trying to calm her racing heart.

As she opened the shower door, the warmth enveloped her. She stepped inside and closed her eyes, letting the hot water cascade down her body, Ramona let the steam envelop her like a comforting blanket, but the warmth did little to soothe the turmoil inside her. Each droplet mingled with her tears, washing away the tension that had built up in her shoulders and neck which she had worn throughout the day. Guilt and fear flooded her mind, each thought sharper than the last.

She felt trapped in a web of her own making, the weight of her decisions pressing down on her like an anchor.

"What have I done?" she whispered to herself, her voice barely audible over the sound of the water. She closed her eyes, trying to block out the images of Mark and the consequences of her choices.

Memories flashed through her mind: the laughter they shared, the trust they had built, all now overshadowed by betrayal. The plans she and Gary concocted felt more sinister with each passing moment, and she realized that there was no turning back.

After dressing quickly, she descended the creaky stairs to the basement, her heart racing with each step. She grabbed the first aid kit, the familiar weight of it a small comfort as she reached the bottom.

The sight of Mark slumped over the chair sent a rush of guilt through her. She hurried to his side, kneeling beside him. "Mark," she whispered, her voice trembling slightly. She opened the kit, her hands shaking as she pulled out gauze and antiseptic.

"Why are you doing this?"

Mark's voice was hoarse, his grip suddenly tightening around her wrist. She looked into his eyes, filled with a mix of pain and confusion, and felt a pang of sympathy.

"You have to trust me," she managed to say, trying to sound more confident than she felt.

"Trust you?" he echoed incredulously.

"You brought me here."

"But it will be over soon. Just hang on."

As she placed a bandage over his left eye, their eyes met for a moment. She saw the hurt, the betrayal, and it made her heart ache. Then, with a sudden rush of strength, she pulled her hand away, leaving him to lick his wounds in silence.

She stepped back, the weight of her choices heavy on her shoulders, knowing she had to follow through with the plan— even if it meant sacrificing everything.

As Jackson was browsing through his social media page, he came across a message from Allison. He paused to read it. "Jackson, I need to see you. We need to talk. Meet me at the warehouse at 3rd and Lombard."

Jackson looked at the time on his cell phone—it was just after midnight. He read the message from Allison again, confused.

They hadn't spoken in weeks, and now, she suddenly wanted to meet him in the middle of the night at a warehouse?

His gut told him something wasn't right, but part of him still cared about Allison. He typed out a quick response, "It's late, we can talk in the morning," and hit send. Jackson put the phone down, rolling over in bed, hoping to forget about it.

Ramona, across town, heard the buzz from Allison's phone inside her handbag. She rushed over, reading Jackson's response. Panic flooded her system. She couldn't afford for Jackson to ignore the message—everything was riding on him showing up at that warehouse.

Quickly, she typed a new message: "I know it's late, but I really need to talk to you face-to-face. Please, it's important."

Back in his room, Jackson's phone lit up again. He sighed as he read Allison's latest plea, feeling uneasy. His thumb hovered over the screen, unsure. "Allison, I haven't heard from you in weeks, and now you want to meet in the middle of the night?"

Ramona could feel the tension mounting as she paced, frantically typing,

"My dad's been drinking again... things are getting bad. I didn't know who else to turn to. Can you please meet me? I really need someone right now."

Jackson stared at the phone, the weight of her words sinking in. He knew Allison's home life had always been complicated. A flood of concern washed over him as he texted back, "Okay, I'm on my way."

Throwing on his sweats, Jackson quietly snuck out of the house, grabbed his keys, and headed for the warehouse.

Ramona, seeing his response, quickly messaged Gary: "He's coming. Get ready."

Gary chuckled on the other end. "Good. Now, let me handle the rest."

Ramona hung up and threw herself onto the bed, exhaustion overtaking her. She closed her eyes, but sleep didn't come easily. The thought of Jackson driving to the warehouse, unaware of what awaited him, haunted her as she drifted off to sleep.

Jackson drives down the cold, dark, and damp streets, unfamiliar with this part of town. His headlights barely cut through the thick fog, and every shadow seemed to flicker as if hiding something. The warehouse address had taken him deeper into an area he wouldn't normally venture into, and after what felt like an hour of searching, he finally spotted it—a looming warehouse.

Jackson's heart pounded in his chest as he stepped cautiously into the dark, damp warehouse. The eerie smell of mildew and decay filled the air, and his instincts screamed for him to turn back. But he couldn't shake the image of Allison's desperate messages, and now that he was here, he had to see if she was okay.

The warehouse was cold, the faint echoes of his footsteps the only sound. As he stepped deeper inside, his eyes adjusted to the dim light filtering through cracked windows. Then, in the faint light, he saw something lying on the floor. His breath caught in his throat.

"Allison?" he whispered, his voice shaking.

She was there, motionless on the cold, hard floor, her body exposed, vulnerable, and utterly still. His pulse quickened, panic overtaking him. He rushed over, kneeling beside her, trying to shake her awake.

"Allison!" he called louder, fear gripping him now.

Her skin was cold to the touch. He frantically checked for a pulse, his fingers trembling. There was none. She wasn't breathing. Jackson's mind raced—how had this happened? Why had she sent him here? And who could have done this?

Meanwhile, Gary was patrolling the warehouse area, anticipating the moment dispatch would notify him about Jackson. Finally, the call came through, providing a description of Jackson allegedly breaking into the warehouse. With sirens blaring, Gary sped toward the location, the adrenaline surging through him as the plan neared its climax.

Arriving five minutes later, Gary quickly enters the warehouse. Jackson felt a chill ran down his spine, and the hairs on the back of his neck stood up as he suddenly realized something. He wasn't alone.

From the shadows, a figure slowly stepped forward. Gary pulled his gun from its holster as he cautiously entered the dimly lit warehouse. The eerie silence was broken only by his commanding voice. The glint of a gun caught the low light. Jackson looked up, his face pale with horror.

Freeze! Put your hands up and back away from the girl!" Gary shouted, his gun steady as he approached Jackson, who stood frozen, unsure of what to do.

Jackson hesitated, confused by the sudden rush of events. "I didn't—"

"On your knees, now!" Gary interrupted, his voice firm and unwavering.

Slowly, Jackson complied, dropping to his knees with his hands raised. Gary swiftly moved in, securing the handcuffs around Jackson's wrists with a sharp click.

"You're under arrest for breaking and entering," Gary said, though his tone hinted that there was more at play than just a routine arrest. Jackson's mind raced, trying to understand how he'd been set up.

Jackson was escorted to the police car, his mind reeling with confusion and fear. As he sat down, Gary discreetly slipped a small brown object into Jackson's pocket. Moments later, Officer Moore began the pat-down.

"You got anything sharp or illegal in your pockets?" Officer Moore asked in a routine tone.

Fear overwhelmed Jackson. "This is a big misunderstanding," he tried to explain, panic rising in his voice and making it choked.

Suddenly, Officer Sanchez, who was assisting with the search, called out, "We found something."

Both officers paused, and Sanchez held up the small object, inspecting it closely. "It looks like expensive jewelry," Sanchez said, his eyebrows raised.

Gary, playing his part, stepped closer and looked down at Jackson, feigning surprise.

Gary pulled out his phone, his fingers tapping swiftly as he typed a message to Ramona: "It's done." He stared at the screen for a moment before hitting send, knowing that this message marked the point of no return.

Around him, the remaining officers were busy securing the warehouse, wrapping the scene in yellow crime scene tape. Flashing blue and red lights reflected off the damp walls of the warehouse, illuminating the grim reality of the plan they had set into motion. Officers moved around, taking pictures, collecting evidence, and noting every detail, completely unaware that it had all been orchestrated by Gary and Ramona.

As the last officer exited the building, Gary took one final look inside, his thoughts momentarily drifting to the weight of what they had done. He inhaled sharply, put his phone back in his pocket, and left the scene, the faint sound of sirens fading into the distance.

"Where did you get this jewelry from?" he demanded.

Jackson's voice cracked as he stammered, "I-I don't know where that came from! I've never seen it before!"

Gary narrowed his eyes, keeping his act together. "Take him to the station," he ordered coldly. "We'll sort this out there."

Jackson pleaded, his voice desperate. "Wait! I'm innocent, I swear!"

But his words fell on deaf ears as the officers led him away.

Meanwhile, Gary moved quickly, his radio buzzing as he called for an ambulance for Allison. EMTs arrived promptly, wrapping her in a blanket as they prepared to transport her to the hospital.

Gary watched the scene unfold, the setup falling perfectly into place, but a shadow of doubt briefly flickered across his face. It was clear that Jackson was in deep trouble, and Gary knew there was no turning back now.

Gary pulled out his phone, his fingers tapping swiftly as he typed a message to Ramona: "It's done." He stared at the screen for a moment before hitting send, knowing that this message marked the point of no return.

Around him, the remaining officers were busy securing the warehouse, wrapping the scene in yellow crime scene tape. Flashing blue and red lights reflected off the damp walls of the warehouse, illuminating the grim reality of the plan they had set into motion. Officers moved around, taking pictures, collecting evidence, and noting every detail, completely unaware that it had all been orchestrated by Gary and Ramona.

As the last officer exited the building, Gary took one final look inside, his thoughts momentarily drifting to the weight of what they had done. He inhaled sharply, put his phone back in his pocket, and left the scene, the faint sound of sirens fading into the distance.

Chapter 15

Jackson Is Arrested

At the Ninth District police station, Jackson was escorted in by Officer Moore, his wrists bound in handcuffs. As they moved down the hall, Detective Miller noticed the commotion.

"What's going on here?" Miller asked, stepping in front of the two.

Moore, stern-faced, replied, "We found him at the abandoned warehouse."

"The one on Third and Lombard?" Miller inquired, raising an eyebrow.

Moore nodded, "Yeah, we found him hovering over the missing Wilson girl.

As Officer Moore led Jackson down the hall, his protests echoed through the station. "I'm innocent! I'm being set up!" he yelled, struggling against his restraints.

Detective Miller watched with a growing unease. He didn't think Jackson fit the profile for something as serious as this. But protocol was protocol.

"Take him to the interrogation room," Miller ordered Moore, who nodded and continued on with Jackson.

Just as the commotion began to die down, Captain Casey stepped out of his office. He approached Detective Miller with a stern look. "I just got a call about Allison Wilson. She's at Cedarwood Hospital. I need you to go talk to her. I'll handle Jackson's interrogation."

Detective Miller crossed his arms, clearly conflicted. "I don't think Jackson has anything to do with the Wilson girl's disappearance," he said quietly.

"We have to go over this case with a fine-tooth comb," Captain Casey responded. "And he was the last person seen with Allison before she went missing."

Miller sighed, running a hand through his hair. "I know, Captain. But Jackson's not that kind of kid. He's soft. But a good kid."

Casey wasn't moved. "It's not the first time a 'good kid' pulled the wool over our eyes. You know that."

Frustrated, Miller reached for his phone. "I'm going to call his mother."

"No," Captain Casey said firmly. "He's of age, so we can question him without his mother. Besides, I don't need a mama bear storming in here, making a scene. Just go talk to Allison and see what she knows."

Detective Miller hesitated but eventually nodded. "Alright. I'll head to the hospital."

He turned and made his way out of the police station, his thoughts racing as he prepared to speak with Allison Wilson, hoping to unravel the truth behind this mess.

Mr. and Mrs. Wilson rushed down the sterile hallway of Cedarwood Hospital, their faces filled with worry and panic. When they reached the nurses' station, Mr. Wilson leaned over the counter, out of breath. "Excuse me, nurse. I was told my daughter is here."

The nurse, busy with paperwork, glanced up calmly. "What's your daughter's name?"

Mrs. Wilson, her voice trembling, said, "Allison Wilson. Please, is she alright?"

The nurse turned to her computer, typing quickly. After a moment, she nodded. "Yes, she's here. Please have a seat in the waiting room. I'll let the doctor know you're here."

Mr. Wilson, his patience wearing thin, slammed his hand on the counter. "I don't want to sit down. I want to see my daughter now!"

The nurse's expression tightened. "Sir, the doctor is with another patient at the moment."

Mrs. Wilson, trying to keep calm, leaned in. "Can you at least tell us how she's doing?"

The nurse exhaled sharply, clearly losing her patience. "If you don't wait in the other room like I asked, I'll have no choice but to call security."

Mr. Wilson was about to protest again, but Mrs. Wilson put a hand on his arm. "Let's wait, honey," she whispered, her voice strained. They both reluctantly walked toward the waiting room, hearts heavy with fear.

Detective Miller walked up to the nurses' station and flashed his badge. "I'm Detective Miller. I was told Allison Wilson is here."

The nurse smiled and nodded. "Yes, the doctor has been waiting for you. I'll let him know you've arrived."

She quickly left to fetch the doctor, leaving the detective standing at the station.

The Wilson family, seated nearby, overheard the exchange. Mrs. Wilson, wide-eyed and frantic, hurried over to Detective Miller, with Mr. Wilson following close behind.

"Detective Miller, we're Allison's parents. Can you please tell us anything about our daughter?"

Before Detective Miller could respond, Doctor Hamilton walked into the room, holding a clipboard.

"I'm looking for the family of Allison Wilson."

Mrs. Wilson quickly stepped forward. "We're her parents," she said, her voice filled with hope and desperation.

The doctor approached them with a calm demeanor. "Mr. and Mrs. Wilson, I'm Doctor Hamilton, and I'm in charge of your daughter's care."

Mrs. Wilson, unable to wait any longer, pleaded, "How is she? Can we see her?"

Dr. Hamilton sighed softly before responding. "Your daughter is severely dehydrated, and we're running more tests to assess her condition thoroughly. Once we've finished, you'll be able to see her."

Mr. Wilson let out a small sigh of relief, his face showing the first signs of hope. "Thank you, doctor," he said softly as Dr. Hamilton nodded and walked away from the parents.

As soon as the doctor was out of earshot, Detective Miller turned to him. "Doctor, may I speak with you for a moment?"

In the cold, dimly lit interrogation room, Jackson sat trembling with fear. His hands, still cuffed, rested on the table as he glanced nervously at the two-way mirror, knowing someone was watching. His heart raced with anxiety, unsure of what was coming next.

Outside, Captain Casey stood observing Jackson through the mirror when Officer Moore walked by. Casey stopped him.

"Any news on the Wilson girl?" Captain Casey asked without taking his eyes off Jackson.

Moore shook his head. "No, sir. Detective Miller is still at the hospital."

Casey gave a quick nod. "Tell him I want to see him as soon as he comes in."

"Yes, Captain," Moore replied before heading down the hall.

With a deep breath, Captain Casey turned and entered the interrogation room. He closed the door behind him and slowly walked toward the table, pulling out a chair across from Jackson. Sitting down, he leaned forward, studying Jackson carefully.

"Jackson," Captain Casey began, his tone calm but probing. "Can you tell me why you were at that warehouse tonight?"

Jackson swallowed hard, his voice shaky. "Allison told me to meet her at the warehouse."

Captain Casey raised an eyebrow, clearly skeptical. "Why would she want to meet you at an abandoned warehouse in the middle of the night?"

Jackson stammered, "She said she wanted to talk to me... about her father."

Casey leaned back in his chair, crossing his arms. "Her father? That's what she told you?" He let the silence hang for a moment before continuing, "Say, Jackson, I've got a problem with your story. You expect me to believe that Allison had no way to contact you except to lure you to some empty warehouse at midnight? No phone call, no regular place to meet?"

Jackson's voice cracked with desperation. "I'm telling you the truth! I got a message from her, asking me to meet her there. I didn't know it was a setup, I swear!"

Captain Casey shook his head slowly, his expression hardening. "I've been doing this a long time, son. And right now, your story just doesn't add up." He paused, letting the weight of his words sink in. "If you know something, now's the time to come clean."

Jackson, on the verge of tears, sat in stunned silence, feeling the walls close in around him.

Captain Casey wasn't letting up on his interrogation. He leaned in closer, his tone unrelenting. "You say you're innocent. Let's go over your story one more time to make sure we're on the same page."

Jackson, still visibly nervous, sighed, "Allison sent me a text to meet her at 3rd and Lombard. I told her I wasn't going to meet her, then she texted me back saying she really needed someone to talk to because her father had been drinking again. She said she left home because of it."

Captain Casey crossed his arms and studied Jackson's face. "So, you're saying she was afraid of her father?"

"I don't know if she was afraid," Jackson replied. "But I know he has a drinking problem."

Casey scoffed. "Let's assume Mr. Wilson has a drinking problem. Why would Allison want to meet you at an abandoned warehouse?"

"I don't know," Jackson said, starting to get frustrated. "You'd have to ask her."

The captain's voice turned sarcastic. "And that's the problem, Jackson. I *can't* ask her anything because she's still unconscious. My officers found you hovering over her half-naked body, and you want me to believe you're innocent?"

Jackson's eyes widened. "She was like that when I found her! I'm telling you, I didn't do anything. I am innocent."

Just then, Officer Sanchez entered the room and whispered something in Captain Casey's ear, handing him an evidence bag. The captain nodded and dismissed Sanchez before turning his attention back to Jackson.

Captain Casey began pacing the room, repeating Jackson's name slowly, over and over again. "This isn't looking good for you, Jackson," he finally said, stopping directly in front of him.

Jackson felt a chill crawl up his spine. "Someone's trying to set me up," he said, his voice trembling. "And I bet Ramona has something to do with this."

Captain Casey raised an eyebrow, then smirked. "Wow. What a coincidence you'd mention Ramona's name." He held up the evidence bag. Inside was a diamond tennis bracelet. "This bracelet was found in your pocket when you were arrested."

Jackson's heart sank. "I've never seen that bracelet before."

"Mrs. Whitmore is on her way to the station to identify it," Casey continued, his tone cold. "If it's hers, you'll be looking at charges for theft, kidnapping, and God knows what else. So, I suggest you start telling me the truth."

Jackson, feeling the walls close in, straightened up and said firmly, "I know my rights. I want a lawyer."

Captain Casey stared at him for a long moment, his face hardening. "Fine. You just lost any chance of a plea deal." He turned toward the door and called out, "Let him make his phone call."

As Captain Casey left the room, Jackson's mind raced. He knew he had to make his call count. He needed someone who believed in him—someone who could help him prove his innocence.

Back at Cedarwood Hospital, Dr. Hamilton and Detective Miller stood in the hallway, discussing Allison Wilson's condition.

Detective Miller asked, "Dr. Hamilton, how is Miss Wilson doing?"

Dr. Hamilton sighed. "Well, she came into the ER severely dehydrated and suffering from hypothermia, but what concerns me more is her mental health."

Miller furrowed his brow. "How so?"

Dr. Hamilton elaborated, "Being kidnapped is traumatic enough, but she doesn't seem to remember any of the events leading up to her being found."

Detective Miller looked stunned. "She doesn't remember being kidnapped?"

Dr. Hamilton nodded, a serious look on his face. "She has amnesia. It's possible she's blocking out the trauma, but I suspect something deeper. I believe she may have been given a drug to distort her memory."

Detective Miller ran his hand through his hair, absorbing the information. "Do you think there's any chance she was sexually assaulted?"

Dr. Hamilton shook his head slightly. "There are no physical signs of sexual assault—no bruising in the lower region. However, I can't perform a rape kit without her consent. She does have bruising on her face and wrists, likely from being restrained."

Miller pressed further. "Is there anything else I need to know about her condition?"

Dr. Hamilton replied, "We're waiting on the blood test results. If there's anything alarming, you'll be the first to know. Now, if you'll excuse me, I need to speak with Allison's parents."

Detective Miller nodded. "Thank you, Dr. Hamilton."

Detective Miller stepped away to make a call to Captain Casey, preparing to update him on Allison's condition when he heard muffled crying coming from the waiting room. Turning his head, he saw Dr. Hamilton entering the room where Mr. and Mrs. Wilson sat anxiously.

Dr. Hamilton began gently explaining Allison's condition, but Mrs. Wilson quickly interrupted, panic in her voice.

"What do you mean she's not going to remember us?"

Mr. Wilson, his frustration boiling over, demanded, "I want to see my daughter now."

Detective Miller took the opportunity to step in, introducing himself.

"Mr. and Mrs. Wilson, I'm Detective Miller, and I'm investigating Allison's case."

Mr. Wilson stepped forward, his face a mixture of concern and anger.

"Where did you find my daughter?"

Detective Miller remained calm.

"Mr. Wilson, I'll fill you in on all the details, but right now, the most important thing is to focus on Allison's health. Here's my card. If you have any questions or need anything, you can contact me at any time."

Mrs. Wilson, her eyes filled with worry, softly replied, "Thank you, Detective."

As Detective Miller headed toward the hospital's entrance to make his call, Dr. Hamilton gently guided the Wilson's toward Allison's room, giving them the moment they desperately needed to see their daughter.

Chapter 16

Who Am I?

In Allison's hospital room, Wilson family stood over their daughter, relieved to see her sleeping peacefully. Mrs. Wilson gently kissed Allison's forehead, but when Allison opened her eyes, she looked startled and confused. Her eyes darted around the room, clearly unsure of where she was.

Mr. Wilson leaned in, his voice soft, "Babygirl, you're awake."

Allison, still disoriented, asked, "Where am I?"

Mrs. Wilson reached out to hold her hand, but Allison pulled away quickly. "You're in the hospital," Mrs. Wilson said tenderly.

Allison's eyes narrowed in confusion. "Who are you?"

Mr. Wilson, heartbroken, replied, "Allison, we're your parents."

But Allison shook her head, trying to process what was happening. "Who is Allison? You're not my parents... I don't know you."

Mrs. Wilson began to cry, devastated by her daughter's words, while Mr. Wilson hurried out of the room to fetch Dr. Hamilton. Inside the room, Mrs. Wilson desperately tried to jog Allison's memory, but Allison grew more agitated, her confusion turning into panic.

Moments later, Dr. Hamilton entered the room with Mr. Wilson, immediately noticing Allison's distress. He calmly approached her, taking out his stethoscope. "Allison, I'm Dr.

Hamilton. I'm in charge of your care. I need you to take a deep breath for me."

Allison pressed her hand to her head, wincing. "My head hurts," she said, her voice tight with pain.

Dr. Hamilton nodded, "I'll have the nurse bring something for your headache. Does anything else hurt?"

Allison shook her head slightly, still trying to make sense of the situation. "I have to get out of here," she muttered, attempting to sit up.

Dr. Hamilton gently but firmly eased her back into bed. "No, you need to rest. I'll need to do a thorough examination. Mr. and Mrs. Wilson, could you wait outside for a moment?"

Allison, clearly panicked, pleaded, "Who is Allison? And why are those people here?"

Mrs. Wilson, her voice breaking, refused to leave. "I'm not leaving my baby."

But Dr. Hamilton remained calm. "It will only be a minute. She's becoming more upset with you here, and we need her to stay calm."

Reluctantly, Mr. Wilson agreed. "Fine, we'll be outside."

He gently pulled his wife toward the door, leaving Dr. Hamilton to care for their confused daughter. As they left, Allison's panicked breaths began to slow under Dr. Hamilton's careful watch.

Later that day, Detective Miller entered Captain Casey's office, feeling the weight of the case already on his shoulders. "You wanted to see me?" he asked.

Captain Casey looked up from his paperwork.

"I just got off the phone with Dr. Hamilton. He informed me that Miss Wilson has amnesia."

Miller sighed, taking a seat across from the captain. "Yes, that's correct."

Captain Casey leaned back in his chair, a concerned frown on his face.

"Her testimony is crucial to this case. Without it, how are we going to connect this to Jackson?"

Detective Miller hesitated. "With all due respect, Captain, I don't think Jackson was involved in Allison's kidnapping."

The captain stood up, pacing around his desk. "I don't know, Miller. His alibi is shaky at best."

"Is he still in lock-up?" Miller asked.

"For now," Casey replied, crossing his arms.

"But I'm going to have to let him go soon. We don't have anything solid to hold him on. However, I want you to call Ramona Whitmore and see if she can identify that diamond tennis bracelet we found in Jackson's pocket."

Miller's brow furrowed. "What bracelet?"

"The diamond tennis bracelet that was found in Jackson's pocket," the captain explained.

Miller looked puzzled. "Don't you think it's a little suspicious that a diamond bracelet was found in his pocket in the middle of the night? It doesn't add up."

Casey walked closer to the door, signaling for Miller to follow.

"We won't know for sure until Ramona comes in and tells us if it's hers."

Miller stood up, following the captain out of the office. As they headed down the hallway, Miller pulled out his phone, scrolling to Ramona Whitmore's contact information. He hesitated for a moment, then dialed her number, hoping that her response would shed some light on the murky case.

The next morning, Ramona arrived at the 9th District Police Station, her nerves on edge. Approaching the front desk, she quietly asked for Detective Miller. Officer Richardson appeared, acknowledging her.

"Mrs. Whitmore, thank you for coming in. I'll let Detective Miller know you're here," he said, escorting her to the detective's desk. "Have a seat, he'll be with you in a minute."

Ramona glanced around anxiously, whispering under her breath, "Why am I here?" Officer Richardson leaned in slightly, whispering back, "Get it together, you're making yourself look guilty." Her eyes darted nervously across the room, and she spotted Officer Sanchez escorting Jackson toward the squad room. Her hands started to sweat as she locked eyes with Jackson, who glared at her. As he dialed a number to make his call, Ramona quickly turned her head to avoid his gaze.

Moments later, Detective Miller approached her with a calm but firm demeanor.

"Good morning, Mrs. Whitmore. Thanks for coming in."

Ramona tried to maintain her composure.

"Good morning, Detective. I'm a bit confused about why I'm here."

Detective Miller nodded. "I need you to identify a piece of jewelry," he explained.

Ramona's expression shifted to concern. "I don't understand what you're talking about..."

Detective Miller hesitated briefly before responding. "The diamond tennis bracelet you reported missing in the robbery."

Ramona's gaze flickered toward Officer Richardson, and then she forced a smile.

"Ah, yes... the tennis bracelet. You'll have to excuse me; I'm still in shock."

Just then, Officer Moore arrived with the evidence bag. He handed it to Detective Miller, who placed it on the desk in front of Ramona. Inside was the diamond tennis bracelet.

"Is this your bracelet?" Miller asked.

Ramona nodded after a moment of silence.

"Yes, it is, Detective."

"Thank you for confirming that," Detective Miller said.

"That'll be all for now. We'll contact you if we need anything else."

Ramona hurriedly left the station, her phone buzzing as she stepped outside. Gary's name flashed on the screen.

"What the hell, Gary?" she hissed into the phone. "You could've warned me about the bracelet."

Gary's voice came back sharp. "You better control your facial expressions, or you'll find yourself under the jail," he barked before hanging up.

Frustrated, Ramona stormed to her car. The phone rang again.

"No more surprises, you bastard," she snapped, but the voice on the other end was silent. After a few seconds, it spoke.

"Is that how you talk to your father?"

Ramona froze, immediately putting her hand to her forehead. "Dad, I'm sorry. I thought you were someone else."

Frank Whitmore's voice was calm but commanding. "Let's do lunch."

Ramona hesitated, trying to gather herself. "I'm sorry, Dad. I have a full schedule today."

"That wasn't a request," Frank replied coldly.

Ramona sighed. "Okay, Dad."

She ended the call, put her keys in the ignition, and drove off, dreading what would come next.

At noon, Allison was sleeping comfortably. Dr. Hamilton had given her a sedative earlier to help calm her nerves. Her parents remained by her side, anxious but relieved she was resting. Dr. Hamilton entered the room to speak with Alison's parents.

"Mr. and Mrs. Wilson, I wanted to update you on Allison's condition," Dr. Hamilton began. "While she's stable today, I don't believe she'll be ready to go home with you right away. She thinks you're strangers. I also want to follow up with a therapist."

Dr. Hamilton nodded. "Yes, I'm afraid it is. Allison is very fragile right now. She's trying to piece together events that are overwhelming and confusing. A therapist can help her with her amnesia. But I must warn you, it's not an easy task. You cannot force her to remember things. Her brain is suppressing the trauma of her kidnapping."

Suddenly, Allison woke up screaming. Dr. Hamilton rushed over to calm her, while Detective Miller, hearing the commotion as he walked down the hall, entered the room.

"Is everything alright?" Detective Miller asked, concerned.

Mr. Wilson was holding his wife, trying to comfort her. Dr. Hamilton administered another light sedative to calm Allison. Detective Miller turned to Dr. Hamilton.

"I came to check on Allison's condition. Any improvement?"

Dr. Hamilton sighed. "I just gave her something to help her calm down. I was telling her parents that it will take time for her to adjust. Her recovery will be slow."

"Dr. Hamilton, is it alright if I ask Allison a few questions?" Miller asked gently. "I promise I'll be brief."

Dr. Hamilton agreed. "Yes, but please keep it short. I'll go prepare her discharge papers."

Once Dr. Hamilton left the room, Detective Miller moved closer to Allison's bedside.

"Miss Wilson, I'm Detective Miller. I'd like to ask you some questions if you feel up to it."

Allison, still groggy from the sedative, nodded. "I don't know how much I can help. I don't remember much."

"That's okay. We can start slow," Miller reassured her. "Do you know a person named Jackson?"

Allison looked confused. "No... is that my brother?"

Mrs. Wilson spoke up, "Allison, you don't have any siblings."

Detective Miller gently intervened. "Mr. and Mrs. Wilson, I know this is hard, but I need Allison to answer on her own."

He turned back to Allison.

"Can you tell me what you do remember?"

Allison furrowed her brow, trying to recall. "Everything is blurry. I only remember bits and pieces. I remember a room and a man's voice."

Miller leaned forward, eager for more.

"Do you remember what the man looked like? Did he have tattoos, a particular hair color, or anything else?"

Allison's voice grew softer. "He was kind to me. He was in the room with me... but I'm sorry, I don't remember more."

Just then, Dr. Hamilton returned with the discharge papers.

"Detective, I need to go over Allison's discharge instructions with her parents."

"Of course, thank you, Doctor," Miller said. He turned to Allison. "If you remember anything else, please don't hesitate to contact me."

As Detective Miller was about to leave, Allison suddenly froze, her eyes wide. She gasped and screamed. "Detective Miller, I remember a woman! I remember her slapping me!"

Miller quickly approached her bedside again. "Allison, can you tell me what she looked like?"

Allison, now panicking, began to curl into a ball, her mind flooded with the terrifying image of the woman who had hurt her. "I don't know, I keep seeing her face, but I can't remember more."

Dr. Hamilton intervened. "Detective, that's enough for today. Allison needs to rest."

Detective Miller nodded, knowing he couldn't push her any further at this moment. But he had something—a critical clue about a woman.

On the other side of town, Ramona canceled her afternoon meetings and reluctantly made her way to meet her father for lunch. Though she dreaded their encounters, she knew that in sticky situations like the one she found herself in now, her father, Frank Whitmore, was always her way out. As she drove through the congested Center City traffic, she wondered why her father had picked the Ocean View Bar and Grill—a spot that was notoriously difficult to reach during lunch hours. The standstill traffic only added to her anxiety, and after receiving a sharp text from her father asking where she was, she chose not to reply, knowing he would only scold her further.

When the traffic finally cleared, she arrived at the restaurant, mentally preparing herself for the inevitable tension. Inside, she spotted her father, a distinguished man with silver hair, sitting in a corner booth. Taking a deep breath, she approached.

"Hello, Dad," Ramona said, trying to keep her tone neutral.

Frank Whitmore glanced up, his expression disapproving. "You're late."

Ramona, already irritated, responded, "I got stuck in traffic."

"Ramona, how many times do I have to tell you—time is money, and money is time?" Frank said sharply.

She recited his mantra back to him, a trace of sarcasm in her voice. "I know, Dad."

"If you know, then you should've left earlier," Frank said, clearly unimpressed.

Ramona rolled her eyes, her frustration barely contained. "Can we just order, please?"

Frank signaled for the waiter, and they ordered drinks. As the waiter walked away, Frank leaned forward, his voice dropping to a more serious tone.

"I heard that Jackson boy got arrested."

Ramona froze, her eyes narrowing in suspicion.

"How do you know about that?"

Frank smirked. "I make it my business to know everything relevant. You're my daughter, Ramona. I have your best interests at heart."

Before she could respond, Ramona's phone rang, displaying Gary's number. She hesitated, but Frank, always in control, gestured for her to answer.

"Answer it," he said, "and put it on speaker."

Ramona reluctantly complied. "Hello?" she said.

Gary's voice snapped through the line, irritated. "Didn't I tell you to answer my calls on the first ring?"

Before Ramona could say a word, Frank interjected smoothly. "And didn't I tell you to handle that Jackson situation?"

There was a long pause on the other end as Gary realized who he was speaking to.

"Mr. Whitmore, I—"

"So, now you have nothing to say?" Frank cut him off.

"I'm sorry, sir," Gary stumbled over his words, his bravado gone.

Frank took a sip of his drink, unfazed. "You will be sorry if I ever hear you talk to my daughter like that again."

"It'll never happen again, sir," Gary promised, his tone almost panicked.

"It better not," Frank replied coldly. "Now, take care of the other problem. Now."

Before Gary could respond, Frank hung up the phone with a calm finality. Ramona, caught between relief and amusement, gave her father a small, appreciative smirk.

Frank looked her over with a critical eye. "Now eat. You're getting too skinny."

Chapter 17

I Remember

Ramona felt a wave of relief wash over her as she left the Ocean View Bar and Grill. Her father had, once again, demonstrated his power by putting Gary in his place, allowing her to breathe a little easier. As she drove away, she thought about how her father always seemed to be one step ahead of everything, effortlessly handling any situation. A small part of her wished she could've seen Gary's face after Frank Whitmore, the powerful senator, scolded him. For now, she felt confident that the issue with Jackson and Allison's kidnapping was no longer her problem.

At the same time, at the 9th District Police Station, Jackson had just been allowed to make a phone call. The first number he dialed was his mother.

At home, Sarah was busy fixing Jackson's favorite breakfast, as she did most mornings. When the phone rang, she wiped her hands on her apron and walked over to the kitchen counter to pick it up, wondering who would be calling so early.

"Hello?" she answered.

To her surprise, she heard Jackson's voice on the other end. "Mom, it's me," he said, his voice laced with panic.

"Jackson? I thought you were upstairs in your room. Where are you?" Sarah asked, confused.

Jackson, his voice trembling, replied, "I'm at the police station."

Sarah's heart skipped a beat. "Why are you at the police station?" she demanded, her tone rising in alarm.

"They're trying to arrest me for Allison's kidnapping," Jackson blurted out, his voice cracking.

Sarah, now furious and panicking herself, shouted, "I'm on my way! Don't say a word to anyone! I'll call your uncle—he's a lawyer." She quickly turned off the stove, leaving the half-cooked food as is, and rushed out the door. Jumping into her car, Sarah sped down the street, frantically dialing her brother, Joe's number as she raced to the station.

A few minutes later, Sarah and her brother, Joe arrived at the police station. As they stepped through the doors, Joe turned to his sister and said firmly, "When we get in here, let me do all the talking." But Sarah, her face flushed with anger, stormed towards the front desk, slamming her hand on the surface. "Where is my son?" she demanded.

The officer behind the desk, maintaining his composure, asked, "Who's your son?"

Before Sarah could escalate the situation, Joe gently pushed her to the side. "Officer, I'm Joseph Lawson, Jackson McKinley's lawyer. I'd like to speak with the person in charge of Mr. McKinley's case."

The officer nodded. "Detective Miller is handling that case. Have a seat, and I'll let him know you're here."

Sarah, still fuming, snapped, "I don't want to sit down!" Joe shot her a stern look, cutting her off before she could make things worse. "Thank you, Officer," Joe said calmly, turning to his sister. "Sarah, I told you—let me handle this."

Just then, Detective Miller appeared, walking into the squad room. The officer at the desk gestured towards him, "Detective, these people would like to speak with you."

Miller turned, immediately recognizing Sarah in the corner. He sighed under his breath, "I feel a headache coming on."

Before he could say anything, Sarah sprang to her feet. "Why did you arrest my son for Allison's kidnapping?" she demanded.

Miller remained calm. "Mrs. McKinley, Jackson hasn't been charged with kidnapping."

"Then why is he here?" she asked, her voice sharp.

"He's been charged with burglary, not kidnapping. Mrs. McKinley, I understand you're worried, but I need you to let me do my job," Miller replied steadily.

Sarah, unconvinced, said firmly, "My son is innocent. He's no thief."

Joe intervened with a pointed glance at his sister, urging her to stay quiet. "Detective Miller, I would like to speak to my client privately before you question him."

Detective Miller nodded, "No problem. Come with me, Mr. Lawson." The two men began walking down the hallway together, but Miller stopped momentarily to address Sarah.

"Mrs. McKinley, you won't be allowed in the interrogation room."

"He's my son!" she protested, her voice trembling with emotion.

Joe placed a reassuring hand on her shoulder. "I'll make sure Jackson is treated fairly," he promised. With that, Joe and Miller continued down the hall, leaving Sarah to anxiously wait in the lobby. As they approached the interrogation room, Joe looked at Miller and said, "I'll need a few minutes alone with my client before you begin questioning him."

Joe walked into the interrogation room and immediately noticed how stressed Jackson looked. When Jackson glanced up and saw his uncle, a glimmer of relief crossed his face. Joe sat down across from him, his expression firm but not unkind.

"Jackson, what is going on with you?" Joe asked, his voice heavy with frustration. "First, dating older women—"

Jackson interrupted, "But you said it was okay to date an older woman."

Joe sighed, "Yes, I did, but not your mother's best friend."

Jackson lowered his head, feeling the weight of his actions. "I know."

Joe continued, his voice taking on a lecturing tone. "Then you get arrested for disorderly conduct. And now you're back here for burglary and, potentially, kidnapping? What the hell, Jackson? Are you trying to give your mother a heart attack?"

Jackson shook his head. "I know, I know I messed up, but I didn't do those things that they're accusing me of!"

Joe took a deep breath, trying to maintain his calm. "Alright. I need you to tell me everything you told the cops and what actually happened. No lies, no missing details. This is serious."

Jackson hesitated but then started to recount the events leading up to his arrest, explaining every detail best as he could remember. Joe listened intently, his eyes narrowing as the story unfolded.

When Jackson finished, Joe leaned back in his chair, giving him a stern look. "Yeah, Jackson, you've definitely screwed up. But, lucky for you, I'm a damn good lawyer. I'm going to talk to the district attorney about getting you out on bail."

Jackson nodded, visibly relieved but still carrying the weight of his mistakes. "Thanks, Uncle Joe. I'm sorry I put you and Mom through this."

Joe stood up, straightening his jacket. "You'll need to do more than apologize, Jackson. You'll need to clean this mess up, and fast. I'll handle the legal side, but you need to get your life together." With that, Joe left the room, determined to negotiate Jackson's release and figure out the next steps.

An hour later, Jackson McKinley and his uncle, Joseph Lawson, stood before Judge Matthew Carson for Jackson's bail hearing. The judge, familiar with Jackson, eyed him sternly.

"Mr. McKinley, we meet again. I told you I better not see you in my courtroom again."

Jackson lowered his head. "I know, Your Honor, but this time it wasn't my fault."

District Attorney Karen Phillips, not missing a beat, added, "Your Honor, Mr. McKinley clearly has no respect for the law or women, for that matter."

Lawson immediately objected, his voice firm. "I object, Your Honor! Do we really need to listen to her male-bashing antics?"

The tension between the two lawyers escalated quickly as they started arguing. Judge Carson, visibly frustrated, banged his gavel on the desk.

"I have a full docket today. Get to the point, Phillips!"

Phillips straightened and said, "We are charging Mr. McKinley with breaking and entering, resisting arrest, and theft."

Lawson shot back, "When did my client resist arrest?"

Phillips, ignoring the interruption, continued, "Additionally, we will be charging him with kidnapping."

Sarah McKinley, Jackson's mother, sat behind her son, her face pale as she listened to the long list of charges. Tears welled in her eyes as the accusations piled up.

Lawson, determined to defend his nephew, countered, "There's no evidence that my client kidnapped Allison Wilson! The district attorney is trying to make a name for herself."

Phillips snapped, "I resent that accusation."

Before the argument could escalate further, Judge Carson slammed his gavel again, his patience wearing thin. "Enough! Either you stop the mudslinging or I'll hold you both in contempt."

Both attorneys quickly apologized, and the judge asked, "Where do the people stand on bond?"

Phillips responded, "The people request no bail, Your Honor. We believe Mr. McKinley is a flight risk."

Lawson, incredulous, exclaimed, "How is he a flight risk? He has strong ties to the community!"

Judge Carson, once again silencing the room with his gavel, stated, "That's enough. The prosecution has presented no substantial evidence linking Mr. McKinley to the kidnapping. Bail will be set at $75,000 cash or bond, and Mr. McKinley will surrender his passport. We are adjourned."

171

As the judge left the courtroom, District Attorney Phillips exited briskly, leaving Jackson, his uncle, and Sarah behind. Sarah, overwhelmed with emotion, whispered, "I can't afford $75,000." She ran out of the courtroom, tears streaming down her face.

Joe turned to Jackson, his voice firm but understanding. "I'll cover your bail, but you're going to pay me back." Jackson nodded, grateful but knowing that his troubles were far from over.

Mid-afternoon, Allison Wilson finally returned home after her traumatic ordeal. Despite Dr. Hamilton's advice, the Wilsons insisted on her discharge, eager to have their daughter home. Allison had agreed to therapy for her trauma and memory loss, but the tension remained thick. As their car pulled up to the house, news reporters swarmed outside, trying to get a glimpse of the girl at the center of a terrifying mystery.

"Welcome home, sweetheart," Mr. Wilson said gently, trying to ease her into the familiar space. "Let me take your coat."

Allison flinched at his touch, unsure and on edge. She stood in the middle of the living room, disoriented. Everything felt foreign, almost claustrophobic. The walls seemed to close in, and she looked at her parents, feeling lost.

"May I go to my room, please?" she asked, her voice quiet.

Her parents exchanged worried glances. Mrs. Wilson said softly, "I'll show you to your room." Together, they led her upstairs, Allison cautiously taking in her surroundings, hoping something might spark a memory.

When they reached her room, Allison opened the door to see a space filled with color—purple and pink hues, bookshelves packed with novels, and a walk-in closet full of clothes and shoes. Her eyes caught on a camera set up on a tripod. She turned to her parents, confused.

"Was I a filmmaker?" she asked.

Her mother walked towards her with a sad smile. "No, sweetheart. You're a fashion influencer."

Allison chuckled lightly, though it didn't feel natural. "Well, that explains all the clothes and shoes," she said, gesturing to the closet.

Her father, trying to be supportive, added,

"We'll leave you alone to rest. If you need anything, we'll be downstairs."

As they stepped out, about to close the door, Allison suddenly screamed, "Leave it open."

The request left her parents even more unsettled. As they walked down the hall, Mr. Wilson hugged his wife, who was on the verge of tears.

"We'll get through this. One day at a time," he whispered.

Hours passed, and Allison sat on her bed, flipping through an old scrapbook of her childhood. The images of birthdays and family trips did little to jog her memory, but suddenly, vivid flashbacks from her kidnapping hit her. She saw a woman, harsh and unkind, slapping her. Panic surged through her body, and she screamed.

Downstairs, Mrs. Wilson had been making dinner, while her husband read the newspaper. Hearing Allison's cry, they rushed upstairs, finding her curled up on the floor, trembling. They tried to comfort her, but she recoiled, not wanting to be touched.

173

Allison, her voice shaky, managed to say, "I remember something. I need to talk to Detective Miller."

As Allison and her parents stepped out of their house, reporters bombarded them with questions, their cameras flashing wildly. Allison, startled and anxious, felt overwhelmed by the barrage of lights and voices. "Is it true you have amnesia?" one reporter shouted. "Allison, is Jackson one of your kidnappers?" another called out. Mr. Wilson quickly shielded his wife and daughter, ushering them toward the car.

"We're happy to have Allison home, but please, no more questions," he said firmly. "Give us our privacy." They hurried into the vehicle, trying to escape the media frenzy.

Meanwhile, at the police station, Detective Miller and District Attorney Phillips were in deep discussion. "How did the bail hearing go?" Miller asked.

Phillips, clearly frustrated, shot him a look. "How do you think it went? We need Allison's testimony. Without her, we don't have a solid case—everything is circumstantial. We need her to remember more."

Miller nodded thoughtfully. "I told you it would be hard to link Jackson to this. I honestly think he's being set up."

Phillips, unimpressed, retorted, "Then get me something solid. I'm not going back into that courtroom without evidence. Talk to Allison again."

Just as Phillips was about to walk away, the Wilson family entered the station. Allison, still fragile, looked uneasy as they walked in. Suddenly, she and Jackson crossed paths. Jackson, desperate, called out to her, "Allison, it's me, Jackson."

Allison looked at him blankly, confused. "I'm sorry, I don't know you," she said quietly.

Jackson's face fell. "Allison, you have to tell them the truth!" he pleaded. His voice grew louder as a police officer led him away. "I didn't kidnap you!"

Allison turned to Detective Miller, her voice shaky. "Is Jackson the one who kidnapped me?"

Miller reassured her, "He's just a person of interest right now. Let me introduce you to the District Attorney." Phillips approached and shook hands with the Wilson's.

"We're going to make sure whoever did this to you is brought to justice," Phillips said, her voice filled with determination. "How are you feeling, Allison?"

Allison sighed, the weight of her memories pressing down on her. "I keep having these vivid images in my head," she admitted.

Mr. Wilson explained, "Allison insisted on coming here to talk to Detective Miller."

Miller pulled up a chair. "Take a seat, Allison. Can you tell us about the images you're seeing?"

Allison hesitated, visibly torn. "Everything is so foggy... I don't want to waste your time." She started to stand, but Miller gently placed a hand on her shoulder.

"Even the smallest details can help," he said kindly.

Phillips signaled for someone to join them. "Allison, this is Melissa Woo. She's with the Behavioral Analysis Unit. Is it okay if she talks with you?"

Allison nodded hesitantly. Melissa smiled warmly, pulling up a chair. "Allison, can you tell us more about these images?"

Allison took a deep breath, then began. "I remember being in a room... it was beautifully decorated. The walls were tan."

"That's good," Melissa encouraged. "Can you describe anyone in the room with you?"

Allison nodded slowly. "There was a middle-aged man. He was... there, but I can't see his face clearly. A woman was yelling at him."

Melissa leaned forward, speaking softly. "Can you tell me about the woman? What did she look like?"

Allison's breathing became erratic, and she started to panic. "I don't want to talk about this anymore. I want to go home."

Melissa immediately guided Allison through calming breathing exercises. After a moment, Allison relaxed and continued. "The woman... she wore expensive clothes. She was beautiful, with a round face and dirty blonde hair."

Allison's face crumpled as tears spilled down her cheeks. "She slapped me so hard on my face," she sobbed, rocking back and forth in her chair.

Mr. Wilson, unable to watch any longer, stepped forward. "That's enough. I'm taking my daughter home."

Detective Miller thanked Allison for her courage. As the Wilson's left the station, the room grew quiet.

Once alone, Phillips turned to Melissa. "What's your take?"

Melissa exhaled slowly. "She's terrified of this woman. Whoever she is, she's likely the kidnapper. We need to find her."

Miller frowned. "She didn't give us much to go on."

"Give her time," Melissa said. "She'll remember more. I've got another appointment, but keep digging."

After Melissa left, Phillips looked at Miller. "Go over Jackson's initial statement. See if you can find this woman Allison described."

As Phillips walked away, Miller muttered to himself, "Is Allison talking about Ramona?"

Around the corner, Gary lurked in the shadows, having overheard the entire conversation.

Chapter 18

Marcus Is Found

As Jackson and Joe arrived back at Sarah's house after the tense bail hearing, the silence in the car was thick with unspoken words. Joe glanced at Jackson through the rearview mirror, disappointment etched on his face. Once they got inside, the weight of the situation seemed to hang in the air. Sarah, still shaken from the day's events, headed to the kitchen. Seeing the mess from the morning, she sat down, overwhelmed, and began to cry softly.

Meanwhile in the living room, Joe sat Jackson down for a conversation that Jackson knew was coming. He tried to cut in, "Uncle Joe, I know what you're going to say," but Joe silenced him immediately.

"See, that's the problem with you Gen Z kids. You think you're invincible," Joe snapped.

Jackson started to protest, "That's not—"

Joe cut him off again, his voice firm. "I know you didn't just interrupt me." Taking off his suit jacket, he leaned in, ready to make his point. "Why on earth would you go up to Allison at the police station? Knowing you were nearly charged with her kidnapping, are you dumb, or just stuck on stupid?"

Jackson didn't answer, avoiding eye contact.

Joe continued, "From now on, I don't want you contacting Allison. Or Ramona. Matter of fact, don't even look at a girl."

"Uncle Joe, I said I was sorry," Jackson shot back, his voice rising in frustration.

Joe reacted swiftly, smacking the back of his head. "Watch your tone! You'll know what sorry is when you're sitting in a prison cell."

Sarah walked in, noticing the tension. "Is everything okay in here?"

Joe, still angry but composed, replied, "Yeah, everything's fine. Jackson was just about to go upstairs and read the Bible—because only God can help him out of this mess."

Jackson stormed off upstairs, slamming his bedroom door behind him. Joe turned toward the noise, fuming.

"I know he didn't just slam that door."

Before Joe could follow him, Sarah intervened. "Don't you think you're being a little hard on him?"

Joe shook his head. "Sarah, this is why he's in this mess. You coddle him. It's time for Jackson to grow up."

Sarah sighed, feeling torn. "Do you want something to eat?" she asked, trying to change the subject.

Joe slipped his suit jacket back on. "No, thanks. I've got to be up early to work on Jackson's case."

As Joe left, Sarah stood there, still in the kitchen, alone with her thoughts, her worry growing heavier by the minute.

Ramona was on top of the world, singing to her favorite song and dancing her way into the house without a care in the world. After weeks of stress, she felt free, liberated, even waving at Maxwell, her unfaithful neighbor, without a second thought. Inside, she danced around the living room, the joy infectious, and her mood so light she couldn't help but hum as she started cooking dinner. Everything seemed perfect, at least for now.

But as she prepared to bring Mark's dinner down to the basement, the TV news interrupted her mood.

"Good Evening, I'm Nicholas Harris. We interrupt your programming to bring breaking news. A body has been found floating in the Schuylkill River. Authorities are currently on the scene and suspect that the individual in question may be Marcus Anderson, the prominent architect who has been missing for four weeks…"

Ramona froze. The tray of food slipped from her hands, crashing to the floor. Marcus Anderson? The news anchor's voice faded into the background as panic set in. Could it be…?

With her heart racing, she sprinted down to the basement. When she reached the bottom of the stairs, her worst fears were realized. Mark was gone. The ropes that had held him were now lying loosely on the floor.

Dropping to her knees, Ramona sobbed uncontrollably. This can't be happening.

As the initial shock wore off, her father's voice echoed in her mind.

"Mark is the problem we need to get rid of."

She had thought he meant taking care of things in a more figurative sense—never this.

The weight of the situation started to sink in. Her father had done this. Ramona's hands shook as she realized the depth of her entanglement in this mess. Everything was spiraling out of control, faster than she could manage.

At the same time, Margaret's world had been turned upside down in an instant. The sound of frantic knocking and flashing police lights outside her window pulled her from a peaceful sleep into a nightmare she never wanted to face. As she slowly made her way to the door, dread filled her chest.

When she opened the door and saw Detective Miller standing there, his somber expression told her everything she feared. His words confirmed it: a body had been found. The possibility that it might be Marcus, her beloved son, struck her like a lightning bolt. Margaret's heart raced, her legs wobbled as the detective explained they needed her to identify the body.

Barely able to breathe, Margaret stumbled back into the house and reached for the phone. She needed someone, anyone. Her hands trembled as she dialed Sarah's number. After several rings, Sarah's groggy voice answered. Margaret's emotions overwhelmed her and the words bubbled out of her, "Sarah, please, I need you to come with me to the hospital. They found a body, and they think it might be Marcus…"

On the other end, Sarah gasped, wide awake now. "Oh, Margaret, I'm so sorry. I'll come with you. Stay strong, I'm on my way."

Margaret didn't bother changing out of her nightclothes. She simply threw on a coat and grabbed her handbag, numb to everything around her.

As Detective Miller helped her into the police car, Margaret asked softly, "Can we stop to pick up Sarah? I can't do this alone…"

Detective Miller nodded, understanding her need for support, and they drove to Sarah's house. As the car approached, Sarah was already outside, anxiously waiting. Margaret felt a small, comforting relief as Sarah climbed into the car, holding her hand tightly. Together, they would face the unthinkable.

At the coroner's office, Margaret Anderson stood trembling, bracing herself for what she feared was the inevitable. Detective Miller led her gently into the room, where the coroner was waiting. Sarah was right beside her, holding Margaret's arm for support.

The coroner explained the process, but Margaret barely heard the words. Her mind was spinning, and her heart pounded with dread. As the coroner slowly lifted the white sheet, Margaret's breath caught in her throat.

One glance at the body was all it took. Her knees buckled, and she collapsed to the floor, sobbing uncontrollably. It was Marcus. Her son.

Detective Miller, though empathetic, had to do his job. In a quiet but firm voice, he asked, "Mrs. Anderson, we need you to confirm. Is this your son?"

Through her tears, Margaret nodded, unable to speak. Sarah quickly guided her out of the room, holding her tightly as they left the sterile, cold environment behind.

Margaret's cries echoed down the hallway as Sarah whispered comforting words, trying to soothe her in this heart-wrenching moment.

Detective Miller stopped in his tracks when the coroner called out to him. "Detective, I found this hair under the victim's fingernail," the coroner said, holding up a small evidence bag containing a strand of hair. "It could belong to the murderer."

Miller's eyes narrowed as he examined the bag. "That's a crucial piece of evidence. Get it tested for DNA as soon as possible," he ordered.

The coroner nodded. "I'll prioritize it, but we won't have results immediately. I'll also perform a full autopsy to determine the exact cause of death. From the initial examination, it seems like blunt force trauma could be the cause, but we won't know for sure until the autopsy is complete."

Miller looked grim, taking a moment to process this new information. "Make sure I'm the first to know when you have the results," he said. He turned to leave, thoughts racing in his mind about who might be responsible for Marcus's death and whether this new evidence would lead them closer to the truth

As Ramona was escorted down the hall by Officer Sanchez, she stumbled upon Margaret, sobbing uncontrollably in Sarah's arms. The sight of Margaret, broken and devastated, made Ramona pause. She hesitated, then softly asked, "Mama Anderson, is it true? They found him in the river?"

Margaret, barely holding herself together, looked at Ramona with disbelief. "Why are you here?" she demanded, her voice strained with anger and grief.

Ramona's voice cracked as she responded, "Marcus was my husband."

Margaret's face twisted with fury. "You bitch! You killed my son!" she screamed, lunging toward Ramona. Sarah quickly pulled Margaret back, trying to calm her down, whispering words of comfort in her ear as Margaret continued to sob.

Ramona, clearly shaken, made her way toward the coroner's office, glancing back at Margaret's pain-filled eyes. Despite Margaret's accusations, Ramona genuinely appeared distraught about Marcus's death. Her face showed traces of grief, and her usual confident demeanor was nowhere to be found.

As Ramona spoke with the coroner about the next steps, Margaret's anguished cries echoed down the hallway. Ramona tried to focus, but the weight of everything—the loss, the tension, and the accusations—seemed to press down on her, making it hard to breathe. The hallway buzzed with a mix of emotions, all centered on the mystery of Marcus's death.

Ramona, trying to maintain her composure, asked the coroner, "Do you know the cause of death?"

The coroner, keeping his professional tone, replied, "We need to perform a full autopsy, Mrs. Whitmore. I can't say much right now, as this is a murder case."

Ramona nodded. "I completely understand. When you're finished with the autopsy, please have Marcus's body sent to Franklin Funeral Home. Mrs. Anderson is too upset to handle the arrangements right now."

The coroner gave a solemn nod. "I'm sorry for your loss, Mrs. Whitmore."

Ramona gave a tight smile and walked out of the room, her heels clicking against the floor in the otherwise silent hallway. As soon as she was outside, she pulled out her phone and dialed her father. When he answered, she didn't wait. "What did you do?"

Her father's voice was cold and commanding on the other end. "Don't question me, Ramona. Just be ready for the press conference in the morning."

Before she could respond, he hung up, leaving Ramona standing there, conflicted and shaken. The weight of her father's involvement in whatever had happened to Marcus was clear now, and she felt the walls closing in on her.

Ramona sat in her car, tears streaming down her face, overwhelmed by the emotions she had tried to bury. Marcus, despite everything, had been a good man. A good provider, and in some ways, a good husband. She didn't want it to end like this. As much as their marriage had become a business arrangement, a part of her still cared for him. In the back of her mind, she hoped he hadn't suffered.

As she neared her house, Ramona saw the crowd of news reporters gathered outside, waiting for a statement. The flashing lights and cameras were a reminder of the scrutiny she was now under. Without hesitation, she drove past her house, wanting nothing to do with the chaos waiting for her there.

She picked up her phone and called Gary. He answered on the first ring.

"Why, Gary?" she asked, her voice trembling with disbelief.

There was a long silence on the other end of the line. Then, Gary spoke, his voice cold and detached. "It had to be done."

Before she could respond, he hung up. Ramona stared at her phone, still reeling from the overwhelming events. She felt trapped, suffocated by the choices that had been made around her, and now she was caught in a web she couldn't escape.

Chapter 19

Political Antics

The next morning, Ramona prepared herself for what would be the performance of her life. Standing in front of her mirror, she carefully wrapped herself in a sleek black dress and donned her black shades. She added a black veil for the perfect touch of mourning, knowing the press would dissect her every move. She wasn't just grieving a husband—she was crafting a narrative.

As she stepped outside, tissue in hand, she dabbed at her staged tears. The reporters swarmed, eager for a story.

"Is it true your husband was killed by the mob?" one asked.

"Mrs. Whitmore, did your husband have a gambling problem?" another shouted.

Ramona's heart raced as she wondered what lies her father had fed the press. She paused for effect, then turned to face them with the air of a grieving widow. "I will be giving an explanation about my husband today at City Hall. I will try to answer all of your questions, but please, respect my privacy during this difficult time. Thank you."

Without waiting for further questions, Ramona got into her car and drove off, leaving the reporters with just enough mystery to keep them hungry for more.

As Ramona arrived at City Hall, she was shocked by the sheer number of attendees and reporters awaiting her arrival. Cameras flashed as Gary helped her out of the car, and she maintained her poised composure despite the tension she felt inside.

"Mrs. Whitmore, I'm sorry for your loss," Gary said softly, guiding her toward the podium.

Her father, Frank Whitmore, swiftly moved to her side, embracing her with a kiss on the cheek before turning his attention to the crowd of reporters. "Please, give my daughter some space," he requested, playing the role of the concerned father. But Ramona knew better—this wasn't just a press conference for Marcus. Frank always had a bigger agenda.

Taking the podium in his pristine black designer suit, Frank commanded the attention of everyone present. "Good morning. I stand before you today with great sorrow. My son-in-law, Marcus Anderson, was found dead yesterday. Ramona and I are grateful to the Philadelphia Police Department for making this case a priority."

His voice held the perfect mix of solemnity and control. Watching on TV, Margaret Anderson, Marcus's grieving mother, was livid. "I can't believe they're standing up there lying. They don't care about my pain or my son," she fumed, her words dripping with hurt and betrayal.

Frank continued, effortlessly transitioning from sympathy to politics. "Philadelphia needs new leadership. The violence in this city, the so-called 'City of Brotherly Love,' has reached unacceptable levels. We are losing too many of our young people. That's why today, I am announcing my candidacy for Mayor of Philadelphia."

In the crowd, Detective Miller and DA Phillips exchanged stunned looks. "Did he just announce he's running for mayor?" Phillips whispered in disbelief.

Before Miller could respond, his phone buzzed. He stepped aside, taking the call from the coroner's office. His expression shifted as he listened, then turned back to Phillips with a sense of urgency. "There's a DNA match," Miller said quietly, the weight of the revelation hanging between them as Frank Whitmore's speech carried on.

Detective Miller, shaking his head in frustration, muttered, "I'm heading over to the coroner's office after this three-ring circus." He watched as Ramona took her place at the podium, dabbing at her eyes with a tissue and putting on a show of grief for the audience.

"I'm speechless right now," Ramona began, her voice trembling as she spoke. "The pain... it's really deep. But I know in my heart that he's at peace." She paused dramatically, and the cameras zoomed in, capturing every tear and quiver in her voice. Margaret, watching from her home, was enraged. She hurled the remote at the TV, her grief and anger boiling over. "When I get finished with you, Ramona, you will know what real pain feels like," she seethed.

Ramona continued, thanking Officer Richardson and the Philadelphia Police Department. "I want to thank my colleagues, friends, and family for all their condolences," she added before stepping aside, letting Frank Whitmore take the spotlight once again.

"Thank you, everyone, for coming out," Frank said smoothly, bringing the press conference to a close. Officer Richardson led Ramona back to her car, guiding her through the crowd of reporters. As Ramona drove off, she felt a strange numbness inside, still in disbelief at how her father had turned the tragic situation into a campaign event.

At this time. Frank turned to Officer Richardson, his voice low but deliberate. "Did you finish cleaning up the loose ends?" he asked. Officer Richardson gave a curt nod before walking away, blending into the sea of people.

From the sidelines, DA Phillips watched the exchange with sharp eyes. "You notice how friendly those two are?" she remarked to Miller, suspicion creeping into her voice. Miller nodded grimly, his mind racing. There was more to Officer Richardson and Frank Whitmore's connection than met the eye, and he intended to uncover it.

As Detective Miller arrived at the coroner's office, Dr. Emily Grant handed him the detailed report. Miller read through the findings, noting the disturbing details of the Marcus Anderson victim. Severe blunt force trauma to the head, defensive wounds, and the presence of foreign DNA under the victim's fingernails pointed toward a violent struggle. The strands of hair clutched in the victim's hand and the particles of skin found suggested that the victim had fought his attacker before succumbing to his injuries.

Dr. Grant began speaking as Miller scanned the report, "The skull fracture led to fatal brain injury. He likely died within a few hours of eating, and the struggle indicates he didn't go down without a fight. The hair and DNA evidence we found are currently being analyzed, and we should have more results soon."

Miller frowned, looking over the notes. "So, we're dealing with a homicide, no doubt. Blunt force trauma... but what's your guess on the weapon?"

Dr. Grant shrugged slightly. "It's hard to say definitively without more information. The fracture is consistent with something like a heavy object—a blunt instrument, possibly a bat or pipe—but we won't know for sure until more investigation is done."

Miller sighed. "And the DNA under the nails and the hair?"

"Still being processed," Dr. Grant replied. "If it's in the system, we might get lucky and find a match. But even if it's not, we'll have a strong lead once it's confirmed. This wasn't random—he fought for his life."

Miller nodded and jotted down some notes. "I'll be back when you have more information. Keep me posted, especially on the DNA and the fibers. This case is turning out to be bigger than I initially thought."

With that, Detective Miller left the coroner's office, his mind already racing with the next steps. The killer had left traces behind, and now it was only a matter of time before the evidence caught up with them.

Detective Miller, standing in front of District Attorney Phillips, continued explaining, "Dr. Grant couldn't pinpoint the exact weapon yet, but she mentioned the skull fracture is consistent with a heavy object—something blunt, like a bat or a pipe. The blood spatter patterns suggest she was struck while standing, then collapsed immediately after the first blow."

Phillips sat back in her chair, her eyes narrowing. "And you said the DNA under the nails and the hair clutched in his hand are still being processed?"

"That's right," Miller nodded. "Dr. Grant is working on it. Once we get the results, we may have a clear suspect. Right now, it's our strongest lead."

Phillips tapped her pen on the desk, her mind racing. "There's something about Officer Richardson that doesn't sit well with me. He's clean on paper, but his connections to Senator Whitmore—and now the way they acted at the press conference—raise red flags. Have you noticed anything off with him?"

Miller hesitated. "I've seen Richardson around, and he's been... close to Whitmore, but nothing solid enough to make a move. I agree there's something fishy, though."

Phillips leaned forward. "Keep a close eye on him. The Senator is clearly using this tragedy for political gain, and I wouldn't be surprised if he's pulling strings behind the scenes. I'll do my part and keep digging from here."

Miller nodded, sharing the suspicion. "I'll follow up on the DNA results, and I'll see if I can find any unofficial leads on Richardson. If he's tied up in this, I'll get something we can use."

"Good," Phillips said firmly. "This case is getting more complicated by the minute, and I want answers before it spirals further."

With that, Miller left Phillips' office, determined to uncover what was really happening behind the scenes.

Dark clouds loomed overhead, casting a gloomy shadow where the sky had once been clear and blue. Ramona drove home in haste, hoping to beat the rain that threatened to fall at any moment. As she pulled into her driveway, her heart sank at the sight of the debris scattered across her yard—remnants of news reporters and curious neighbors who had been there earlier, feeding on the tragedy that now surrounded her life.

She sighed, her fingers still gripping the steering wheel, feeling the weight of everything pressing down on her. Slowly, she turned off the ignition and sat there for a moment, staring at the mess in front of her. Empty coffee cups, discarded papers, and even a few broken pieces of camera equipment littered the ground. It was as though the chaos of the past few days had left a physical mark on her home.

Maxwell looked up from picking up the trash, meeting Ramona's gaze. He hesitated for a moment before speaking, his voice soft. "He really did love you, you know."

Ramona stood there, her hand still on the car door, uncertain how to respond. The whirlwind of emotions she had been suppressing came rushing back, but she maintained her composure. "Well," she finally said, her voice tinged with bitterness, "he had a strange way of showing it."

As she started walking toward her house, the sound of Max dragging the trash can caught her attention again. She paused and turned back to see him struggling slightly with it. With a sigh, Ramona stepped toward him and, without saying a word, picked up a broom from the ground and began sweeping up some of the litter scattered across the sidewalk.

Max was surprised by her unexpected gesture. "You don't have to do that," he said, walking over to her. "I've got it."

Ramona shook her head. "It's fine. I need something to take my mind off things. Besides, it's about to rain. You can't finish all this before it pours."

As lightning flashed across the sky, Ramona and Max worked together in silence, quickly sweeping up the remaining debris. The first few drops of rain began to fall, but they continued, both determined to finish before the storm hit in full force. Thunder rumbled in the distance as they hurried to clear the last of the trash.

Just as the downpour began, Max grabbed Ramona's arm gently, leading her toward his house. "Come on, you don't want to get caught out here," he said, his voice just loud enough to be heard over the sound of the rain.

Ramona hesitated for a moment, weighing her options. She didn't want to seem vulnerable, especially not to Max, the man she had once seen as part of her husband's betrayal. But as she looked at her drenched clothes and felt the cold rain soaking deeper, the idea of a warm drink and dry clothes seemed more appealing. She finally nodded and said, "Alright, but just for a little while."

Max smiled and gestured for her to follow him inside. His house was warm, the scent of coffee already brewing in the kitchen. "I'll grab you a towel and something dry to change into," Max said as he hurried down the hall. Ramona stood by the fireplace, staring at the family photos and the quiet elegance of the room. It felt oddly comforting, a stark contrast to the whirlwind of emotions she'd been living through.

Max returned with a soft towel and a pair of his college sweatpants and a hoodie. "It's not much, but it's dry," he said, handing her the clothes and pointing toward the guest bathroom. Ramona smiled faintly, appreciating his kindness, and headed to change.

As she emerged from the bathroom in his oversized clothes, she found Max had set up two mugs of steaming coffee and a small plate of sandwiches on the coffee table. He looked up at her and grinned, "I didn't know what you'd like, so I kept it simple."

Ramona sat down and wrapped her hands around the warm mug. She took a sip and let the warmth spread through her. "This is... nice," she admitted, feeling a strange sense of calm settle over her.

They sat in comfortable silence for a few moments before Max broke the ice. "You know, Marcus... he had his faults, but I know he cared for you in his own way."

Ramona looked at him, surprised by his openness. "We had a complicated relationship," she said quietly. "But in the end, it wasn't enough."

Max nodded, understanding more than she expected. "People are complicated. Relationships are messy. But that doesn't mean there wasn't love there."

Ramona sighed, staring into her coffee. "I suppose," she said, though her heart felt heavy. She took another sip, grateful for the distraction and the warmth of the moment.

Before she knew it, an hour had passed. Ramona glanced at her watch, realizing how late it had gotten. The warmth of conversation and the shared moment of peace had distracted her from the outside world. She stood up, excusing herself from the table with a soft smile. "I really should be going," she said, her voice gentle but firm.

Maxwell stood as well, offering a polite nod. "Of course," he replied, understanding in his eyes. "Thank you for staying. It was nice to talk, really."

Ramona returned the smile, feeling a strange sense of comfort in his words. As Ramona stepped outside, the rain had slowed to a soft drizzle, and the once-dark sky had lightened slightly. She took a deep breath, feeling a weight lift from her shoulders. The evening with Maxwell had been unexpectedly pleasant, a stark contrast to the chaos of her morning. She walked back to her house, still warm from the coffee and the company, her mind replaying the moments they shared in conversation.

Maxwell stood at his door, watching Ramona as she made her way home. He couldn't help but smile, realizing that beneath her strong exterior was someone just as vulnerable and human as anyone else. For a moment, all the tension and unspoken judgments between them seemed to dissolve.

As Ramona reached her front door, she paused, taking one last glance back at Max, who waved before heading back inside. She entered her house, closing the door behind her, feeling an unfamiliar sense of peace. Maybe, just maybe, not everything in her life was as broken as it seemed.

Inside, Ramona changed out of Maxwell's clothes and settled on the sofa, wrapping herself in a blanket. For the first time in a long while, she didn't feel completely alone. She wasn't sure what the future held, but tonight, in the midst of tragedy, she had found a small moment of solace.

The storm outside continued to rumble in the distance, but inside, Ramona felt a little less like it was tearing her apart. Little did she know, however, that she was still being watched.

Detective Miller sat in his unmarked car across the street from her house, eyes fixed on her every move. The shadows of suspicion had started to creep into his mind, and though there were no solid answers yet, something about Ramona's demeanor and the events surrounding Marcus's death didn't sit right with him. As she pulls to Maxwell's house, he noted the time, taking in the detail of her quiet exchange with the neighbor.

"Why are you so calm, Ramona?" he muttered under his breath. He jotted down a few notes, then leaned back in his seat, watching the lights fade, as she enters the house, thinking there was more to this widow than met the eye.

With the storm still raging, Miller knew he had to stay sharp. The case was full of shadows and unanswered questions, and Ramona Whitmore was at the center of it.

Chapter 20

Concealed Dirty Weapons

At the 9th District police station, Captain Casey and District Attorney Karen Phillips were deep in conversation about Senator Whitmore's press conference. Phillips, clearly frustrated, recounted how the senator had hijacked the event, turning it into a campaign promise. "His own daughter was mortified," Phillips said, shaking her head.

Captain Casey leaned back in his chair. "I saw the coverage on TV. Turned the whole thing into a spectacle."

Phillips's expression darkened. "Detective Miller believes Officer Richardson is the mole in your camp," he said, her voice measured but serious.

The captain raised an eyebrow, visibly surprised. "Richardson? A five-year veteran with a squeaky clean record? The man's up for a promotion. I don't think he'd do anything to jeopardize that opportunity."

Phillips crossed her arms. "I don't trust him. He's too close to Senator Whitmore for my liking. And you know how the senator plays—dirty politics. Richardson's alignment with him raises red flags. We need to be careful."

Captain Casey remained quiet for a moment, his mind processing the implications. "I understand your concern, but we need solid evidence before we go down that road. Squeaky clean or not, if Miller has suspicions, it's worth looking into. But tread lightly. If Richardson is involved, we need to handle this carefully—Whitmore won't make it easy."

Phillips nodded in agreement. "I'll keep digging on my end. We can't let Whitmore play us like puppets. If there's a mole, we'll find him."

"Look, Casey, this is a high-profile case, and we can't afford any mistakes," DA Phillips said, frustration evident in her tone.

Captain Casey, leaning against his desk, nodded, but kept his voice calm. "I want to nail Senator Whitmore too, but we have to tread lightly. He's powerful, and one misstep could blow everything."

Phillips paced the room. "Where are we with the DNA and the murder weapon?"

Casey crossed his arms. "We still haven't found the murder weapon."

Phillips' face tightened, her patience thinning. "And the DNA from under the victim's fingernails?"

Captain Casey was about to respond, but Phillips cut him off, yelling, "Is everyone just sitting on their ass?"

Casey stepped forward, his voice firm. "Karen, my officers are working around the clock. This city is under attack. We've got more guns on the streets than officers, and every time we lock someone up, your office lets them out. So don't lecture me on how to do my job."

Phillips froze for a moment, realizing how far she had pushed. She let out a deep sigh, rubbing her temples. "I'm sorry. This case... It's frustrating. I'm just... feeling the pressure. We need answers, Casey. We need to take this senator down, and I can't afford another high-profile case slipping through our fingers."

Captain Casey softened slightly, recognizing the shared stress. "I get it, Karen. We're all feeling it. But let's not let it cloud our judgment. We need to move smart, not fast. We'll get the DNA results soon. When we do, we'll know who's involved. But until then, we need to stay steady."

Phillips nodded, the tension between them easing. "Alright, keep me updated. We have to win this one, Casey."

As Phillips turned to leave Captain Casey's office, Detective Miller's call came in. Casey gestured for Phillips to stay, putting the call on speaker.

"Miller, did you find the murder weapon?" Casey asked, sounding hopeful.

"No, sir," Miller replied, frustration evident in his voice.

Casey kept calm, switching gears. "What about the DNA results?"

"Dr. Grant's swamped," Miller explained, "but she said she'll make it her first priority."

"Do you have anything new on this case at all?" Casey pressed.

Miller took a deep breath. "Not exactly, but I'm following a lead. Sir, I need a search warrant for Ramona's house."

Casey raised an eyebrow, skeptical. "Judge Carson isn't going to issue a warrant on a gut feeling, Miller."

Phillips cut in. "Miller, it's Phillips. Where are you now?"

"I'm at Ramona's house. She was acting strange at the press conference today, and Allison told me she remembered hearing trucks and drilling sounds around the time of the kidnapping."

Casey, confused, leaned forward. "What the hell are you talking about, Miller?"

Miller tried to explain quickly. "There's a construction site down the street from Whitmore's house. It could be connected."

Phillips sighed. "That's something, but not enough for a warrant."

Casey nodded in agreement. "Miller, I need more than a hunch. Here's what we're going to do—head back to the warehouse. Search the area thoroughly—expand it to a 100-yard radius. Look for anything we missed. And take Officer Richardson with you."

"Richardson?" Miller sounded unsure.

"Yes, Miller," Casey continued. "Take him with you. Keep an eye on him, see if he slips up. Phillips and I will talk to Allison ourselves, see if she remembers anything else. Keep us posted."

"Understood, Captain," Miller replied before the line disconnected.

Phillips glanced at Casey, tension still lingering in the air. "We're going to need more than this if we want to get ahead of Whitmore."

"I know," Casey agreed, grabbing his coat. "Let's hope Allison has something solid for us."

Captain Casey and District Attorney Karen Phillips followed Mr. Wilson inside the Wilson home, the warmth of the house contrasting with the cold night outside. Mrs. Wilson appeared from the back of the house, wiping her hands on a towel.

"Who's at the door?" she asked, her voice carrying curiosity and concern.

"It's Captain Casey and..." Mr. Wilson paused, unsure of Phillips' name.

"I'm District Attorney Karen Phillips," she said, extending her hand toward Mrs. Wilson, who shook it politely.

"Well, come on in from the cold," Mrs. Wilson invited.

"We appreciate it," Phillips said, stepping inside. "We won't take too much of your time, I promise. We just need to ask Allison a few questions."

Mr. Wilson looked hesitant but spoke, "I'm not sure how much she's going to be able to tell you. The therapist said she's still struggling to remember much from that night."

As he finished speaking, soft footsteps echoed down the staircase. Allison appeared at the bottom, looking fragile but composed. She held the banister tightly, her face a mix of apprehension and curiosity.

"Allison, sweetie," Mrs. Wilson called gently, "these people would like to talk to you."

Captain Casey and Phillips exchanged a glance before stepping closer. Phillips crouched slightly to meet Allison's eye level and gave her a warm smile.

"Hi, Allison, I'm Karen Phillips, and this is Captain Casey. We're working hard to find out what happened, and we were hoping you could help us. We know it's not easy to remember, but anything you can tell us might be helpful."

Allison hesitated, glancing at her parents before speaking softly. "I... I don't remember much, but there was... a noise."

Casey leaned forward, encouraging her. "What kind of noise, Allison? Take your time."

Allison bit her lip, clearly nervous. "There was... like trucks. I heard them... and... something else, like... like drilling or banging."

Phillips exchanged a glance with Casey, their instincts telling them this could be important. "Did you see anything, Allison? Or anyone who looked suspicious?" Phillips asked gently.

Allison shook her head, her eyes clouded with frustration. "No, I just heard things. I was too scared to look."

"That's okay," Casey reassured her. "You're helping more than you know."

Phillips nodded. "Yes, you're doing great, Allison. Can you think of anything else? Maybe something unusual before everything happened?"

Allison furrowed her brow, thinking hard. "There was... a car. I think... it was dark-colored, and I remember seeing it pass by a few times, like it was circling. I didn't think much of it then."

Phillips smiled kindly. "That's really helpful, Allison. You've done great. Thank you so much for talking with us."

Allison's parents stood nearby, looking relieved but still worried about their daughter's fragile state. Captain Casey stood up, giving the family a nod. "We appreciate your cooperation. We'll keep in touch if we need anything else."

The Wilson's escorted them to the door, and as they stepped outside, Phillips looked at Casey. "That's something to work with. Trucks, drilling, a circling car. We'll need to check with the construction site near Whitmore's house."

Casey nodded, pulling out his phone to make a call. "We'll follow up on this. Let's hope it leads us somewhere."

Captain Casey looked at his phone, dialing the necessary contacts. "I need a forensic team at 247 Monastery Road ASAP," he ordered. "And someone get in touch with the construction foreman. I want him on-site as soon as possible."

Phillips, standing beside him, added, "Get Miller and Richardson to help with the search."

Casey hesitated for a moment. "I'm not sure it's a good idea to have Richardson at the site. If he's the mole, we might be tipping him off."

Phillips crossed her arms, her gaze steady. "Exactly. If Richardson is the one leaking information, we can catch him in the act. He won't expect we're onto him. Besides, we'll have other eyes on him."

Casey sighed, nodding reluctantly. "Alright, but make sure you watch him closely."

Phillips continued, "We also need Allison to come down to the station and look at some mugshots. Maybe she can recognize someone."

Casey agreed. "I'll have Moore and Sanchez go back to the warehouse while Miller and Richardson begin the search at the construction site."

As Phillips turned to walk back to her car, Casey called after her, "You're not going to the site with us?"

Phillips shook her head. "I've got to tie up some loose ends. And I have to wake up Judge Carson. We're going to need that search warrant for both the construction site and Mrs. Whitmore's house. I'll catch up with you later."

Casey watched her drive off, knowing they were all racing against time. With a quick glance at his watch, he barked more orders into his phone, preparing his team for the long night ahead.

Captain Casey watched Karen walk back to her car with a mixture of concern and persistence. He knew she was right; the investigation needed to move quickly and carefully, but having Richardson involved felt like playing with fire.

"Moore, Sanchez," he barked into the receiver after dialing. "I need you both back at the warehouse immediately. Miller and Richardson are handling the construction site. Keep your eyes open and report anything suspicious. We're tightening the net."

Hanging up, Casey stood for a moment in the rain, processing everything. The case had become more convoluted than he ever anticipated—politics, murder, and corruption seemed to be intertwined, and it felt like they were still only scratching the surface.

Karen, meanwhile, was speeding down the road, her mind focused on the next step. She needed to get Judge Carson on board to secure the warrants for both the construction site and Mrs. Whitmore's house. Karen knew the senator's daughter might be hiding something, or at the very least, she was involved more deeply than she let on.

As Karen approached the courthouse, she felt a sense of urgency growing. Time was ticking, and every delay could mean more evidence slipping through their fingers. She parked and rushed inside, heading straight for Judge Carson's chambers.

Moments later, she was seated in the judge's office, explaining the situation. "We need these warrants, Judge. There's a high probability that the evidence we're looking for is at both the construction site and Mrs. Whitmore's house."

Judge Carson looked over the documents she had prepared. "Karen, I understand the gravity of this case, but I'm going to need a solid reason to grant a search warrant for the senator's daughter's residence. You know how delicate this situation is."

Karen leaned forward, her voice steady but firm. "Judge, if we don't get these warrants now, we risk losing vital evidence. Mrs. Whitmore could be directly involved in covering up the murder. Her father is already under scrutiny, and we have reason to believe that the murder weapon or something tying them to the crime could be in her home."

Carson sighed, rubbing his temples. "I'll grant you the warrant for the construction site immediately, but Mrs. Whitmore's house is going to need more concrete evidence than a suspicion."

Karen pressed her lips together, knowing this was the best she could get for now. "I understand. Thank you."

As she left Judge Carson's office, Karen pulled out her phone and dialed Captain Casey. "We've got the warrant for the construction site. I'll keep working on Mrs. Whitmore's place, but we need more before we can get in there."

Casey responded, "That'll have to do for now. I'll let Miller know. We're heading to the site. Hopefully, we find something that can push this investigation forward."

Karen hung up, feeling the weight of the investigation pressing down on her.

Two hours later, Captain Casey and a few dozen officers arrived at the construction site, their headlights cutting through the darkness. The air was heavy with the recent rainfall, the ground slick and muddy. Fifteen minutes after the forensic team started setting up, the foreman, Giovanni Lopez, pulled up in a truck. He stepped out, his face a mix of frustration and exhaustion.

"What is the meaning of this?" Lopez demanded, walking briskly toward Casey. "This couldn't wait until morning?"

Captain Casey's patience was wearing thin. He took a step closer to Giovanni Lopez, lowering his voice to a dangerous tone. "You also have the right to remain silent, Mr. Lopez. I suggest you exercise it before you find yourself in deeper trouble than you realize."

Lopez stiffened, his arms still crossed, but his defiance wavered. He glanced over at the forensic team already setting up near the muddy construction site, a sign that things were serious. His jaw clenched, and he glared at the officers spreading out across the site. "You can't just barge in here in the middle of the night! I have rights, and you can't search without a warrant."

At that moment, District Attorney Karen Phillips arrived, walking briskly towards the group with a document in hand. "Did somebody say we needed a warrant?" she called out, waving the paper in the air.

Lopez snatched the warrant from her hand, his eyes scanning the document quickly. Realizing the situation was beyond his control, he grudgingly stepped aside. "Fine. Do what you have to do," he muttered, clearly irritated but not willing to argue further.

Captain Casey nodded to the officers and the forensic team. "Let's move in," he ordered. The team spread out across the site, careful to avoid disturbing anything unnecessarily, as they began searching for evidence.

As they dug through the wet, muddy ground and inspected the equipment, Phillips stayed close to Lopez, asking him questions. "Who owns this property?"

Lopez, still clearly irritated, replied, "Anderson Corp. And do they have to make such a mess? There's mud everywhere."

Phillips paused, surprised. "What did you say? Anderson Corporation?"

Lopez nodded. "Yeah, the company owned by Marcus Anderson—the man you all fished out of the river. His company is building the condos here."

Phillips exchanged a look with Captain Casey, the pieces of the puzzle beginning to align in a way that made her uneasy. She glanced toward Officer Richardson, who was lingering near the edge of the search area, his gaze occasionally drifting toward the officers working in the mud.

Just then, one of the officers near a small creek called out. "I got something!" Everyone turned to see him holding up a four-inch pipe, its surface coated in mud.

Detective Miller carefully lifted the four-inch pipe, caked in mud, from the ground. The weight and shape of it made his heart race—it could very well be the missing murder weapon. He handed it off to the nearest forensic officer, who bagged it meticulously.

Phillips stared at the pipe, a sinking feeling growing in her stomach. "Do you think that's the murder weapon?" she asked, her voice low.

Miller stood up, wiping the mud off his hands. "It looks like it. And given the location, something definitely went down here."

Karen Phillips watched as the forensic team took photographs and marked the area. She glanced toward Officer Richardson, who stood at the edge of the site, watching the proceedings with what seemed like growing tension. She didn't like the way he was keeping his distance, almost too calm in the face of a discovery like this.

Richardson noticed her gaze and started walking over, forcing a neutral expression on his face. "I think we've gathered everything we need, ma'am," he said, his tone professional but clipped.

Phillips, with a hint of suspicion, responded casually, "It looks like it. Richardson, what color is your car?"

Richardson blinked, caught off guard by the question. "Navy blue," he replied, nodding towards a dark Honda parked on the far end of the construction site.

Phillips nodded slowly, her mind already racing. "Right," she murmured. Her eyes lingered on Richardson as he turned away, her instinct telling her there was more to him than met the eye. Something was off, but she would bide her time.

As Detective Miller walked back toward his car, Phillips intercepted him. She handed him a folded piece of paper. "I think you're going to need this," she said cryptically. Miller took it without a word, gave her a nod, and headed toward his vehicle, the night still thick with unanswered questions.

Monetarily, the forensics team secured the scene, taking photos of scattered blood spots and gathering every potential piece of evidence. The construction site, now illuminated by the floodlights, was buzzing with activity, but it felt cold, ominous even, as if the ground itself was holding secrets no one had yet uncovered.

Detective Miller returned from his car, walking briskly toward Phillips. "What's on that paper you gave me?" he asked.

Phillips smiled faintly. "Just a reminder of a few things I need you to check with Judge Carson. We're going to need more than this pipe to tie everything together. Also, get Allison down to the station to look at some mugshots. We need to see if anyone from the site or anyone around Whitmore's circle matches what she remembers."

Miller nodded. "I'll take care of it. You think Richardson's involved?" he asked, lowering his voice.

Phillips hesitated for a moment before replying. "It's possible. There's too much lining up—his connection to Whitmore, his proximity to the case, and now this car description. But we need proof. We can't tip him off before we're sure."

Miller frowned, thinking it over. "I'll keep an eye on him, but you're right—we need to be careful."

Just then, Captain Casey approached, his boots caked in mud. "We've sent the pipe to the lab. If this is the murder weapon, we might be closer to cracking this case wide open."

Phillips nodded, but her mind was still on Richardson. "Let's hope so. But until then, we need to keep our cards close to our chest, especially with Richardson around. If he's the leak, he could destroy evidence before we even realize it."

Casey grimaced. "I'll talk to Judge Carson about keeping this under wraps for now. We can't afford to blow this investigation wide open until we're sure who's involved."

Phillips agreed, her mind already formulating the next steps. "Good idea. Let's play it smart. I'll follow up with the lab on the DNA under the victim's fingernails. It might give us more clues."

As the rain began to fall lightly again, Phillips and Miller exchanged a final glance before heading their separate ways. Both of them understood that the stakes were now higher than ever, and any mistake could undo all their hard work.

Chapter 21

Funeral Chaos

The next morning, Officer Sanchez burst into Captain Casey's office with a laptop in hand, looking both excited and anxious.

"I've got footage from outside Tasty Treats Bakery," Sanchez said, setting the laptop on the captain's desk. Casey leaned forward, his fingers drumming on the desk as Sanchez played the video.

"When was this taken?" Casey asked, his eyes glued to the screen.

"About two days before Allison went missing," Sanchez replied, stepping closer. "You can see Allison talking to Mrs. Whitmore."

Casey frowned, studying the footage. "This is circumstantial at best," he said, a trace of frustration in his voice. "Mrs. Whitmore already said she took Allison to see some properties."

Suddenly, something on the screen caught his eye. "Wait," Casey leaned in. "Is that a dark-colored car?"

Sanchez quickly zoomed in on the grainy footage. "Yes. It looks like it could be a 2014 Honda Civic."

Captain Casey's face lit up with recognition. "Zoom in on the license plate."

Sanchez frowned. "It's a bad angle from this side. But I'll get Jose from the computer lab to clean it up and bring up the plates." Just as he finished, a knock sounded at the door.

"Come in," Casey called.

Officer Moore stepped inside. "Captain, the Wilson family is here."

Casey straightened his suit jacket and nodded. "Good. Put them in Interrogation Room Three. I'll be there shortly."

As Moore left, Casey turned back to Sanchez. "Get me those plates, Sanchez. If we can tie that car to Richardson or Whitmore, we've got a solid lead."

Sanchez nodded, already heading for the door. Casey stood up, straightened his jacket again, and prepared himself for the conversation ahead. The Wilson family had been through enough, but he needed to see if Allison remembered anything more that could help break the case wide open.

Captain Casey, DA Phillips, and Detective Miller sat down with the Wilson family in the interrogation room — the tension thick in the air.

"Good morning, Mr. and Mrs. Wilson," Captain Casey said, nodding gratefully. "Thank you for bringing Allison to speak with us today."

Detective Miller sat straight with a warm smile. "Can I get you something to drink? Allison, would you like some water?"

"Yes, please," Allison replied quietly.

Mr. Wilson shifted in his seat, his arms crossed. "I don't understand why we're here again. Allison already told you she doesn't remember much," he said, frustration clear in his voice.

DA Phillips spoke gently but firmly, "We understand, Mr. Wilson. Allison, we know this is difficult and frustrating, but we're very close to solving this case. However, we need your help with just a few more details."

Mr. Wilson shook his head, standing up. "You can't force her to remember. I've had enough of this nonsense — let's go," he said, pulling at Allison's arm.

"Please, honey, sit down," Mrs. Wilson pleaded, holding his hand. "Let her speak."

Allison looked up at her parents, her face calm but determined. "Mom, Dad, I'm okay. I'm starting to remember more details every day." She turned to the officers. "I want to help."

Detective Miller gave her an encouraging nod. "That's great, Allison. We appreciate it. We're going to show you some photos now. Just take your time. Tell us if anything stands out."

He spread a series of photos across the table, a mixture of random people, a picture of Officer Richardson in plain clothes, and a photo of Ramona.

Allison scanned the photos slowly. She didn't seem to recognize Ramona, moving her gaze past her without a second glance. But when she reached the photo of Officer Richardson, her brow furrowed. She stared at it for a moment longer than the others.

"This one..." she whispered, pointing at the picture of Richardson. "Something about him seems... familiar. I can't place it, but I feel like I've seen him before."

Detective Miller exchanged a glance with Captain Casey and DA Phillips. They had what they needed — a connection, even if faint, to Officer Richardson. It was enough to push forward with more suspicion.

"Thank you, Allison," DA Phillips said gently. "You've been a great help today."

Allison hesitated for a moment, her eyes shifting as she searched her memory. "I... I remember the room being small, not much in it. Just a bed, some kind of lamp, and... I think there was a window, but it was covered. The walls were dark, maybe a deep gray or blue."

Detective Miller leaned forward, listening intently. "And the person, Allison? Was it a man or a woman?"

Allison closed her eyes, trying to piece together the memory. "It was a man, I think. His voice was low, but he didn't talk much. He didn't come close to me, but I could feel him watching. There was something cold about him... like he didn't care."

Miller nodded, sensing the importance of her recollection. "Did he say anything? Or was there something about him that stood out? Any features you can remember?"

Allison bit her lip. "I remember... he wore dark clothes, and I think he had a hat, but I couldn't see his face clearly. He always stayed in the shadows. The only thing I remember is the sound—he had something in his pocket that jingled, like keys or coins."

Detective Miller's mind raced, each detail potentially leading to new clues. "That's very helpful, Allison. Thank you. Was there anything else? Anything unusual about the room or something he did?"

She shook her head slightly. "No, but... the room smelled strange. Like chemicals or something. It made me dizzy sometimes."

Miller's eyes narrowed. "Chemicals? That could mean something. You've done a great job, Allison. Every detail helps."

He exchanged a quick glance with Captain Casey and DA Phillips, knowing they were closer now to figuring out who was behind this.

Karen said, "I think we have enough for a warrant. Go ahead out to Mrs. Whitmore's house, and I'll meet you there with the warrant."

Captain Casey and Detective Miller arrived at Ramona's house. The air felt heavy with anticipation as they pulled up to the quiet suburban home, the weight of the on-going investigation pressing on their minds. Detective Miller got out of the car first, scanning the property as if trying to piece together what might lie within.

Just as they approached the front door, Karen Phillips pulled up behind them, stepping out of her car with the warrant in hand. "Let's make this quick," she said, her voice firm.

Detective Miller knocked on the door, and moments later, Ramona answered, looking flustered and surprised. She was dressed in somber attire, clearly ready to attend her husband's funeral. Her brow furrowed as she saw the officers standing before her.

"What is this?" Ramona asked, her voice barely hiding the tremor of unease.

Captain Casey stepped forward, holding up the warrant. "Ramona Whitmore, we have a warrant to search your house. We're looking for evidence related to an ongoing investigation."

Ramona's face fell, her hands trembling as she clutched the door frame. "You can't be serious," she whispered. "Not today of all days. My husband's funeral…"

"We understand the timing is unfortunate," Karen said, stepping beside Captain Casey, "but this is crucial to the case we're investigating."

Reluctantly, Ramona stepped aside, allowing them into her home. As the team entered, the tension in the air thickened. Detective Miller and Captain Casey moved swiftly, beginning their search while Ramona followed them anxiously.

They worked their way through the rooms, eventually descending into the basement, where Detective Miller had previously noticed the unusual repainting of the walls. The vibrant blue hue still seemed out of place, and now, with the warrant in hand, the officers had the authority to dig deeper.

Ramona stood at the top of the stairs, watching nervously. "What are you looking for?" she asked, her voice trembling.

"We'll know when we find it," Captain Casey replied, his focus unwavering as he examined the basement floor.

Detective Miller found his way to the hatch they discovered during the Search. Without hesitation, he opened it, revealing the crawl space underneath. The air down there was damp and still, as though it hadn't been touched in some time.

As Miller climbed down, Casey followed. The narrow space was dark and unsettling. Karen and Ramona remained upstairs, tension building between them as they waited for any sign of discovery.

"There's something down here," Miller's voice echoed from below. Casey's flashlight revealed faint marks on the ground, something that seemed hastily covered or buried. The crawl space felt like it held secrets long kept.

Karen glanced back at Ramona, whose expression was now one of dread. "What are you hiding, Ramona?"

Ramona didn't answer, her eyes wide with fear.

Moments later, the door swung open, and Frank Whitmore stormed into the house. His face was filled with confusion and anger as he noticed the police cars parked outside his daughter's home. He immediately spotted Ramona standing near the stairs, her eyes red from stress.

"What's the meaning of this?" Frank demanded as he walked briskly toward her.

Ramona, filled with panic and desperation, quickly ran into her father's arms. "Oh, Father, they think I'm involved in kidnapping and murder!" she cried.

Frank's face turned pale, and his eyes widened in disbelief. "You're accusing my daughter of killing her own husband? How dare you!" he barked, turning to glare at the officers.

Karen Phillips, standing calmly by, held up a hand to deescalate the situation. "We did not accuse her of anything, Frank."

"So, why are you here?" Frank shot back, his voice filled with skepticism.

"We're just following up on a lead," Karen responded, showing him the warrant. Frank snatched it from her hand, his face hardening as he read it over.

"Karen, this is bullshit!" he spat, his voice filled with venom. "I know the law — you forget I used to be a prosecutor before I became a senator. You think you can just barge in here with some flimsy warrant?"

Karen remained unshaken, her tone measured but firm. "I haven't forgotten, Frank. Which is why you know how this goes. So, let me do my damn job."

Frank's face flushed with anger. "You listen to me — by the time I'm finished with you, you'll be asking 'paper or plastic'!" he threatened.

Detective Miller, who had been quietly observing the confrontation, finally spoke up. "Let's wrap this up. Mrs. Whitmore has a funeral to attend," he said, looking at Karen for approval.

Karen gave a small nod and turned back to Frank and Ramona. "We'll be out of your way soon enough, but until then, we are going to complete this search."

Frank held Ramona protectively, glaring at the officers as they continued their investigation. The tension in the room was palpable, and Ramona's sobs echoed through the house, a stark reminder of the chaos and suspicion that now surrounded her family.

As the forensic team packed up to leave, DA Karen Phillips turned to Captain Casey and Detective Miller. "Did you find anything in the crawl space?" she asked, her frustration evident.

Detective Miller shook his head. "The strange smell is probably bleach or ammonia. We sprayed the room with luminol to detect any blood spatter, but there's nothing there."

Karen clenched her jaw. "I know Allison was held here. She described everything to a T. And they repainted the walls?"

Captain Casey nodded. "Frank's a smart man. He's always going to be one step ahead of us. Where's Richardson?"

Miller replied with a shrug, "I sent him on a wild goose chase. There's no way he knew about this warrant."

As they descended the stairs, Phillips glanced at Casey. "It's time for you to clean house. You've got more than one mole in your station," she warned.

Meantime, outside, Frank Whitmore locked up Ramona's house. She leaned in close, her voice a hushed whisper. "How did you know about the warrant?"

Frank's face twisted into a wicked grin. "There's more than one way to skin a cat," he said with a smug chuckle. "Besides, Richardson is an idiot."

While the police searched Ramona's house for evidence of her involvement in the case, the funeral continued on the other side of the city. The church was filled with somber faces, a heavy air of grief hanging over the room. Family, friends, dignitaries, and co-workers had gathered to pay their last respects to Ramona's husband, a military man who had served his country with honor. The somber procession of soldiers approached Ramona, each saluting her with reverence. One soldier presented her with a folded flag, a symbol of her husband's ultimate sacrifice. Ramona, still in shock, accepted the flag with trembling hands.

The minister began to address the congregation, speaking words of comfort and offering solace to those mourning. Detective Miller and DA Phillips sat in the back, observing the funeral quietly. Though they were there for official purposes, the weight of the occasion was not lost on them.

Margaret Anderson, Marcus Anderson's mother, sat in the first row, her face a mask of grief as she mourned her son. Maxwell.

Marcus's close friend, sat beside her, providing silent support. He glanced occasionally in Ramona's direction, his expression unreadable. Jackson and Sarah were also in attendance.

As the minister's words continued to echo through the sanctuary, a sense of unease settled over Miller and Phillips. They exchanged glances, both knowing that despite the sorrow in the room, they couldn't let their investigation rest — not even at a funeral.

The church fell silent as Detective Miller's voice echoed through the somber atmosphere. The gathered mourners, who had come to pay their respects, turned in shock as Miller approached Jackson with a grim demeanor.

Jackson stood frozen, disbelief washing over him as Miller continued, "Jackson, you are under arrest for the murder of Marcus Anderson."

Margaret Anderson gasped from the front row, her hand flying to her mouth. Ramona, already grief-stricken from the loss of her husband, could barely comprehend what was happening. The soldiers who had just honored her with a flag now stood at attention, unsure how to react.

"You're making a mistake!" Jackson exclaimed, his face pale as Miller stepped closer, handcuffs in hand.

DA Phillips, standing nearby, spoke up, her voice firm. "We have the DNA evidence, Jackson. It's over."

Jackson looked around, his eyes landing on Margaret, who stared back at him, wide-eyed and devastated. He shook his head, stepping back as if the weight of the accusation was too much to bear. "I didn't do it. I swear, I didn't kill Marcus."

But it was too late. As Miller led Jackson away in handcuffs, the whispers began to spread through the church, and the air, once filled with grief, was now thick with shock and disbelief.

Ramona sat motionless, the folded flag still in her hands, her world spiraling further into chaos.

As the minister's words filled the church, Margaret Anderson suddenly slumped forward, unconscious. Panic spread across the front row as Maxwell, a family friend, rushed to her side to catch her before she fell completely. The crowd gasped, but before anyone could fully react, Jackson erupted into a fit of rage.

"No! This can't be happening!" Jackson screamed, his voice echoing off the walls as he pushed past mourners. His face was flushed with anger and fear, and his movements were erratic. Sarah, his mother, ran after him, shouting, "My son is innocent! He didn't do anything!" Her voice cracked with desperation as she followed him, but not before throwing a venomous glance at Ramona, who stood frozen, clutching the flag tightly to her chest.

Detective Miller wasted no time, moving quickly to detain Jackson before the situation could escalate further. As Jackson continued resist, Miller led him to the police car waiting outside. Jackson thrashed, his anger not subsiding as he yelled, "You've got the wrong man! I didn't do it!" But the evidence told a different story.

Right after the chaos outside the church, DA Phillips tried to calm Sarah down. "Mrs. McKinley, please, we're just following the evidence. Let us do our job." But Sarah was inconsolable, her tears mixing with her rage. "You people are making a mistake! My son is innocent!" she wailed, but Phillips remained firm, her voice steady despite the chaos.

As Jackson was placed in the back of the police car, Sarah's cries echoed through the air, while inside the church, the once peaceful funeral had descended into confusion and grief. Ramona, still in shock, watched everything unfold, knowing the storm was far from over.

Chapter 22

Twisted Reality

Jackson had just gone through the full intake process — fingerprints, mugshot, and a humiliating strip search. Despite the overwhelming evidence, he clung to his innocence, repeating, "I didn't do it!" at every opportunity. His defiance did little to quiet the storm brewing outside the interrogation room.

Joseph Lawson, Jackson's uncle, and Sarah McKinley, his mother, burst into the police station, their faces red with anger and frustration. Joseph, a seasoned defense attorney, stormed up to the front desk, demanding to see District Attorney Karen Phillips. "Where is she? I want to see this so-called evidence you have on my nephew!" His voice boomed through the station, catching the attention of several officers. Sarah, eyes swollen from crying, stayed by his side, her hands trembling with rage.

Moments later, Karen Phillips emerged from the interrogation room, composed and professional. "Joseph," she greeted, her voice calm yet firm, "always a pleasure." Joseph, not in the mood for pleasantries, cut straight to the point. "Karen, I don't know what kind of game you're playing, but I want to see the evidence you're basing this ridiculous arrest on. You and I both know Jackson isn't capable of murder!"

Sarah, unable to hold back any longer, shouted, "I want to see my son!" Her voice cracked with desperation. Karen glanced at her sympathetically but shook her head. "I'm sorry, Mrs. McKinley, but your son is still being processed. You'll be able to see him later." Sarah, visibly distraught, turned to Joseph, pleading, "I don't want to go home, Joseph. I need to be here."

Joseph sighed, his face softening as he gently tried to comfort her. "Sarah, you should go home and rest. This is going to take time. Let me handle this."

Karen stepped closer to Joseph and pulled him aside, lowering her voice. "Joe, I know you believe your nephew didn't do this, but the evidence points somewhere else. We're not rushing this, and we're giving him every chance to prove otherwise." She handed him a paper — a copy of the preliminary findings, including DNA evidence and witness statements. "Take a look at this. It's not as clear-cut as you think."

As Karen walked away, her heels echoing down the long hallway, Joseph stood there, staring at the paper in his hand, his face etched with concern. He knew that Karen wasn't one to play games, but this was his nephew — his family. He would fight tooth and nail to get to the truth, no matter how long it took.

As Dr. Grant approached, Captain Casey, Detective Miller, and DA Phillips were deep in conversation about the DNA findings. Karen asked Miller, "What did Dr. Grant say about the hair sample under the victim's nails?" Before Miller could respond, Dr. Grant interrupted, her face serious.

"I need to talk to you about that hair sample," Dr. Grant said, her voice calm but urgent. Phillips nodded. "Please, clear up any confusion we might have."

Dr. Grant wasted no time. "First, I have some new information for you," she began, causing all three officials to lean in, listening intently. "I pulled a partial fingerprint off the pipe we found at the construction site. I sent the print to the crime lab, and Jose and I have been working closely on this case because certain things just don't add up."

Captain Casey raised an eyebrow, "How so?"

Dr. Grant continued, "The partial print belongs to Mr. McKinley, and the hair found on the victim also matches his DNA profile."

Detective Miller's eyes widened. "So, we have our murderer?"

But Dr. Grant quickly raised her hand. "Not so fast. There's something off. The partial fingerprint looks... placed, almost like it was too conveniently found on the pipe. The alignment of the print, the clean nature of it — it feels tampered with."

Captain Casey frowned. "Are you suggesting someone is framing McKinley?"

Dr. Grant nodded. "It's a possibility we need to consider. The evidence seems to point to him, but the way it's presenting itself feels orchestrated. We need to dig deeper before drawing any conclusions."

Karen Phillips exchanged a glance with Miller. "If this is true, then we're dealing with more than just a simple case of murder. Someone wants McKinley to take the fall."

Captain Casey's jaw tightened. "We need to go over everything again — every piece of evidence, every statement. If someone's setting him up, we're missing the real killer."

Captain Casey's voice echoed through the hallway, "Where the hell is Richardson?" His tone was sharp, clearly irritated by Richardson's unexplained absence. The team dispersed as ordered, each heading in their assigned direction.

Karen caught up with Casey as they walked towards Interrogation Room One. "You think Jackson's going to crack?" she asked.

Casey sighed, "We'll see. We've got enough to hold him, but if Dr. Grant's right, something about this doesn't sit well with me. I need to hear Jackson's side. And make sure his lawyer is present."

As they reached the room, Karen opened the door. Jackson McKinley was sitting at the table, his face tense, with Joseph Lawson beside him, his attorney. Jackson looked up, his eyes weary but defiant.

"Mr. McKinley," Casey started as they entered the room, "we're here to clear some things up. We're not here to play games, and I don't want to force you into anything. But we need to get the facts straight."

Joseph Lawson leaned forward. "Captain Casey, let's keep this professional. My client is innocent, and I expect you to treat him as such."

Karen sat down next to Casey, her gaze fixed on Jackson. "Jackson, we know the DNA evidence ties you to the crime scene, but Dr. Grant believes the prints may have been planted. That's why we're here. You're saying you're innocent, and if that's true, we need your cooperation."

Jackson's eyes flickered with something — fear, or maybe guilt — but he remained silent, looking between his lawyer and the officers.

Immediately after, Detective Miller headed out to track down Ramona Whitmore, knowing her involvement was critical. As for Sanchez and Moore, they were already on their way to bring Allison back to the station, hoping that she might recall something more that could break the case wide open.

But one thing gnawed at the back of Casey's mind — where was Richardson? His absence in a moment like this was more than suspicious.

An hour later, Allison arrived at the police station with Moore and Sanchez. Margaret and Sarah are sitting in the lobby.

Allison's voice was soft as she greeted Margaret Anderson, her eyes filled with uncertainty. Margaret looked up, her grief-stricken face showing a brief moment of recognition. She forced a weak smile and nodded, but didn't say anything.

Allison turned away quickly, walking past them, her mind racing. Why do I know her? She thought, the connection just beyond her grasp.

Moore gently guided her to a seat at his desk. "Mrs. Wilson, please sit. I'm going to let the captain know you're here."

As Moore and Sanchez walked off, Allison's heart began to race. Something about seeing Margaret was stirring memories deep inside her. Flashes of places, faces — things she couldn't quite put together. She squeezed her hands together nervously, trying to calm herself.

At this time, Sarah was still pleading with Margaret. "Margaret, you know Jackson didn't do this. He loved Marcus like a father! You have to believe me."

Margaret, her voice shaky and her gaze distant, whispered, "I don't know what to believe anymore, Sarah. I've lost everything."

As she stood up, preparing to leave, she gave Allison one last glance. Allison, noticing the look, felt another wave of anxiety. She recognized something in Margaret — something that was pulling at the edges of her memory. Her heart began to pound faster, and a sense of panic started to rise.

Suddenly, she mumbled under her breath, "I know her... but from where?"

Moore and Sanchez returned, noticing the change in Allison's demeanor. "Allison, are you okay?" Sanchez asked, concern evident in his voice.

She looked up, her eyes wide with confusion.

Senator Whitmore stormed into the station, his face flushed with anger. "This is outrageous!" he shouted as he guided Ramona inside. His daughter looked pale and shaken, clearly overwhelmed by the mounting pressure. "First, you show up at her home right before her husband's funeral, then you arrest someone at the funeral itself, and now you drag her back here? Have you no decency?"

Detective Miller, who had been quietly observing, stepped forward. "Senator, we're following leads. This investigation is about more than just your daughter."

Senator Whitmore's eyes blazed with fury. "Leads? You're harassing her! My daughter has done nothing wrong! This is a witch hunt!"

Amid the commotion, Allison, seated at Moore's desk, started to feel uneasy. She glanced over at Ramona, her eyes lingering on Senator Whitmore as her mind scrambled to make sense of the fragments of memories flashing back. The sight of the senator, his harsh tone, and the presence of Ramona sent her spiraling into a mix of anxiety and fear.

"I remember... something about him," Allison muttered under her breath, her voice barely audible.

Moore, catching the hint of recognition in Allison's voice, turned to her with concern. "What do you mean, Allison? Can you remember something specific?"

Allison swallowed hard, her eyes darting between Ramona and Senator Whitmore. "He was there... or someone connected to him. I don't know how, but I know him. I remember that voice... yelling at someone."

As Moore absorbed what she was saying, he glanced toward Captain Casey, who had just stepped out of his office after hearing the raised voices.

"Captain, I think Allison's starting to recall more. She recognized Mrs. Anderson and now... I think the senator's presence is triggering something."

Senator Whitmore, hearing part of the exchange, shot a sharp look at Allison. "This is absurd!" he snapped. "You're basing an investigation on the confused ramblings of a girl, who can't even remember what happened? My daughter is innocent! You're wasting time!"

Captain Casey, maintaining his composure, addressed the senator calmly. "We're doing our due diligence, Senator. No one's accusing Ramona of anything... yet. We just need her cooperation."

Ramona, who had been quiet all this time, finally spoke up, her voice trembling. "Dad... please. Let them do what they have to do. I just want this to be over."

Senator Whitmore turned to her, his expression softening, but his anger remained palpable. "They have no right to drag you through this, Ramona. No right at all."

As the tension in the room grew, Allison, still seated at the desk, began to tremble. Sanchez noticed her distress and quickly knelt beside her. "Allison, focus on your breathing. You're safe here. Try to stay calm."

But the more Allison focused, the more the pieces of her fragmented memories seemed to collide. She looked at Ramona, then at the senator, her mind struggling to connect the dots.

"I think I remember something else... a man. He was with them. He had a cap... he was... watching me," Allison stammered, her voice shaky.

Captain Casey and Karen exchanged glances, knowing that every small detail Allison remembered could be crucial. They just needed to help her put it all together. All the while, Senator Whitmore stood by, his face hardening as the weight of the situation pressed down on him.

Allison's sudden scream echoed through the station, startling everyone. "I remember!" she shouted, her voice filled with panic. The memory hit her like a flood — she saw the man who had been mean to her, hidden in the shadows, wearing a baseball cap. Overwhelmed, she bolted out of the police station, running blindly into the street.

A red car screeched to a halt just inches from her. Sanchez, quick on his feet, dashed out after her and pulled her back onto the sidewalk before the car could hit her.

Allison sat on the curb, shaking and clutching her knees, her breaths shallow and erratic. Sanchez knelt beside her, trying to calm her down, his voice gentle. "Allison, you're safe now. It's okay, just breathe."

Moore and a few other officers rushed out of the station, forming a protective barrier between Allison and the onlookers. Detective Miller, hearing the commotion, came outside with Captain Casey and Karen close behind. They exchanged worried glances as they saw Allison, visibly shaken, rocking back and forth.

"Get her inside," Captain Casey ordered. Sanchez and Moore carefully helped Allison to her feet and escorted her back into the station. Inside, they led her to a quiet room, away from the chaos, and sat her down.

Karen knelt in front of Allison, speaking softly. "Allison, can you tell me what you remember? It's important, but take your time. You're safe here."

Allison's eyes darted around the room, her voice trembling. "I... I remember the man... the man with the baseball cap. He... he was mean. He was there, in the room, where I was held. He said things, threatened me." She paused, trying to catch her breath. "I... I saw Senator Whitmore. I think... I think he was the one who came to the house that day."

Karen and Captain Casey exchanged looks, their suspicions deepening. The mention of Senator Whitmore added a new layer to the investigation, one that could have serious implications. They knew they needed to tread carefully.

Simultaneously, in the lobby, Senator Whitmore was still berating Detective Miller. Ramona stood by, silent and anxious, while her father continued to defend her.

"You're all making a mistake! My daughter is innocent in all of this!" Senator Whitmore barked. "Arresting people at funerals, traumatizing my family — this is a disgrace!"

Detective Miller remained calm but firm. "Senator, we're just doing our job. We have questions that need answers. Your daughter is a key witness, and we need her cooperation."

Ramona, looking increasingly uncomfortable, glanced towards the interrogation room where Allison had just been taken. Her eyes filled with fear and uncertainty, as if she knew that everything was unraveling.

Captain Casey walked back into the lobby. "Senator Whitmore," he said, his voice level but authoritative, "your daughter is not under arrest. But we need to question her further. There's more going on here than you realize."

The senator glared at him, but there was a flash of hesitation in his eyes. He was losing control of the situation, and he knew it.

Back in the room, Allison was still trembling but had calmed slightly. Karen gave her a reassuring nod. "You're doing great, Allison. Just a little more. Can you tell us anything else about the man with the cap? Was he someone you recognized?"

Allison shook her head slowly, her voice barely a whisper. "I don't know him... but I think he knew Senator Whitmore."

Karen's heart sank as the pieces of the puzzle began to fall into place. They were inching closer to the truth, but it was a truth that could shake everything.

As the scene outside the police station became chaotic with reporters swarming around Senator Whitmore and his political antics, Sanchez discreetly informed Captain Casey. The captain, already frustrated, muttered, "Of course, Whitmore would call the media." He had no desire to face the press after an intense interrogation with Jackson McKinley, who still claimed his innocence.

Moments later, Jackson's uncle, Joseph Lawson, emerged from the interrogation room, his face somber. He approached Sarah, Jackson's mother, and broke the news, "Jackson's bail is set at a quarter of a million dollars." Sarah's eyes widened in disbelief. "A quarter of a million? I don't have that kind of money. Why is it so high?" she asked, panic creeping into her voice.

Joseph explained grimly, "He's accused of killing the senator's son-in-law, and the DA is using this case to boost her career. Plus, Jackson's recent arrests don't help."

Margaret Anderson, still grieving her son Marcus, spoke quietly, "And he's been arrested three times this month, Sarah."

Sarah, visibly upset, turned to Margaret. "Mrs. Anderson, you don't really believe my son killed your son, do you?"

Margaret put a hand on Sarah's shoulder, her voice soft but firm. "For a moment, the thought crossed my mind. But I know your boy, and I don't believe he killed Marcus."

Sarah, filled with tenacity, began walking toward the exit. "Where are you going?" Joseph called after her.

"I'm going to get the deed to my house. My son won't spend another night in this hellhole," she replied, her voice resolute as she stormed out of the station.

Inside, Captain Casey decided it was best for Allison to leave through the back to avoid the media frenzy. As she was being escorted down the hallway, she suddenly spotted Jackson being led out of the interrogation room. In a surprising turn, Allison ran to him and hugged him tightly as if nothing had ever happened.

The officers, including Detective Miller and Officer Moore, exchanged bewildered looks. "Jackson, did that woman hurt you?" Moore asked, confused by Allison's behavior.

Detective Miller, sensing the strangeness of the situation, signaled Sanchez to take Jackson back to holding. Something about Allison's sudden attachment to Jackson didn't sit right, and Miller knew they needed to get to the bottom of it.

Chapter 23

I Spy

Captain Casey stormed back into his office, his frustration barely contained as DA Phillips followed him inside. "I want to nail that slum bucket to the wall," Casey fumed, pacing around his desk.

DA Phillips, her voice sharp with impatience, added, "Whitmore is up to his neck in this. I know he's connected to all of it." Before they could continue, a knock on the door interrupted the tense atmosphere.

"Come in," Casey called, still bristling with anger.

Detective Miller stepped in, looking uneasy but determined. "Sir, I don't think Jackson has anything to do with Allison's kidnapping," he said.

DA Phillips, her patience worn thin, exploded. "We are running out of time! The public is outraged, the mayor is on my back, and you two better get your act together."

Casey slammed his hands on the desk, his voice steady but dangerous. "Don't tell me how to do my job, Karen. The witness is just starting to put pieces together. We have to give it time."

Phillips took a step closer to him, her voice lowering with emotion. "My heart goes out to the Wilson family, but they have their daughter. Mrs. Anderson's son was murdered, brutally. And you're telling me to let you do your job, when we know his ex-wife might be involved? His body was unrecognizable, and it's my job to put the bastard responsible behind bars."

Detective Miller intervened, trying to cool the heated exchange. "Alright, everyone just calm down. We're all on the same side here."

Casey, exasperated, turned to Miller. "Miller, do you have any ideas?"

Miller's eyes lit up, a glint of decidedness returning to his expression. "Yes, I do. The Whitmore's are always one step ahead of us, but it's time for us to flip the script."

Karen, intrigued, leaned closer. "Alright, what do you have in mind?"

Miller outlined his plan. "We know Richardson is working for Whitmore, but he's not the only one. We need to flush out the other moles. I think we should use Jackson as an informant — leverage him to get inside information."

Casey frowned, uncertain. "I don't know, Miller. Jackson's becoming a liability. His mother's getting unhinged, and his uncle is a nightmare to deal with."

Karen, suddenly smiling, leaned forward. "Wait a minute, this could actually work. Jackson knows more than he's letting on."

Miller, encouraged, began explaining the finer points of the plan. Casey's frown slowly turned into an evil grin as he listened intently, the wheels turning in his mind.

Captain Casey picked up the phone, dialing Jackson's uncle, Joseph, explaining the plan and what they needed Jackson to do to clear his name. Though initially resistant, Joseph eventually agreed, understanding it was Jackson's best chance to avoid more serious charges and potential jail time.

A few minutes later, Jackson was escorted into Casey's office. Casey, DA Phillips, and Detective Miller were all waiting, their expressions serious. Jackson slouched into the room, his face tense and unsure.

Casey leaned forward, speaking bluntly. "Jackson, here's the deal. We need you to go undercover for us. Get information from anyone close to Whitmore, especially Richardson. We know he's been working for the senator, but we need proof — and we need you to help us get it."

Jackson shook his head, his face a mix of fear and frustration. "You're asking me to spy on people who could ruin my life if they found out."

Phillips stepped in. "Look, Jackson, I get it. This isn't easy. But if you want to clear your name and avoid a murder charge, this is your shot."

After a long pause, Jackson reluctantly nodded. "Fine. I'll do it."

Just as Jackson agreed, Casey slammed his hand down on his desk, the sound startling everyone in the room. "One more thing, where the hell is Richardson?"

Miller's eyes darted to the door, his expression darkening. "I haven't seen him since this morning. I'll find him, Captain."

Casey nodded, his jaw set. "Do that. And Jackson," he added, turning back to him, "you'd better get this right. One slip-up, and we all go down."

Jackson finally realized he was out of options, and his uncle's words echoed in his mind, making it clear that cooperating was the only chance he had to avoid a long prison sentence.

Detective Miller carefully attached the wire to Jackson's shirt, testing it and giving him a reassuring nod.

Captain Casey leaned in, his voice steady and direct. "Follow the script exactly, Jackson. Ramona is smart; she'll pick up on anything unusual. Don't push too hard, just keep her talking, and let her lead the conversation if you need to." Jackson listened closely, nodding, though his heart pounded with nerves. He knew the risk he was taking.

Jackson picked up his phone and dialed Ramona's number, swallowing his anxiety as he waited for her to answer. After letting it ring once, she declined the call, and he could feel the weight of the operation start to crumble. He tried again, and finally, she picked up on the second ring, her tone cautious. After some convincing, Ramona finally agreed to meet him at Pete's Bar, though her reluctance was evident.

Hours later, Jackson sat alone in a dim corner, watching the door, palms sweaty as he rehearsed his lines over and over in his head. When Ramona finally arrived, she paused outside, her eyes meeting his through the window. She hesitated, then picked up her phone and dialed him, her voice uncertain. "Jackson, it's late. I don't think this is a good idea for us to meet tonight."

Jackson fumbled to pick up his phone, feeling every pair of eyes in the bar turn to him for a second before looking away. Detective Miller's voice came through the earpiece, calm but firm. "Get it together, Jackson. You're about to blow this."

Taking a deep breath, Jackson forced a smile, letting out a casual laugh as if nothing was wrong. "Hey, sexy," he said, his voice light. "I knew you weren't gonna stand me up. You know you miss me."

Ramona paused but eventually let out a reluctant chuckle. "I do miss you, but... with everything going on, it just doesn't feel right for us to be seen together."

Jackson leaned back, working to keep his voice steady. "It's just for a minute, I swear. Come on inside, let's talk."

After another pause, Ramona sighed, "Alright, but just for a minute." She turned off her car engine, taking a quick look around to make sure she wasn't being watched. With a final glance over her shoulder, she opened the bar door, stepping inside. Her eyes quickly scanned the room, landing on Jackson sitting in the booth at the far end.

Jackson felt his heart race as she approached. He knew this could be his only chance.

Detective Miller, barely recognizable in his disguise, settled at a small table with a menu propped up as cover, his eyes discreetly fixed on Jackson and Ramona. He strained to hear their conversation, hoping Jackson would steer it the way they needed without raising Ramona's suspicion. The bar had a quiet, almost tense energy as they hunched in their seats toward one another, speaking in hushed tones.

Back at the station, Captain Casey's office door swung open, and Richardson walked in. The captain looked up, adjusting his glasses and giving Richardson a sharp once-over.

"Richardson, where the hell have you been?" Casey's voice was a mix of suspicion and frustration.

"I swapped shifts with Sanchez this morning, so I could study for the lieutenant's exam," Richardson replied calmly, handing a stack of forms to the captain. "Here's the form you requested, sir."

As Captain Casey scanned the paperwork, he noticed Richardson's gaze drifting to some files on his desk. Richardson looked at them a beat too long before catching himself and looking away.

Casey gave him a hard look. "That'll be all, Richardson."

"Yes, sir," Richardson nodded, quickly exiting the office. As he walked down the hall, his hand slid into his pocket, pulling out his phone. Glancing around, he pressed it to his ear, his voice low and hurried as he spoke, making sure he was out of earshot. The tension back at the station was rising, and Captain Casey's suspicions were far from settled.

In a dimly lit back room of an upscale restaurant, Frank Whitmore sat with two other city council members, leaning in as they discussed "arrangements" with a group of local business owners. Stacks of paperwork and glossy brochures promising "new opportunities" cluttered the table, concealing the real purpose of the meeting: persuading these business owners to exchange "favors" for expedited city permits and approvals.

Whitmore's phone buzzed repeatedly, flashing a name he chose to ignore. He shot a quick glance at the screen, frowning before muting it. He couldn't afford to have anyone overhear this call right now. Seated beside him, the two council members nodded and gestured to emphasize the urgency and advantages of their proposals, each one more dubious than the last.

Across the room, a handful of gamblers were deep into a game, oblivious to the meeting in the corner. The small, illegal gambling ring had long been one of Whitmore's secret revenue streams — a "hidden gem" that let him bypass pesky oversight. His reputation as a respectable public servant had kept suspicions low, and he intended to keep it that way.

Yet, as his phone buzzed again, he couldn't shake the nagging feeling.

Whitmore excused himself from the table with a tight-lipped smile, muttering, "Gentlemen, I'll be right back." Once out of earshot, he snatched his cell phone out of his pocket and snapped, "This better be important. I'm in the middle of a high-stakes deal."

There was a pause on the other end before Richardson's voice came through, low and tense. As Whitmore listened, his face paled. "You're sure?" he demanded, his voice barely above a whisper. The news left him rattled; he muttered a curse under his breath, then hung up without another word.

Steeling himself, he returned to the table, drained the last of his drink, and forced a polite smile. "Gentlemen, I'm afraid I have to cut this short," he said. "Family emergency." Ignoring their confused glances, he gathered his things, muttering an apology before making a swift exit.

Outside, he jumped into his car, gripped the wheel, and sped off. Frustration and panic churned inside him, and he clenched his jaw, muttering under his breath, "This girl is going to be the death of me."

Back at Pete's Bar, Gary Richardson strolled in casually, oblivious to Jackson and Ramona seated in the shadowed corner booth. As he made his way toward a young woman seated near the bar, Detective Miller, who had been discreetly keeping tabs on Jackson, noticed Richardson's familiar voice. He lowered his menu just enough to get a good look and was startled to see Richardson with a young woman he recognized but couldn't immediately place.

Miller pulled out his phone, quickly snapping a photo of Richardson and the woman and sent it to Captain Casey. He dialed the captain and, keeping his voice low, said, "Sir, I just sent you a picture of Richardson with an unknown woman."

A moment later, the captain responded, his voice tinged with realization. "That's Veronica from forensics."

Miller's eyes widened. "We've found our mole," he whispered.

"Keep an eye on them," the captain ordered firmly. Miller pocketed his phone and settled back into his seat, his eyes trained on Richardson and Veronica, ready to catch any slip-up that might confirm their suspicions.

Miller encouraged Jackson to keep Ramona talking. "Stretch this out. Keep her engaged," Miller's voice buzzed in Jackson's earpiece.

Ramona leaned in, her voice barely above a whisper. "This better be quick," she said, her eyes scanning the room. "You know the risks we're taking just being here."

Jackson forced a casual laugh, hiding his anxiety. "Relax, babe. Just needed to see you. Felt like things were... unfinished."

Ramona narrowed her eyes, crossing her arms. "Unfinished? Or is it something else? You're not getting yourself into anything messy, are you?"

"Ramona, you know me. I'm not the messy one," Jackson replied, steadying his voice. "But things are getting tight. I need to know you've got my back."

She glanced around uneasily. "Look, Jackson, my father's already asking questions. I don't know how much longer I can keep him out of this," she said, her gaze hardening. "What exactly do you need from me?"

Jackson took a careful breath. "I need information, Ramona. Just a few names. People who can make things go away. I… I love you, Ramona."

She paused, studying him before pulling back. "I don't know what you're talking about," she said tersely, glancing at her phone as it buzzed. The name on the screen made her freeze — her father was calling. She quickly grabbed her handbag, and without another word, dashed out of the bar.

Across the room, Richardson noticed her hasty exit, slamming his fist on the bar in frustration. Watching this unfolds, Miller muttered under his breath, "Got you."

Miller immediately called the captain. "Sir, Ramona just bolted out of here like a chicken with her head cut off."

Captain Casey's voice was firm. "Gary must have called Senator Whitmore. Richardson was probably tipped off too. Take Jackson back to holding. We'll figure out our next move in the morning."

Miller nodded to himself and slipped out of the bar quietly, making sure not to draw Richardson's attention. Once outside, he took a steadying breath before signaling Jackson. "Come on. We're done for tonight." Jackson followed, clearly tense but relieved to leave.

As they reached the car, Miller glanced back one last time at the bar, his mind racing with the events of the night.

Chapter 24

The Mole

The morning was tense at the district police station as District Attorney Karen Phillips and Detective Miller sat across from Captain Casey in his office, piecing together the events from Pete's Bar, the night before.

DA Phillips broke the silence. "I heard we've identified the mole?"

Captain Casey cleared his throat, visibly uneasy. "Yes. Turns out, she works in the forensics lab."

Phillips's eyes narrowed. "Who is she?"

Detective Miller stepped forward, holding a manila folder. "Her name is Veronica Wayne. But that's her alias — her real name is Veronica Richardson."

Casey ran a hand through his hair, his face clouded with frustration. "Don't tell me she's related to Officer Richardson."

Miller nodded grimly. "Yes, sir. She's his niece."

Phillips looked incredulous. "Please tell me you're joking."

"I wish I were," Miller continued, his tone serious. "And it gets worse. Veronica, A.K.A. Veronica Richardson, served two years at Rikers Island."

Phillips's expression turned stormy. "Did no one screen her before she was hired? How long has she been in forensics?"

Miller opened the file and glanced at the details. "Six months. She transferred here from the New Jersey police department."

Captain Casey rose from his chair, connecting the dots. "Six months ago... that's around the same time Marcus Anderson went missing."

DA Phillips leaned forward, urgency in her voice. "Where is she now?"

"Veronica is currently in Interrogation Room One, along with Officer Moore," Miller replied.

Captain Casey grabbed the phone on his desk. "Tell them to bring Ms. Wayne to my office. I'd like to have a word with her."

Ramona was jolted awake by loud, persistent banging at her door. She groggily checked the time — 7:00 AM. Irritated, she grabbed her robe and slippers and made her way down the stairs. Peeking through the peephole, she recognized her father, Frank, his expression livid.

She opened the door just a crack. "Do you know what time it is? What are you doing here at 7:00 AM?"

Ignoring her question, Frank pushed the door open and stormed inside, his face tense with frustration. Ramona watched as he paced, feeling her own nerves rise.

"They're onto us!" he hissed, his tone low and angry. "How could you be so reckless? I gave you everything — the best schools, the best life. And this? This is how you repay me?"

Ramona scoffed, crossing her arms. "Oh, spare me, Dad. You were hardly father of the year."

Frank's face flushed with anger. "Watch your tone, Ramona. For someone so 'smart,' you've made idiotic choices. Parading around town with that Jackson boy, putting everything at risk. And now? Veronica's being questioned at the police station as we speak, and Richardson will likely be next."

Ramona's face fell as she realized the gravity of the situation. "What are you saying?"

"We need to leave. Now," he commanded, his voice firm. "You don't have time to pack anything. We're not sticking around for this to blow up in our faces."

Frank's frustration was evident as he clenched his jaw. "There I was, about to close the deal of a lifetime, and I get a call from Veronica and Gary telling me you're at Pete's Bar... with Jackson!"

Ramona's face went pale, panic creeping into her expression. "How was I supposed to know Veronica would get involved? I didn't tell her to do anything!"

Frank's patience snapped. He grabbed her arm firmly, forcing her to look at him. "You're not hearing me, Ramona. Detective Miller was at Pete's Bar last night. He saw everything. He knows."

Ramona's pulse quickened. "I just need a few things, Dad. Just let me grab my stuff, and we'll go," she pleaded, voice shaking.

"No!" he barked, his grip tightening. "We don't have time. Every second we waste here brings us closer to getting caught."

Back at the Captain's office, officer Moore nodded at Captain Casey and DA Phillips, recounting his earlier conversation with Veronica. "She had a bright future ahead of her, graduated top of her class in computer forensic science at Princeton. But everything changed when she got mixed up with Chance Rodriguez."

DA Phillips looked up, eyebrows raised. "And who is Chance Rodriguez?"

Moore explained, "Rodriguez was involved in a local chop shop in the Bronx. Stealing cars wasn't enough, so he turned to robbing banks. He's currently serving time at Williamsburg Prison."

Turning to Veronica, DA Phillips spoke firmly, "Ms. Wayne, I suggest you start talking. This isn't looking good for you."

Veronica's voice wavered as tears started to form. "I don't even know where to begin. None of this is my fault."

Captain Casey leaned forward. "Then start from the beginning."

Veronica hesitated, then whispered, "I can't. He'll kill me."

Detective Miller pressed, "Who are you afraid of?"

"Mr. Whitmore," Veronica answered, trembling.

DA Phillips leaned forward. "We can help you. But you have to talk. How did you get involved in this scheme?"

Veronica took a deep breath. "Like Officer Moore said, I dated Chance Rodriguez. I didn't know he was involved in crime until it was too late. After doing two years for that, I promised myself I'd stay out of trouble. But I couldn't find a job, so my Uncle Gary stepped in to help me. He used my mother's fingerprints, and I started working under her maiden name, Wayne."

DA Phillips folded her arms, impatience showing. "And Whitmore?"

Veronica continued, "I was leaving the forensics lab one day when Mr. Whitmore approached me. He handed me a glass with fingerprints on it, along with some hair samples. I refused, but he threatened to reveal my true identity."

Casey nodded, urging her to continue. Veronica's eyes filled with tears as she confessed, "I was shadowing Dr. Gray in the morgue. When he wasn't looking, I planted the hair under the victim's fingernails."

Everyone in the room was visibly shocked. DA Phillips leaned forward. "And the pipe?"

Veronica sighed, "I used tape to lift the prints from the glass and tried to transfer them to the pipe. But before I could finish, Jose walked into the lab, and I only managed to put partial prints on it."

Captain Casey shook his head, disappointment evident. "It's a shame you couldn't use your skills for good. Officer Moore, get her out of here."

Suddenly, the door opened, and a man walked in — Jonathan Wayne, Veronica's father. "Veronica, don't say another word," he said.

DA Phillips glared. "Please, tell me you're not her Father?"

"Mr. Wayne, sorry! I can't help you with that question. However, you know you can't speak to Ms. Wayne without counsel present."

Karen rolled her eyes. She whispered under her breath, "Freaking believable."

Jonathan retorted, "Are you officially charging my client?"

DA Phillips exchanged a look with Captain Casey. "No, not yet."

"Then we're leaving," Jonathan said, guiding Veronica out of the office.

As they left, DA Phillips turned to Casey, her frustration mounting. "I need to call Judge Carson. We're going to need some warrants."

The same day saw Sarah woke to the rich aroma of honey hazelnut coffee drifting through the air. She'd fallen asleep on the couch, and Margaret hadn't had the heart to wake her. Stretching her back, she felt a twinge of pain from the awkward position she'd slept in. When she finally made her way to the kitchen, her hand on her lower back, Margaret greeted her with a warm smile and a steaming coffee pot in hand.

"Good morning, sweetie! Would you like some coffee?" Margaret asked.

Sarah's eyes widened as she noticed the breakfast spread on the table. "Margaret, you didn't have to do all this! You're a guest in my home."

Margaret just waved her to sit down. "Have a seat before the food gets cold."

Sarah pulled out a chair, glancing at her friend apologetically. "I'm sorry, I fell asleep on you. That was so rude of me."

Margaret joined her at the table. "Oh, don't worry about that. I just grabbed a blanket and laid back in the La-Z-Boy. Quite comfortable, really. Besides, you need your rest."

Sarah chuckled, shaking her head. "That old chair! You could've slept in the guest room."

Margaret gave her a playful but stern look. "Not another word about that chair. Now, eat up! You'll need your strength, if you're going to dance with the she-devil."

As Sarah ate, she checked her phone, hoping for an update from her brother Joe about Jackson. Seeing no missed calls, she felt a pang of worry. Margaret reached over, squeezing her hand.

"Don't worry, sweetie. We'll get through this together. Remember, God doesn't give us more than we can handle."

They enjoyed a delightful breakfast together, sharing a warm conversation. When they finished, Sarah got up to clean the kitchen while Margaret rested her swollen ankles.

Once they were done, they walked into the living room, only to be met with a mess of scattered papers from Sarah's search for the house deed the previous day.

Sarah sighed, "Oh, my…"

Margaret put her hands on her hips, eyeing the room with determination. "Well, you take the left side, and I'll take the right. Let's get this place in order!"

With smiles and laughter, the two friends set to work, tackling the mess as a team.

At the morning briefing, Captain Casey and DA Phillips entered the room, each carrying a stack of papers. Captain Casey clapped his hands to gather everyone's attention. "Listen up, officers. We've got a lot to cover in this meeting."

As Casey began passing out the papers, a hand shot up from the back of the room. "Captain, shouldn't we wait for Officer Richardson?" an officer asked.

Casey froze momentarily, exchanging a glance with Phillips, who raised a single eyebrow. Clearing his throat, Casey replied, "Officer Richardson won't be joining us today. He's...taking the lieutenant exam."

The room filled with murmurs, and another officer started to raise her hand, but Phillips stepped forward sharply. "Please, hold your questions until after the meeting," she said curtly, cutting off any further inquiries.

Casey shot Phillips a hard look but continued. He walked to the front of the room and pointed to the whiteboard, which displayed a web of names:

Jackson McKinley

Ramona Whitmore

Senator Frank Whitmore

Victims: Allison Anderson and Marcus Anderson

Each name was circled, connected by lines and arrows showing relationships and potential motives.

"Alright, officers," Casey said firmly. "Time is of the essence. We need to solve this case and do it quickly. The pressure's on, and the public is watching. We can't afford any more missteps."

Phillips chimed in, her voice icy and precise. "This case is critical. Every single one of these names ties into an intricate web of corruption, betrayal, and violence. We have suspects, we have victims, but what we don't have is clarity. Your job is to give us that clarity."

Casey nodded. "We'll be working leads on multiple fronts. Forensics, interviews, surveillance — we need everything airtight. Officer Banks, you're taking lead on Ramona's financials. Officer Carter, dig into the senator's recent dealings. Everyone else, focus on compiling connections between the victims and suspects. I want a full timeline on my desk by the end of the week."

The room buzzed with tension as the officers quickly jotted down notes. Phillips glanced at the whiteboard one more time before addressing the group. "Let me make one thing clear. We're not just solving murders—we're unraveling a conspiracy. Eyes on the prize. No mistakes."

Casey crossed his arms, his tone final. "Let's get to work."

As the officers began gathering their things to leave, DA Phillips raised her voice, stopping them mid-stride. "One more thing," she said, her tone sharp. "As you're all aware, this department is currently under investigation by Internal Affairs."

The room grew tense, and Officer Carter spoke up. "Why is Internal Affairs investigating us? This station has the best officers in Philadelphia!"

Another officer chimed in, "I heard it's about Veronica Wayne in forensics!"

The room erupted into a mix of murmurs and speculative chatter.

Captain Casey clapped his hands loudly to regain control. "Hey! Settle down! Yes, this department has an outstanding record. But—"

Phillips interrupted Casey, her voice commanding the room's attention. "Yes, the 9th District does have excellent officers. However, as with any institution, there are occasionally bad apples. As for Ms. Wayne, my office is not at liberty to discuss an ongoing investigation. Now, focus on your work."

Casey's jaw tightened, but he held his composure. "If there are no further questions, this meeting is adjourned. Get to it."

As the officers dispersed, Casey grabbed Phillips' arm and pulled her aside, his frustration boiling over. "Don't you ever undermine me like that in front of my team again."

Before Phillips could respond, Mayor Washington entered the room, his presence commanding immediate attention. "Good morning," he said brusquely. "What's going on with the case?"

Casey straightened up, his tone measured. "I'm sure DA Phillips will bring you up to speed on all the details, Mayor. I have other business to attend to."

Without waiting for a response, Casey turned on his heel and walked out of the squad room. As he passed the doors, he saw a throng of reporters waiting eagerly outside. He smirked and turned back to Phillips.

"Looks like your fan club is here," he quipped, his tone dripping with sarcasm before striding confidently past the cameras, leaving Phillips to handle the media circus.

After the mandatory morning meeting with Captain Casey and his officers, Casey returned to his office with Detective Miller. Dark circles lined Casey's eyes, and a look of exhaustion was evident in every step he took.

Miller gave him a knowing look. "You look like hell, sir. Did you sleep here all night?"

Casey sighed, rubbing his temple. "I didn't mean to. I was following up on a lead, and I must've dozed off at some point."

He glanced at his phone, noticing three missed calls from his wife. "And now I've got three missed calls from the missus. She's going to chew me out when I get home."

Miller chuckled, crossing his arms. "That's why I'm not married — don't need the extra drama."

Casey laughed, despite himself. "Well, you have to find a woman first."

The two exchanged a smirk, their shared exhaustion temporarily lifted by the bit of humor.

There was a firm knock at the door. Casey immediately stood up, straightening his shirt and jacket, then called for the person to come in. DA Phillips strode in, a grin on her face as she waved a stack of papers in the air.

"Good afternoon, gentlemen," she greeted, her tone brisk. "Hope you're ready for an all-nighter. Judge Carson just granted us a stack of warrants to go after some serious players."

Casey, already charged with adrenaline, grabbed his gun and holster. "What about Veronica?" he asked, adjusting his gear.

"We'll offer her leniency for her cooperation, but she'll still face some time," Phillips replied.

Detective Miller raised an eyebrow, intrigued. "So, who are we putting the silver jewelry on?"

Karen's grin widened. "With the testimony from Allison and Veronica, we're bringing in Richardson. And with Sanchez's excellent undercover work, we can finally charge Frank Whitmore with extortion, money laundering, and bribery."

Miller looked surprised. "What? Whitmore's not being charged with Anderson's murder?"

Phillips met his gaze sternly. "Don't look a gift horse in the mouth, Detective. Judge Carson was generous enough to issue a warrant for the senator. We finally have enough on his underground gambling ring to hold him, and once we get him into interrogation, I have a feeling he'll start talking. Especially, if he knows his daughter might face charges, too."

"Ramona's got pending charges for kidnapping," Phillips continued. "We'll bring her in, make her believe she's facing murder charges. That might just be enough leverage to get her talking about her father."

"Got it," Miller nodded. "What's our plan?"

Casey spoke up. "I want to be the one to put the cuffs on Richardson. Miller, take Sanchez and Moore and pick up Whitmore, and bring Ramona in as well. And alert the airport, trains, and bus stations to be on the lookout. Whitmore's not slipping away."

Phillips chimed in, "Already done. We've got all exit routes monitored."

As Miller, Sanchez, and Moore hurried out, Karen pulled Casey aside. "One more thing, Casey. Internal Affairs is investigating the department."

Casey's face darkened. "You've got to be kidding me, Karen. I don't need this right now."

Phillips crossed her arms, her tone more serious than ever. "Don't shoot the messenger, Casey. This is beyond me. The mayor's involved, and it's election season. He's determined to clear out anything that looks like corruption."

Casey clenched his fists

"They think you're dirty as well," Karen said, her voice cutting like ice.

Casey's face flushed with anger. Without another word, he slammed the door open, leaving Karen standing there, momentarily speechless.

He strode down the hallway, his mind racing. Years of service, all the cases he'd cracked, and now this shadow of doubt hanging over him. He clenched his fists, jaw set, as he muttered to himself, "After everything I've done..."

Just outside, Miller, Sanchez, and Moore were waiting, gear ready. Miller raised an eyebrow, sensing Casey's anger. "Everything alright, sir?"

Casey took a deep breath, forcing a smirk. "Just a little more fire under our feet. Let's bring these guys in and make sure our work speaks for itself."

Casey glanced at his phone, seeing Karen's name on the caller ID. He sighed, muttering to himself, "What does she want now?"

Looking at his team, he gave a quick nod. "Y'all go ahead and pick up the Whitmores. I'll catch up."

Turning his back to his team, he answered the call. "What now, Karen? You got a problem with my driving?"

Karen's tone was firm on the other end. "Cut the sarcasm, Casey. You left before I was finished talking to you."

Casey rolled his eyes, leaning against the wall. "Say what you have to say, Karen. I have a job to do."

Karen's voice sharpened, her tone demanding his attention. "I was about to tell you, Casey, that Judge Carson released Mr. McKinley to his uncle, Mr. Lawson."

Casey's shoulders tensed. "McKinley's out already? Great," he muttered, glancing away as his team prepped to head out.

"There's more. Judge Carson insisted on a gag order for McKinley. Make sure Jackson doesn't breathe a word to his mother about being an informant," Karen continued, her voice steady but insistent.

Casey exhaled sharply. "Is that all?"

"That depends," Karen replied, a hint of warning in her tone. "Just do your job, Casey — and do it right."

He didn't respond, just ended the call, shoving his phone back into his pocket. The weight of what lay ahead pressed on him, but he turned back to his team with a firm expression. "Alright, let's get this done. You all know your roles — Whitmore, his daughter, and Richardson. We move fast, and we don't leave any loose ends."

The team exchanged a determined look, knowing this wasn't just about the warrants anymore — it was about restoring trust in their team, no matter what.

Chapter 25

Full Disclosure

An hour later, after finishing up the living room, Margaret spotted a small wooden box tucked under the table. She bent down and picked it up, brushing off the light layer of dust that had settled over the years. "Looks like we missed something," Margaret said with a gentle smile, handing the box to Sarah.

Sarah's face softened with surprise. "Oh my goodness, I haven't looked in this box in years." She held it carefully, almost reverently, as if it contained a fragile part of her past.

Margaret's curiosity was piqued, but she didn't want to intrude. She simply watched as Sarah slowly lifted the lid, revealing a small stack of old, worn letters inside. Sarah's eyes immediately began to fill with tears as she recognized the familiar handwriting.

Margaret reached over, resting a hand on Sarah's knee. "Are those... happy tears?"

Sarah nodded, a bittersweet smile on her face. "These are love letters from my husband... back when he was in the service."

Margaret's own eyes softened with empathy. "He sounds like he was a wonderful and romantic man."

As Sarah began reading the letters aloud, memories filled the room. The warmth of her husband's words wrapped around her, comforting and yet stirring up emotions that had been tucked away for years.

Sarah's expression shifted, a hint at of confusion crossing her face as she held up one particular letter. "I don't recognize this one," she murmured, her voice barely above a whisper. Margaret leaned in, watching Sarah's reaction closely.

Sarah unfolded the letter, her hands trembling slightly, and began to read aloud, her voice shaky:

Sarah's hands trembled slightly as she unfolded the unfamiliar letter. Taking a deep breath, she began to read aloud:

My Dearest Mona,

These last few weeks with you have been nothing short of wonderful — moments filled with laughter, stolen glances, and an intimacy I never thought I'd experience. You've illuminated parts of my life that had long been hidden, and for that, I will always cherish you.

But this must come to an end. I'm in love with you, but I also love my wife, Sarah. With the news of her pregnancy, my priorities have shifted, and I must honor the commitment I made to her and to the family we're about to start.

Please, understand that this is not a reflection of your worth. You'll always hold a special place in my heart, and I hope you can forgive me and remember our moments together. You deserve someone, who can fully devote themselves to you, and I can no longer be that man.

With all my love,

Jake

Sarah felt her throat tighten as she read Jake's words, each line piercing deeper than the last. Margaret, noticing the shift in Sarah's expression, gently touched her shoulder. "Oh, Sarah..."

Sarah's face drained of color, her hand clutching the letter as if it might slip away. "How could he…?" she whispered, her voice breaking. The room felt heavy with silence, her heart shattering as she realized her husband had been hiding something all along.

Margaret reached out, her hand resting gently on Sarah's shoulder. "Sweetie…" she began, her voice full of concern.

But Sarah's gaze was already hardening, her mind racing as shock and betrayal settled into something deeper and darker.

Sarah dropped the letter, her voice barely a whisper. "I can't believe this. He cheated on me, while I was carrying his child." Her hurt quickly turned into fury as she stood, her hands clenched. "He betrayed me and our family for her."

In the bottom of the box there was a gun. Sarah's hands trembled as she held Jake's gun, the weight of it pressing into her palm. She stared at it, lost in a whirlwind of emotions — rage, betrayal, grief. The very idea of holding a gun was foreign to her; she had always despised them, considering them tools of violence and destruction. But now, in her mind, it was the one tangible thing connecting her to the man she thought she knew and the deception that shattered her life.

Margaret moved quickly to intercept, grabbing Sarah's hands. "Sarah, please, take a breath. Let's think this through."

Sarah's face was red with anger, her hand still clutching the gun tightly. "She took everything from me, Margaret! She took my husband's love while I was carrying his child. How can I let that go?" Margaret placed both hands on Sarah's shoulders, looking her straight in the eye. "If you go after her, it won't bring you peace, Sarah. It'll only make things worse. Think about your son, your life — you're stronger than this." Sarah walks closer to the door. "I'm sorry, Margaret, but I have to go."

Margaret stood frozen in the doorway, her heart pounding as she watched Sarah's car disappear down the street. She knew how deep Sarah's pain ran, but she feared what Sarah might do in her rage.

Moments later, Jackson and his Uncle Joe approached Jackson's house, the afternoon air filled with an unusual stillness that made the hairs on the back of Jackson's neck stand up. As they walk up to the front porch, Jackson noticed the door was slightly open, just enough to prompt a knot of worry to form in his stomach.

"Uncle Joe, the door's open," Jackson whispered, his voice barely rising above a whisper.

Joe nods slowly and gestures for Jackson to stay back. He approaches the steps with a serious footstep, his hand reaching for the door. With a careful push, he nudged the door open wider, the creak echoing through the quiet house.

Inside, their eyes met a little old woman with frazzled gray hair and oversized glasses walking around the living room, picking up stray papers and fluffing pillows. Margaret Anderson, look up at the sound of the door creaking and picks up the lamp.

Margaret put her hand on her chest. "What, are y'all trying to give me a heart attack?" Joseph gave Mrs. Anderson a hug. "I'm sorry, I didn't mean to scare you. I just saw the door open, and I thought somebody was breaking in."

Margaret steadied herself, lowering the lamp. She looked at Joseph and Jackson, her expression a mix of relief and worry.

"Thank goodness, you're both here," she said, glancing nervously around the room. "Sarah... she found something she shouldn't have, some old love letters from Jake. She didn't take it well. When she left here, she was... she was furious."

Jackson's heart dropped. "Where did she go, Mrs. Anderson?"

Margaret took a deep breath. "I think she went to find Ramona. She's not thinking straight, Jackson. I'm worried she might do something she'll regret."

Joe and Jackson's faces dropped in shock. Joe took a deep breath, saying, "I have to find my sister. I was afraid this day would come when she found out."

Jackson stepped forward. "I'm going with you, Uncle."

Joe held up a hand. "No, I need you to stay here with Mrs. Anderson. She needs someone to keep her safe."

Jackson shook his head. "Uncle, I'm going with you. You need backup, and you know it."

Joe sighed, looking torn. Finally, he gave in. "Fine. But stay close and let me handle things, when we find her."

Joe put a steadying hand on Margaret's shoulder. "We'll find her, Mrs. Anderson. Stay here, keep the door locked, and don't worry. We'll bring Sarah back." Margaret, left alone, whispered under her breath, "Please, Lord, keep them safe... and help Sarah find her way back. She is not an OG like me."

Without wasting another second, the two men rushed out, climbed into the car, and sped off into the unknown, hoping they weren't too late.

Jackson and Joe drove in tense silence, each man consumed by worry. Joe gripped the steering wheel, glancing occasionally at Jackson, whose jaw was set, his expression unreadable.

"Uncle Joe," Jackson finally broke the silence, "why didn't you ever tell me? About the affair?"

Joe sighed heavily, his eyes focused on the road. "I tried my best to make sure that she'd never find out. I didn't want to hurt either of you, and especially not Sarah." He hesitated, guilt flickering in his eyes. "I was afraid something like this would happen if she ever did."

As they approached Ramona's neighborhood, Joe's phone rang. It was Margaret. Her voice was tense as she whispered, "You better hurry, Joe. Sarah's in a dangerous state of mind."

Joe hung up, his knuckles white against the steering wheel. "Hold on, Jackson. We're almost there."

They sped down the street, hearts pounding, hoping they weren't too late.

At Ramona's house, Frank was yelling up the stairs, frustration thick in his voice. "What are you doing up there? Frank clenched his fists, muttering under his breath. "We're not going to have time for your backtalk, Ramona," he snapped. "They're closing in on us, and you're worried about that dog."

Ramona finally appeared at the top of the steps, carrying a suitcase in one hand and her little dog, Coco, in the other. She descended slowly, looking unimpressed. "Will you stop yelling?" she retorted. "You're so jumpy. They don't have anything on us."

Frank pointed a finger at her, his face tense. "They've been watching you for two months, Ramona. I warned you to keep a low profile, but you just had to keep showing up in public like you are untouchable."

She looked around the living room, double-checking to see if she'd forgotten anything, as Frank shook his head and turned toward the door. "Where do you think you're going with that overdressed mutt?" he sneered.

Ramona's expression hardened. "Coco is coming with me, and don't be mad because she looks better than that toupee you call hair." Frank sighed, exasperated. "Fine. But once we're out of here, you follow my lead. No questions, no arguments."

Just then, a loud bang on the front door made both of them jump. Frank grabbed Ramona's arm, pulling her toward the back exit. "We need to go. Now."

But Ramona pulled her arm away and squared her shoulders. "We're Whitmores. We don't run." She strode to the door and swung it open.

Sarah stood there, anger blazing in her eyes. Without a second thought, she slapped Ramona across the face, the sound echoing through the hall. Ramona stumbled back, her hand flying to her cheek, shocked. "How dare you?!" she spat, regaining her balance.

Sarah's face was flushed with fury. "How dare I? How dare *you,* Ramona! You tore my family apart while I was carrying his child. I trusted him, and you—" her voice wavered, but her anger didn't.

Ramona straightened, her eyes narrowing. "You think you're the victim here? Jake came to me, Sarah. If he really wanted you, he wouldn't have—"

Before she could finish, Sarah stepped closer, points the gun at them, but Frank stepped between them. "Ladies, enough!" he barked, glancing nervously toward the door. "Sarah you don't wanna do something you might regret."

Sarah's hands gripped the gun tighter, her voice trembling with rage. "Don't you dare twist this, Ramona. You were supposed to be my friend, someone I could trust. But you've proven you'd do anything to get what you want."

Ramona crossed her arms, her face cold and unapologetic. "Oh, Sarah, get over it. Maybe if you weren't so insufferable, he wouldn't have come to me in the first place."

Sarah's face flushed, her breath coming faster. "You were with him while I was pregnant, Ramona. And now you're dragging my son into your mess? Have you no shame?"

Ramona's smirk widened, unfazed. "It's not my fault you couldn't keep him satisfied, Sarah. Maybe it's time you stopped blaming everyone else."

Ramona saw her chance as Sarah's attention wavered, and lunged for the gun in Sarah's hand. Underestimating Sarah's resolve, they grappled furiously, both refusing to let go. The struggle intensified, until suddenly — a loud bang echoed through the room. Frank staggered back, clutching his arm as blood began to seep through his fingers. He dropped to his knees, gritting his teeth in pain.

The commotion drew the attention of neighbors, who immediately called 911. Dispatch crackled through the police radio as Detective Miller and Moore were driving nearby.

"All available units: shots fired at 234 Montgomery Avenue. Repeat, shots fired at 234 Montgomery Avenue."

Moore's eyes widened as he turned to Detective Miller. "Isn't that Ramona's address?"

Miller's expression hardened. "Yeah, it is. This just became a little more interesting."

Chapter 26

Who's In charge?

Captain Casey, accompanied by two senior officers, arrived at Copperwood Training Facility in the early afternoon. The sprawling complex was surrounded by tall pines, their rustling leaves the only sound as they approached the main entrance. The facility, with its modern architecture and state-of-the-art design, stood out starkly against the wilderness that enveloped it.

"Impressive," one of the officers remarked as they stepped into the main lobby, where a receptionist greeted them.

"Captain Casey, welcome," the receptionist said politely. "Are you here to observe the training exercises or oversee the lieutenant exams?"

Casey gave a curt nod. "I'm here to check on Officer Richardson. He was supposed to be taking the lieutenant exam today."

The receptionist consulted a digital tablet. "Officer Richardson is registered for the exam. Let me confirm if he's in the exam room."

As they waited, Casey glanced around the lobby. The walls were adorned with motivational posters, photographs of past graduates, and plaques highlighting the facility's achievements. The atmosphere was both professional and intense, reflecting the rigorous training that took place within its walls.

After a moment, the receptionist looked up, her brow furrowed. "It appears Officer Richardson didn't sign in for the exam this morning, Captain. I can check with the proctor to see if he arrived late or left early."

"Please do," Casey replied, his voice tight.

The receptionist made a call while Casey's officers exchanged uneasy glances. Within minutes, the proctor arrived — a stern-looking man in his fifties, wearing the Copperwood Training Facility logo on his jacket.

"Captain," the proctor greeted him. "I understand you're looking for Officer Richardson. He's on the attendance list but didn't show up for the exam today."

Casey frowned. "When was the last time you saw him?"

"Yesterday," the proctor said. "He attended the briefing for the exam candidates. He didn't mention anything about not showing up today."

Casey's jaw tightened. "Did he leave anything behind? Any indication of why he might not be here?"

The proctor shook his head. "No, sir. His behavior seemed normal during the briefing."

Casey turned to his officers. "We need to find out where Richardson is. This doesn't sit right."

One of the officers nodded. "Should we check his house or contact his family?"

"Not yet," Casey said. "I want to keep this quiet for now. If Richardson's absence is tied to anything bigger — like the Whitmore case — we don't want to tip anyone off."

As they left the facility, Casey's gut told him this wasn't a simple case of an officer skipping an exam. Copperwood's serene surroundings suddenly felt ominous, as if the dense forest around them held secrets they had yet to uncover. He pulled out his phone and dialed Phillips.

When she picked up, her tone was curt. "What is it, Captain?"

"Richardson's gone," Casey said bluntly. "He didn't show up for the exam, and no one's seen him since yesterday."

Phillips sighed, clearly annoyed. "And what do you want me to do about it, Casey? Track down your officer? He's your responsibility."

"I don't think you're grasping the situation," Casey said, his voice low and measured. "If Richardson's disappearance is connected to the Internal Affairs investigation — or worse, the Whitmore case — we've got a serious problem on our hands."

There was silence on the line for a moment before Phillips replied. "Fine. I'll send someone to start looking into it. But you'd better make sure this doesn't spiral out of control, Casey."

As he hung up, Casey turned to his officers. "Let's head back to the precinct. If Richardson doesn't want to be found, we're going to have to dig deeper to figure out why."

Detective Miller tries to call Captain Casey, but the call goes straight to voicemail. The phone reception was bad at Copperwood Training facility. He slips his cell phone back into his pocket and says, "I'll let Captain Casey know to meet us there."

He quickly left a message, briefing him on the situation as he and Moore sped toward the scene, sirens blaring.

269

The screeching of tires outside barely registered over the tension that filled the room. But as Joe and Jackson rushed inside, their faces quickly turned from alarm to horror. The gunfire had just ended, and now a new nightmare was unfolding before their eyes.

Joe stepped forward, his voice calm but unyielding. "That's enough! Both of you, stop this right now."

Jackson's face was a mixture of fear and confusion as he looked at his mother. "Mom, this isn't the way," he said softly, taking a step toward her. But suddenly, his eyes went wide, and he stumbled backward, clutching his chest before collapsing onto the coffee table.

"Jackson!" Sarah's scream tore through the room, her voice breaking as she rushed to her son. Ramona, now frozen in shock, dropped to her knees, her hands covering her mouth. "Oh my God" she whispered, unable to look away.

Sarah cradled her son's face, panic in her eyes. "What did you do?" she demanded, her voice shaking with disbelief. Ramona stammered, "I didn't mean to… I didn't… it just happened."

Frank tried to steady his daughter, holding her close as Ramona began to tremble. Joe knelt beside Jackson, his hands pressing against Jackson's chest, desperately trying to stop the bleeding. "Hold on, nephew. Help is on the way. Just stay with us."

Jackson's eyes fluttered as he took one last shallow breath, his voice barely a whisper. "I love you, Mom." He slowly closed his eyes, and then he was gone.

Sarah's scream shattered the silence, raw and filled with unimaginable grief. Joe wrapped his arms around his sister, holding her as she shook uncontrollably. "She killed him. He was my son. My son…" she repeated over and over, her words echoing in the hollow silence as the EMTs finally arrived to carry Jackson's lifeless body out of the house.

Sarah's sobs filled the air, an unending torrent of anguish, as she clung to Joe, broken and devastated.

Detectives Miller and Moore arrived just as the EMT were carefully wheeling Jackson's body out, a grim procession that silenced the small crowd of onlookers gathering outside. The two detectives entered the house, taking in the chaos — a living room that now looked more like a battlefield.

Before they could process the scene, Frank rushed over to Officer Moore, gripping his injured arm. "I'm glad you're here, Officer. Sarah's completely lost it! The crazy woman shot me!" he groaned in pain.

Moore reached into his pocket, pulling out a set of handcuffs. "Franklin Whitmore, you're under arrest for larceny, bribery, and a long list of other charges." Frank's face twisted in anger and pain. "You can't do this! I need a doctor!" he yelled.

As Moore motioned for the officers to handcuff Ramona as well, she approached him with a desperate plea. "You can't arrest him! He needs medical attention!" she insisted. But Moore held firm. "Mrs. Whitmore, we've got a set of these for you too."

Detective Miller decides to call the Captain once again. His phone buzzed insistently in his pocket. He glanced at the screen — Detective Miller. His gut tightened; Miller didn't call unless something urgent was unfolding.

Casey answered, his voice brisk. "Miller, talk to me."

"Captain, we've got a situation," Miller said, his tone tense. "There's been a shooting at Ramona Whitmore's house."

Casey stopped in his tracks, his officers exchanging concerned looks. "A shooting? You gotta be bullshiting me? Who's involved? What happened?"

"Reports are still coming in, but it's a chaotic scene," Miller replied. "Multiple witnesses reported hearing gunfire. EMT is on-site, and Frank Whitmore was shot in the arm. And, Captain... Ramona's in custody. She tried to pin the shooting on Sarah, but the evidence doesn't add up."

Casey's jaw clenched. "Is Sarah there?"

"Yes, but her brother Joseph is inside the house as well," Miller said. "Witnesses say it got ugly — Jackson was killed in the scuffle."

Casey froze, the weight of Miller's words sinking in. "Jackson's dead?"

"Yes, sir. Shot during a struggle between Sarah and Ramona. Witness accounts say the gun went off accidentally, but we need forensics to confirm," Miller said grimly. "Ramona's trying to spin the story, but her credibility's shot — literally and figuratively."

Casey exhaled sharply, his mind racing. "All right. Secure the scene and make sure forensics collects everything. I'm on my way back now. Call Phillips — she needs to get ahead of this before the media runs wild."

"Already done," Miller replied. "But Sir, FBI just arrived on the scene." Casey's grip on the phone tightened. "Figures. Keep everyone focused. We can't afford to screw this up. I'll be there soon."

Ending the call, Casey turned to his team, his expression grim. "Change of plans. We're heading straight to Ramona

Whitmore's house. This just got a hell of a lot more complicated."

As they piled into their vehicles, Casey couldn't shake the feeling that everything was spiraling out of control — and the threads tying it all together were starting to unravel faster than they could grasp.

Few minutes later, Ramona and Frank were led out of the house, Frank's shouts echoed down the driveway. "I am innocent! I'll have your job for this!" Captain Casey pulled up just as Moore was placing Frank in the police car, smirking as he approached. "Those cuffs look good on you, Senator."

Frank glared. "You can't do this. I'm Frank Whitmore!" he spat, but Casey merely chuckled. "Save it for the judge."

The scene outside grew more chaotic as reporters swarmed Casey. "Captain Casey! Is it true Mrs. Whitmore killed her young lover, Mr. McKinley?" one reporter called out. Another added, "Is it true Internal Affairs is investigating your department?"

Before the captain could respond, DA Karen Phillips pulled up. Exiting her car, she quickly addressed the reporters. "I'm DA Phillips. This is an active investigation. Captain Casey, his officers, and his department will update the public once all details are confirmed. For now, please allow the officers to work."

Casey directed officers to put up crime scene tape as the DA and he entered the house. Inside, they were shocked at the state of the living room, shattered furniture and bloodstains painting a dark picture. Forensics moved through the scene, snapping pictures and collecting evidence.

Detective Miller was trying to talk to Sarah, who sat in shock, barely acknowledging him. Her brother Joe, now firmly in lawyer mode, intervened. "Detective, my client needs medical attention. These questions can wait under the circumstances."

Without waiting for a reply, Joe helped his dazed sister up, escorting her out of the house, while leaving Miller, Casey, and the DA speechless.

As the rain poured outside, the atmosphere inside the house grew tense. Sarah, trembling and in shock, was gently guided by Joseph to the waiting ambulance. The EMTs quickly wrapped her in a blanket, their faces reflecting concern as they assessed her condition. At the same time, inside, the arrival of Agent Christian Walker and Agent Melinda Harris turned an already chaotic scene into a battleground of authority.

Captain Casey, standing in the middle of the crime scene, clenched his jaw as soon as his eyes landed on Walker. The two had a history of disagreements, and Walker's reputation as a narcissist with a penchant for undermining others only added to the tension.

"Casey," Walker drawled, his tone dripping with condescension, "once again, I have to clean up your mess."

Casey took a deep breath, trying to keep his composure. "Agent Walker, why are you here? This is my investigation."

Walker smirked and stepped closer, with Agent Harris following closely behind. "Not anymore. You and your men are officially off this case," he declared with smug finality.

Karen Phillips, standing beside Casey, quickly stepped in to introduce herself. "Hi, I'm Karen Phillips," she said, her tone professional but firm.

Walker barely spared her a glance. "We know who you are," he said curtly, brushing past her as if her presence was irrelevant.

Casey squared his shoulders, his voice rising slightly. "Listen, Walker, my team has been working this case for months. You don't just get to waltz in here and—"

Walker interrupted with a cold laugh. "Casey, you're out of your depth. This isn't just a homicide anymore. It's tied to a federal investigation, and we don't need local cops muddying the waters."

Agent Harris, who had been silent until now, added with a pointed glare, "If you'd done your job properly, we wouldn't even be here cleaning up after you."

Detective Miller bristled at the insult. "Excuse me? We followed every protocol. Don't come in here and act like—"

Before Miller could finish, the room erupted into a shouting match. Officers and agents alike exchanged heated words, their voices echoing through the house.

Officer Sanchez, sensing the situation spiraling out of control, stepped forward in an attempt to diffuse the tension. "Hey, we're all on the same side here. Let's focus on solving this case instead of—"

Walker cut him off with a sneer. "Mind your business, Sanchez, unless you want to end up as a security guard at the local supermarket."

That was the final straw for Casey. He stepped forward, his voice dangerously low. "Don't you dare talk to my officers like that."

The captain turned to the rest of the room. "Everyone, out. Now. I need a word with Agent Walker. Alone."

Karen hesitated, concern etched across her face. "Casey, are you sure? Walker's not—"

"It's fine, Karen," Casey interrupted, his tone resolute. "I've got this."

Reluctantly, Karen signaled for the others to leave. "Miller, make sure we have all the witness statements, especially Ramona's neighbor, Maxwell," said Casey.

Detective Miller walked out, Captain Casey turned his full attention to Agent Walker, his jaw clenched. "Okay, Walker, we're alone now. Cut the theatrics. Why are you really here?"

Walker smirked, his hands in his pockets as he strolled casually around the room. "You know, Casey, you should really take advantage of that department therapist. You've got some serious anger issues building up. It's not healthy."

Casey didn't bite. "Save it. Answer the question."

Walker stopped pacing and faced him, his expression smug. "Fine. You want the truth? We've been investigating the Whitmore's for over a year now. Frank Whitmore isn't just some corrupt senator dabbling in shady deals. He's running underground gambling rings, and we have evidence linking him to human trafficking."

Casey's eyes widened slightly, his usually calm demeanor faltering. "Human trafficking? You were sitting on this whole time, and no one thought to loop me in?"

Walker chuckled darkly. "Why would we? Your job was to handle the petty crimes and keep your officers out of trouble.

But now it's escalated, and your case — this *homicide* — is directly connected to ours. Which means, Captain, you're officially sidelined."

Casey crossed his arms, standing his ground. "This is still my jurisdiction, Walker. And I've been tracking the Whitmore's just as long as you have. This isn't your playground to take over."

Walker took a step closer, lowering his voice. "Your jurisdiction means nothing when it comes to federal crimes. This is bigger than your little homicide case, Casey. And let's not forget, I've got an informant — Ramona's neighbor, Maxwell — ready to spill everything."

Casey's jaw tightened. "Maxwell? You think he's credible? He's a weasel, and you know it."

Walker smirked. "He's credible enough for me. And speaking of him, I've got a meeting to attend. If you'll excuse me."

Without waiting for a response, Walker turned on his heel and headed for the door.

The rain intensified, Captain Casey stood alone in the dimly lit living room, his mind racing after the confrontation with Agent Walker. His hands tightened around his phone as he dialed. The ringing felt like an eternity before a familiar voice answered.

"Casey, what's going on?" Karen Phillips' voice was calm but concerned.

"Karen, we have a problem," Casey said, his voice low and sharp. "Walker just dropped a bombshell about the Whitmore's. They've been investigating Frank for a year — gambling rings and human trafficking. He claims this whole mess is connected."

Karen let out a deep sigh. "Human trafficking? That's a new level of chaos. Why didn't they loop us in earlier?"

"Because Walker's an egotistical maniac, who thinks his team is the only one capable of cracking a case," Casey snapped. "He's already claimed jurisdiction over the homicide investigation. He also said he's working with Maxwell — the Whitmore's' *neighbor*. That makes things even messier."

Karen paused, processing the information. "Maxwell? The guy who called in half the noise complaints? He's a key witness?"

Casey nodded, even though she couldn't see him. "Apparently, he's also an informant for Walker. But something doesn't sit right. Walker's too smug, and I don't trust him."

Karen's tone grew serious. "We need to tread carefully, Casey. If Walker's playing games, it could jeopardize everything. But if Frank Whitmore's really tied to trafficking, this case is bigger than any of us thought."

"I agree," Casey replied. "But I'm not backing down. This is my team's case, and I'm not gonna let Walker undermine everything we've worked on. We'll keep our distance, but I want you to quietly dig into Maxwell. If Walker's hiding something, we need to know."

Karen hesitated. "What about the homicide? We still need to secure Sarah's statement and ensure Ramona doesn't weasel her way out of this."

"I've got Miller working on that," Casey said firmly. "For now, just focus on Maxwell and see what you can find. And Karen... be discreet. If Walker catches wind, he'll bury us before we have a chance to move."

"You've got it," Karen said. "Be careful, Casey. Walker's dangerous when he feels threatened."

Casey ended the call and slipped the phone back into his pocket, his jaw tightening. He glanced out the window, watching the rain cascade down the glass.

The storm outside felt like a mirror to the chaos brewing in the investigation. One thing was clear — this was no longer just about murder. It was about unraveling a web of corruption that stretched far deeper than he'd anticipated. And Casey wasn't about to let Agent Walker or anyone else get in his way.

Chapter 27

New Beginning

Three months after Jackson's death, the high-profile trial of The State of Pennsylvania vs. The Whitmore's began. The courtroom was packed each day as the Whitmore's sought to shift blame, claiming Officer Richardson had masterminded the entire scheme. During all this, the notorious Gary Richardson was nowhere to be found, with rumors suggesting he had fled the country.

The District Attorney office scheduled a press conference along with other city officials.

Mayor Washington stepped up to the podium, adjusting the microphone as he addressed the crowd. "Good morning, everyone. Today is indeed a difficult day for the city of Philadelphia and for the Anderson family. We are deeply disappointed in the court's decision to dismiss key charges against Frank and Ramona Whitmore. However, I stand here to assure you that the safety and justice for our citizens remain our top priority."

He paused, glancing at Margaret Anderson, who stood silently behind him, her hands clasped tightly together. "District Attorney Phillips and Captain Casey have my full support as we continue to seek justice. This fight is far from over, and together, we will bring accountability to those who think they are above the law. This city will not tolerate corruption and abuse of power."

Margaret Anderson, wiping tears from her face, slowly stepped forward. The crowd mayor gave her a reassuring nod as she approached the podium. The crowd quieted, their attention fully on the grieving mother.

She took a deep breath, steadying herself. "My son, Marcus, was a kind, loving soul. He didn't deserve what happened to him. To see the people responsible for his death walk free is a nightmare I wouldn't wish on anyone. But I will not rest until justice is served — not just for my son but for every family, who has suffered because of corruption and greed."

The crowd murmured in agreement as Margaret stepped back, tears streaming down her face. Karen Phillips returned to the podium, her tone firm and resolute. "Thank you, Mrs. Anderson, for your courage. Let me make this clear: we are not giving up. My office is exploring every legal avenue to hold Frank and Ramona Whitmore accountable. This fight isn't over."

Just as Karen was about to conclude, Agent Christian Walker appeared unexpectedly, walking up to the stage uninvited. The crowd's whispers grew louder. Karen shot Captain Casey a questioning look, but he appeared just as caught off guard.

Walker took the microphone without hesitation, his commanding voice cutting through the tension. "Good morning. I know many of you are frustrated by today's developments. Let me assure you, Senator Whitmore is not off the hook. What you don't know is that this case is part of a much larger federal investigation — one that's been ongoing for over a year. The Whitmores are just one piece of a deeply entrenched network of crime and corruption."

Karen stepped forward, clearly irritated. "Agent Walker, this press conference is for the local authorities to address the community."

Walker ignored her, continuing, "We're playing the long game here, ensuring that when justice is served, it's final. I understand your frustration, but trust me, the work we're doing will have a greater impact than you realize."

The media erupted with questions, but Walker dismissed them with a wave, stepping off the stage. The crowd of reporters' cameras flashing was loud and insisent as they tried to capture every reaction.

The press conference descended into chaos after Agent Walker's abrupt and uninvited appearance. The crowd of reporters shouted overlapping questions, cameras flashing as they tried to capture every reaction.

Karen Phillips tightened her grip on the podium, her frustration barely concealed. She glanced at Captain Casey, who shook his head in disbelief. Margaret Anderson stood frozen, her prepared words forgotten in the whirlwind of Walker's interruption.

Karen leaned toward the microphone, her voice sharp and commanding. "Ladies and gentlemen of the press, I appreciate your patience. As I was saying before the interruption, this case is far from over. My office remains dedicated to securing justice for the victims and their families. Any further questions regarding Agent Walker's statements should be directed to his agency, not my office. Now, if you'll excuse me, we have work to do."

She stepped back, gesturing for Captain Casey and Mayor Washington to follow her away from the podium. Margaret, still visibly shaken, was gently escorted by an aide.

As they moved away from the crowd, Karen muttered under her breath, "Who does Walker think he is, hijacking a press conference meant to reassure the public?"

Casey nodded grimly. "He's making a power play, trying to undermine us, while boosting his own narrative. It's Walker's

MO — grandstanding and making sure everyone knows he's in charge."

Mayor Washington, keeping his voice low, added, "This doesn't look good. The public's already skeptical, and now it seems like we're not unified. Walker's stunt just added fuel to the fire."

Karen took a deep breath, her mind racing. "We need to control the narrative. I'll hold another press conference tomorrow to clarify our position, but for now, let's regroup. Casey, I want updates on every angle of this case. And find out what Walker's agency is really up to. He's hiding something."

Casey nodded. "Consider it done. We'll expose him if we have to."

As they moved to their cars, Margaret Anderson approached Karen, her voice trembling but resolute. "Don't let them get away with this," she said. "My son deserves justice."

Karen placed a reassuring hand on Margaret's shoulder. "I promise you, Mrs. Anderson, we won't stop until we bring them all to justice. For your son, and for everyone else they've hurt."

The group dispersed, the weight of the moment pressing heavily on all of them. Though, Agent Walker drove away, a smug smile on his face, knowing he had planted seeds of chaos and uncertainty in the hearts of the press and public.

This is just the beginning; desperate to reduce his sentence, Frank Whitmore turned on his former allies, providing damning evidence against several city officials and individuals within the police department. His testimony uncovered a web of corruption and misconduct that sent shockwaves through the community. Ramona, pled guilty to stalking Jackson, though the state was unable to tie her to his murder or a conspiracy to harm her former husband, Marcus Anderson. Key testimony from Alison was dismissed, proving too fragile to convict the Whitmores on the most serious charges.

Throughout the trial, Sarah chose not to attend. She was on a journey of healing, grappling with the grief of her son's loss and coming to terms with the betrayals of her past. Therapy became her refuge, and she leaned on the support of Margaret and Alison. Over time, the three women grew closer, meeting weekly for lunch, finding solace in each other's company and shared experiences.

A year later, the women channeled their pain into a powerful initiative. Together, they launched *Women Against Violence*, an organization dedicated to supporting women impacted by violence and betrayal. Their cause quickly gained momentum, drawing on their own stories to inspire others to speak out, heal, and stand up against violence and corruption.

Epilogue

The sun dipped low on the horizon, casting a golden hue across Eastbridge, but shadows loomed larger than ever over those left standing after Marcus's shocking demise. The once-vibrant town now felt more like a stage, with its residents playing characters in a tragedy that unfolded without warning. Whispers swirled like autumn leaves in the wind, and the question on everyone's lips was the same: Who killed Marcus?

In the days following the tumultuous events that sent shock waves through their lives, Ramona Whitmore found herself grappling with the fallout. Each morning, she woke up to the chilling reminder of the chaotic night that had unraveled everything. As the FBI continued to investigate, her anxiety twisted tightly around her heart. Officer Gary Richardson, whom she had trusted implicitly, seemed to have vanished into thin air. The last image she retained of him was his steely gaze meeting hers in the chaos — what had happened to him? Was he in hiding, or had he become another player in this dangerous game?

Meanwhile, Agent Walker had slipped into the role of the puppeteer, commanding the investigation from the shadows. With a reputation for being two steps ahead, Walker was known for playing his cards close to his chest. As he sifted through the evidence, he plotted his next move, determined to uncover the truth that lay cloaked behind a veil of deceit. Did he know more about Marcus's murder than he let on? Were his intents purely justice-driven, or did he have personal scores to settle within this tangled web?

Frank Whitmore and Ramona faced the daunting prospect of prison time. Their fates now depended on how much they would divulge to the authorities. The corrupt schemes that had linked them to both crime and betrayal hung over their heads like a dark cloud, threatening to rain down misery. While Frank clung to the hope that his connections could somehow avert disaster, Ramona felt the weight of her choices pressing down on her conscience. Could they spin their story to escape the long arm of the law? Or would the truth finally entrap them?

In a dimly lit interrogation room, the tension was palpable. Frank sat across from Agent Walker, a calculating glint in his eyes. "You think you can pin this on us?" he sneered, the bravado half-hearted and shaky. The air crackled with unspoken threats as Agent Walker leaned in, a sly smile creeping onto his face. "Oh, Frank. This is just the beginning. I'm not after you for Marcus's death," he said smoothly, "I want everything you've been hiding. Everything."

With a flick of his wrist, Agent Walker revealed evidence that sent a jolt through Frank — photos of money transfers, clandestine meetings, and a well-documented trail of betrayal that led right back to him. Unbeknownst to Frank, Walker had been building a case long before Marcus's untimely end — a case that could bring down the Whitmore empire.

As Ramona paced back at home, she couldn't shake the nagging feeling that danger lurked around every corner. The life she envisioned, filled with luxury and success, felt as elusive as the autumn breeze. The truth began to trickle in, like the first drops of rain before a storm. Her heart raced as she pieced together the fragments of the puzzle. Irrevocable decisions loomed large, and the consequences of their actions were catching up faster than she had anticipated.

And as winter approached, so did the chilling realization that life as they once knew it was gone. For Ramona, a reckoning awaited — not just with the law, but with her own heart and the choices that had led her to this moment. Would she finally confront the shadows of her past, or would she let them consume her whole?

As the sun set over Eastbridge and the interrogation room filled with shadows, Frank faced off against Agent Walker, and one question lingered in the air: Would justice prevail, or was this just the beginning of a deeper conspiracy that would bring them all to their knees?

And so, as darkness settled over Eastbridge, the answers awaited, shrouded in mystery but inevitable as the dawn. The saga was far from over; the stage was set for a showdown that would determine the fates of not just one, but many.

JenniferJackson©2025